The
BAD UNICORN TRILOGY

Bad Unicorn
Fluff Dragon
Good Ogre

GOOD OGRE

·BOOK THREE OF THE BAD UNICORN TRILOGY·

BY *Platte F. Clark*

ALADDIN
New York   London   Toronto   Sydney   New Delhi

This book is a work of fiction. Any references to historical events, real people, or real places are used fictitiously. Other names, characters, places, and events are the product of the author's imagination, and any resemblance to actual events or places or persons, living or dead, is entirely coincidental.

ALADDIN

An imprint of Simon & Schuster Children's Publishing Division
1230 Avenue of the Americas, New York, NY 10020
First Aladdin paperback edition April 2016
Text copyright © 2015 by Straw Dogs LLC
Cover illustrations copyright © 2015 by John Hendrix
Also available in an Aladdin hardcover edition.
All rights reserved, including the right of reproduction in whole or in part in any form.
ALADDIN is a trademark of Simon & Schuster, Inc., and related logo is a registered trademark of Simon & Schuster, Inc.
For information about special discounts for bulk purchases, please contact Simon & Schuster Special Sales at 1-866-506-1949 or business@simonandschuster.com.
The Simon & Schuster Speakers Bureau can bring authors to your live event. For more information or to book an event contact the Simon & Schuster Speakers Bureau at 1-866-248-3049 or visit our website at www.simonspeakers.com.
Cover designed by Jessica Handelman
Interior designed by Karina Granda
The text of this book was set in Bembo.
Manufactured in the United States of America 0216 OFF
2 4 6 8 10 9 7 5 3 1
Library of Congress Cataloging-in-Publication Data
Clark, Platte F.
Good ogre / by Platte F. Clark. — First Aladdin hardcover edition.
pages cm.—(The bad unicorn trilogy; book 3)
Summary: After saving three worlds, Max has trouble settling back into middle school and life at home, but when he tries to return to the magical planet of Magrus, the evil Maelshadow begins changing humans into monsters in an effort to take over the planet.
[1. Wizards—Fiction. 2. Magic—Fiction. 3. Adventure and adventurers—Fiction. 4. Ghouls and ogres—Fiction. 5. Unicorns—Fiction. 6. Humorous stories. 7. Fantasy.]
I. Title.
PZ7.C55225Goo 2015
[Fic]—dc23
2014017688
ISBN 978-1-4424-5018-9 (hc)
ISBN 978-1-4424-5019-6 (pbk)
ISBN 978-1-4424-5020-2 (eBook)

To my father, Platte Evans Clark,
who tolerated a twelve-year-old's love of comic books,
fantasy novels, and long games of Dungeons & Dragons

PROLOGUE

DWAINE WAS AN OGRE, BUT NOT IN THE LUMBERING, FOOTBALL-PLAYING, knocks-your-lunch-tray-off-the-table-when-he-walks-by kind of way. Dwaine was an ogre in the green-skinned, humongous, not-a-human-being kind of way. Although, admittedly, Dwaine wasn't a particularly accomplished ogre: He had only earned a participation ribbon at the elf-smashing games (everyone who entered got one); his war howl sounded more like an old Volkswagen trying to start on a cold morning; and on career day his counselor gave him a pamphlet entitled *Armor Testing and You!* Worst of all, he'd only scored 7 percent on the MEE (Magrus Evil Exam). Seven percent ranked him as only slightly more evil than an annoyed woodchuck. Dwaine's parents did their best to hide their shame, but when his older brother,

Dolrug, scored a whopping 97 percent evil, they threw Dolrug a party and sent him to law school. The chances of Dwaine ever getting a party thrown in his honor were slim to none.

When graduation day arrived at Moldy Cave Middle School, Dwaine cleaned out his locker and followed the other students outside. His class was eager to get to the recruitment fair, so they hurried across the field to assemble at the various career booths. It was the ogre custom that as soon as one graduated from middle school, he or she was expected to choose an occupation. And so it was that the recruiters were out in force.

The biggest booth belonged to the ogre army, sporting a large banner that read COME SMASH FOR CASH! Other trades were represented as well, such as blacksmithing, culinary arts, and animal husbandry (also known as marriage counseling). Those with exceptionally high Magrus Evil Exam scores were immediately marked for a career in politics. Dwaine was not one of them, however. In fact, he was the only ogre not excited by the fair—not with his pathetic test score. So he lumbered around the field and watched as students listened to the speeches from recruiters, checked the minimum MEE scores for that vocation, and if interested, signed their contract. It was how things were done in the ogre community.

Dwaine sighed. With a score of 7 percent there was no sense stopping at one of the colorful booths. Even the army required a minimum 15 percent evil. That left only one option, and Dwaine shuddered at the thought. At the far end of the field he saw the armor-testing stand, its old and tattered banner proclaiming ARMOR TESTERS— PROTECTING THE ONES WHO MATTER. It was supposed to be inspirational.

Dwaine began his slow walk across the fairgrounds and consigned himself to his fate. He was to be an armor tester, then, which amounted to putting on various bits of ogre armor and getting whacked by an assortment of weapons. It wasn't the kind of career that even bothered to offer a retirement plan. He passed the other ogres in silence as they celebrated their choices, but as he made his way across the field he noticed something odd—a small, black booth standing apart from the others. Stranger still, while the other booths had crowds of young ogres around them, not a single ogre stood before the black one. Dwaine hesitated, unsure what to do. He knew getting his hopes up was a dangerous thing—disappointment always followed, and he'd learned it was easier to just accept that the worst was going to happen and get on with it. But still . . . what did he have to lose? He shrugged and approached the structure, finding a solitary human sitting inside. The old man wore black robes, seemingly cut from the same black fabric as the booth, and watched Dwaine with a bemused grin.

"Uh, are you part of the recruitment fair?" Dwaine asked looking around. The man rose from his seat in response.

"Could be. Ever hear of the Maelshadow's Minions?"

Dwaine scratched at the side of his large, green head. "I don't think so."

"Not many have," the man answered. "We're a select group. Very particular."

"Ah, well, it was nice talking to you," Dwaine replied, turning to walk away. He knew words like "select" and "particular" meant he should be on his way. But the man called back to him.

"Not so fast there. You've already passed the first test."

"I have?" Dwaine asked, turning around.

"There's a reason nobody else is standing here," the man answered. Just then a group of students walked by.

One of them, an ogre named Brokug, pointed at Dwaine. "Hey, you lost or something? You're supposed to find a booth." The group laughed and continued on their way. Dwaine turned back to the old man, who was smiling at him.

"They can't see you, can they?" Dwaine asked, not really understanding what was going on.

"Clever," the old man said. "Too clever a head to test helmets all day."

"The only thing that can do *that* is magic," Dwaine continued, the words sounding strange in his mouth. He'd learned about the Wizard's Tower and its order of magic users, although there were rumors that the Tower in Aardyre had fallen. But why would the Tower care about ogres? Or, for that matter, him?

"I don't suppose you see a lot of magic out here," the old man replied. "But to answer your question, yes—my booth and I are completely invisible. Well, invisible to most."

"I don't understand. Why come to a recruitment fair to not be seen?"

"It's a test," the man said, waving his hand. "We're looking for those who are, how do I put this . . . *slightly* evil. I'm cloaked in a spell that keeps me hidden from everyone else."

Dwaine had never heard of a recruiter looking for somebody who wasn't mostly evil. "But didn't you say you worked for the Maelshadow?"

"That's right."

"And isn't the Maelshadow the most powerful and *evil* being in all of the three realms?"

"All that and more," the man nodded. "He is the Ruler of the Shadrus! The Lord of Shadows!"

Dwaine scratched at his head again as he tried to work it out. "I don't think I understand why someone like that would be interested in me."

"Look, I'm going to share a secret with you," the man said, motioning for Dwaine to lean closer to him. "Evil isn't all that difficult to master when you really think about it. I mean, how hard is it? Stomp around and destroy some pretties? Swipe things that don't belong to you? Bonk a few innocents on the head? The great weakness of evil is that it's, well . . . *predictable*. And predictable is exactly what you don't want to be when you're trying to take over the universe."

The old man paused, watching as his words sank

in. Dwaine had never heard anything like this before. Everything that mattered in an ogre's life was centered around being as evil as possible.

The old man brought his hand up to his head. "Boom!" he exclaimed as he opened his fingers. "Kind of mind-blowing when you think about it."

"I suppose so."

"See, if you're the Maelshadow and you're as evil as evil can get, you have to stop playing by the rules if you want to win. So the Lord of Shadows is looking for special recruits to carry out important missions—recruits with enough good in them to throw everything off. Recruits just like you."

Dwaine had never been called special. "I only scored seven percent on my evil exam."

"Seven percent?" the man said, beaming. "That's the lowest yet! My friend, let me officially offer you a job!"

Dwaine wondered what his parents would think of that. Maybe he'd get that party after all. The old man pushed a solid black parchment forward and handed Dwaine a white feather. "Just sign at the bottom."

Dwaine squinted at the black document.

"I can't read anything," he finally admitted.

"Well, of course you can't," the old man said, as if it were the most sensible thing in the world. "Standard procedure for a Maelshadow contract is black ink on black parchment. Cuts through all the nonsense of having to read and understand it."

"Oh," Dwaine said, slightly confused. But then again, what did it matter? Joining the Maelshadow was his way out. He took the white feather and pressed it against the parchment, feeling it vibrate in his hand as he scrawled his name across the bottom.

"Congratulations," the black-robed man announced, snatching the contract back. "You, my friend, are going to go places. And by that, I mean right now, because your ride is here."

"It is?" Dwaine asked. Then he heard the sound of approaching hooves and turned to see a black horse galloping through the woods toward them. Only it wasn't like any horse Dwaine had seen before. For one, it was much bigger. And when it snorted, flame and smoke bellowed from its flared nostrils. It was so black, in fact, that even in the sun the beast looked as if it had been peeled from the darkest night sky. It leapt across the open field, startling Dwaine's classmates and scattering them in all directions.

The creature galloped forward, then skidded to a stop in front of the black booth. Its mane fell around the huge neck in a tangle of thick hair, and two burning eyes stared down at Dwaine. The scent of smoke and sulfur rolled off the beast, and the sunlight seemed to pull away from it as if such a thing had no business being in the world.

"That . . . ," Dwaine said doing his best to speak. He was having a hard time finding his voice. "That's a *nightmare!*"

"Yes, so I wouldn't keep her waiting if I were you," the man said. "They have been known to eat riders that annoy them."

Dwaine swallowed. All around him the other ogres were pointing, their heavy jaws hanging in disbelief. Then he realized that if there was ever a moment he could let the whole school know that they had misjudged him, it was now. Dwaine took a breath and reached for the thick black mane. He might have been one of the most unpopular ogres in school, but he was an ogre nonetheless, and his powerful legs propelled him up and onto the beast's back. The nightmare reared, pawing at the air with black hooves that seeped a tarlike substance, which smoldered when it hit the ground.

There were gasps from all around the fairgrounds,

and Dwaine nearly tumbled off the creature's rear (which would have been a bit embarrassing, all things considered), but he managed to stay on.

"My name is Dwaine!" he shouted as the nightmare thundered back to the ground. "And I am *not* an armor tester!" And with that the nightmare galloped off, flame igniting around its hooves as it charged forward. The great beast flew across the grounds and into the forest, burning hoofprints marking the path behind it.

There was a stunned silence as the remaining ogres caught their breaths. Syndy, one of the more popular females on the cheerleading team, turned to her boyfriend.

"What did he say?" she asked, her voice filled with awe.

"I think he said his name was Dave," the ogre answered thoughtfully. "And he's an armor tester."

Meanwhile, Dwaine was holding on to the nightmare for all he was worth, quickly losing any thoughts of parties and such. They were doing more than traversing the lands of his ancestral home—they were descending from the Magrus into the Shadrus, the Shadow Realm. The nightmare was able to cross the border between the two realms as few other creatures could.

Day turned to night, and Dwaine had to tie the heavy

cords of the nightmare's mane around his arms or risk falling off. He lost all sense of time, noting only that the world grew darker the farther they traveled. He finally gave in to exhaustion and slept.

He woke to a black sun burning against a gray sky. The nightmare had ceased running, and instead walked purposefully toward a giant fortress that rose from the cracked, dry ground. Ragged, seemingly chaotic pillars of rock climbed over one another to form the palace of the Maelshadow. An impossibly large wall encircled the structure, while rivers of thick, putrid water snaked along the ground. Dwaine wondered what else was on the other side of the wall—a city, perhaps?

They continued traveling along the well-worn road. On either side numerous statues emerged from the earth—clay creatures that crawled away from the Maelshadow's domain, their expressions locked in horror. Definitely not the kind of thing you'd see on a postcard and think, *Now that's a place I'd like to visit.*

It wasn't long before the nightmare deposited Dwaine at the main gate. The ogre was met by a sullen, emaciated creature whose dark skin was covered in ivory tattoos. The strange symbols crawled around the manlike limbs and chest, disappearing behind the folds of a loose-fitting robe.

"Are you a wizard?" Dwaine asked, his muscles aching from the long ride.

"Wizard? I should certainly say not!" the creature coughed, and Dwaine had a sudden feeling that he had a cold coming on. "I am a plague—a bringer of disease and pestilence. You'd better learn the way of things down here if you want to live long enough to be useful. Now, follow me." Dwaine had never met a plague before, and decided it was probably not a good idea to shake hands.

The two of them passed under the gate and walked toward the palace in the distance. "I imagine you're the Black Death, then," Dwaine said, thinking that maybe the two of them had gotten off to a bad start. "You hear a lot about the Black Death. Very impressive."

"Oh, sure, it's *bubonic* that gets all the attention," the being said, waving a skeletal hand at the gray sky above. "I suppose it's the fashionable way to go if you want to be part of the in crowd."

"I didn't know plagues could be popular," Dwaine continued, doing his best to keep the small talk going.

"We're no different from anybody else, you know," the plague replied. "Bubonic—as if there's any challenge in that.

Do you know how difficult it is to start a bubonic outbreak?"

"I've never really thought about it."

"Give me a rat and a couple of peasants and I can whip up the Black Death in no time."

"So what kind of plague are you, if you don't mind my asking?" Dwaine pressed. He'd decided to keep his eyes forward and concentrate on the conversation. Around him the Shadrus city, comprised of oddly twisted buildings and even stranger inhabitants, seemed to press in with an almost palpable sense of foreboding.

"I am tonsillitis," the plague answered with a sinister glint in its eye.

Dwaine walked in silence for several moments. "Is that an actual plague? I thought it was just swollen glands or something,"

"It's from the pharyngeal family if you really want to know," the plague said, sounding defensive.

"I see," Dwaine replied.

"Sure, I know what you're thinking," the plague continued. "A sore throat and intermittent cough isn't a big deal. But if you don't get it looked at, it can turn into rheumatic fever. Very nasty, that."

"Sounds like it," Dwaine agreed. He didn't think

ogres got rheumatic fever, but it probably wasn't a good time to bring that up.

"Beware the Red Swelling!" the plague suddenly exclaimed. "Sounds scary, doesn't it? Like the Black Death, much better than bubonic plague. Every good disease needs a catchphrase." Suddenly the plague started chuckling. "Get it? A *catch*phrase about a virus . . . sometimes I crack myself up."

Dwaine forced a laugh just to be polite. Thankfully, the plague was content to walk the rest of the way in silence.

He was led into the spacious palace and taken to a temple where the Lord of Shadows was waiting. Once Dwaine was in his presence, he felt icy fingers wrap their way around his insides. The Maelshadow was every bit as terrifying as in the stories he'd heard, and when the Lord of Shadows spoke, his voice filled the place with a deep rumble, as if some giant had awoken beneath the earth.

"Listen," the Maelshadow commanded, "and I will tell you how Max Spencer, the boy who can read the book, will doom his world."

CHAPTER ONE

RETURN OF THE CONQUERING HERO

MAX STARED AT THE OBJECT OF DREAD HANGING IN FRONT OF HIM AND realized there was nothing to do but face it. It was bad enough that Parkside Middle School's husky-sized PE shorts had remained unchanged and out of fashion since 1976, but now everyone was staring at him too. And that included the older kids. From Max's perspective it looked as if the entire ninth grade were sitting in the bleachers, watching him. Kids with actual facial hair were giving him the eye.

"Spencer, Max," a deep voice grumbled for the second time. A hush settled over the gym as Max finally raised his hand.

"Here."

Coach Mattson put his clipboard aside and raised his

whistle to his mouth. He wore his United States Marine Corps T-shirt and was probably the only guy in the world trained to use a dodgeball ball as a deadly weapon. "On my mark," he grunted through clenched teeth.

Max slowly stepped forward, craning his neck in an effort to see how high the rope stretched. It was the first day of the new school year, and how Max performed on the rope climb would determine his fate. He'd either be going into regular PE (where they played games that involved actual score keeping), or remedial PE (where Coach Mattson ran his special military-inspired torture routines). Max had heard the whispered tales of woe that came from remedial PE: pain, humiliation, and guaranteed barfing. Max really, *really* wanted to be in regular PE, but if there was one exercise he was especially bad at, it was the rope climb.

Max looked at the students in the bleachers and the line of others waiting impatiently behind him. Maybe he could fake a seizure? Only he wasn't a particularly good actor, and if he got it wrong, it would just make things worse. Everyone knew you could only play the seizure card once, so you had to make it count.

"Come on, Max, you can do it!" a familiar voice

cried out. It was Dirk, his oldest and best friend. Dirk was the kind of kid who ate nothing but junk food and still managed to scuttle up the rope like gravity had left the building. He was also the fastest runner in the entire school, which was a good thing given his tendency to say things that made people want to kick him—even girls.

"Yo, don't break it, Spencer!" another voice shouted, and behind it came a chorus of cackles. That voice belonged to Ricky "the Kraken" Reynolds, and he was about as scary a kid as you could imagine. Undefeated as a wrestler, he'd gained his nickname for all the bones he "cracked" on the mat. It also gave him the kind of reputation perfect for bullying. But Max had seen something even more terrifying when the Kraken had been transformed into something else—a hulking beast with red skin and glowing eyes. *That* had been in a different time and in a different world, but the memory remained.

Max jumped for the rope, and the burning in his arms began much too quickly. He struggled to pull himself up, and he imagined he looked like a fish flopping around at the end of a fishing line. Thankfully he managed to find the big knot at the bottom with his feet.

"Hey, Spencer, you're supposed to go *up!*" another wrestler called out. There were more laughs.

"Yeah, even I got higher than that!" a squeaky voice followed. It was Melvin Jenkins, head of the Live Action Role-Playing group, or LARPers. They dressed up as fantasy characters and ran around with cardboard swords and threw tennis balls as spells. Online gaming was different—your character had truly heroic abilities. LARPers simply ran around and pretended to do things. So if *Melvin* was mocking him, his life had hit an all-time low. In response, the gym broke out into howls of laughter.

Max gritted his teeth and shoved off the knot. For a moment—a very brief moment—he managed to hold himself on the rope. But the burning in his arms became a fire and his hands were sweating way too much. It occurred to him that he should at least try for a graceful dismount. He let go, but he ended up sliding too fast, and his feet got tangled up in the rope. He somersaulted forward, the rope flying through his hands. And if that wasn't bad enough, the large knot at the bottom whipped around and smacked him squarely in the face. His glasses flew off as he tumbled forward. Max landed with a loud slapping sound that seemed to reverberate off the old gym's walls. There was a moment of stunned silence before the entire gym exploded in laughter. It was, without a doubt, the most humiliating moment in Max's life—and that was saying a lot.

"Okay, that's enough," Coach Mattson said, blowing his whistle and bringing the place back to order. He marked something on his clipboard. "We'll be seeing you in remedial PE, Mr. Spencer," he announced. Max picked himself up off the mat and retrieved his glasses. "Don't worry son," the coach continued. "I'll toughen you up."

There's a place where I'm tough enough already, Max said to himself. He wiped his glasses off and limped back toward the locker room. Dirk ran to catch up to him.

"Dude, you're not very good at rope climbing," he announced, stating the obvious.

"Really?" Max replied, trying not to sound bitter. He hadn't bothered to put his glasses on—that way he wouldn't have to see the laughing, judging eyes of everyone in the gym.

"Don't worry about those dweebs," Dirk said as if reading his mind. "Jocks might rule the schools, but nerds rule the world. That's why they're so angry at us."

Max smiled at that. He knew plenty of people who thought he and Dirk were nerds. But so what if they liked computers and role-playing games and reading all the sci-fi and fantasy they could get their hands on? Max knew a truth that very few others did—that the universe was made up of three different realms, and magic, heroes, and monsters really did exist. It turned out the nerds weren't so far off after all.

"Meet me in the lunchroom," Dirk said, slapping Max on the shoulder. "I hear we're getting new tater tots this year."

That afternoon Max rode the bus in silence. Dirk was going on about an online game he was excited about, but Max wasn't paying attention. Instead, he watched as the houses of Madison passed by the window. Madison was a small town that was, as the mayor liked to say, "not too close or too far from anything important." But everyone knew that was just code for being in the middle of nowhere.

Max looked up and saw Ricky Reynolds standing in the aisle, staring down at him. The bus driver gave a quick disapproving glance in the mirror, but refrained from saying anything. Ricky was big enough that even adults thought twice about making him angry.

"I liked how you cried in gym today," Ricky taunted, saying it loud enough that everyone could hear. "I liked it so much I was thinking that maybe you should cry some more."

"Don't go using all your big words at once," Dirk shot back. "You might want to save some for tomorrow."

Someone near the back of the bus started to laugh, but when Ricky shot an angry look in that direction, it quickly became a cough.

"Come on, Spencer," Ricky continued, turning his attention back to Max. "I hear you had an exciting first day at school today. Let's see, you were tripped in the hallway, wet-willied between classes, had your chocolate milk taken at lunch, towel snapped in the locker room, and, oh yeah, you humiliated *yourself* in front of the entire school. I'm just worried you might think you're a loser or something. Oh wait, you totally *should* feel like a loser, because you are one."

Ricky began to howl with laughter, and the rest of the bus followed his lead. Thankfully Sarah didn't ride the bus home, because she was the kind of person who'd stand up to Ricky. She'd done it before, in fact, last year. She was an expert in judo and had sent Ricky flying in the school hallway. Ricky avoided her now, but that only seemed to make him more venomous toward Max and Dirk.

"Dude, we get it, okay?" Dirk said. "You're big and bad and you've proved it once again. So maybe cut him some slack?"

It was, unfortunately, the wrong thing to say to a kid like Ricky Reynolds. Ricky didn't look at weakness as an opportunity to step back and declare victory. Ricky saw weakness as an opening for total annihilation. He lifted his hand and pointed at Max. "Look, everyone, I see a tear. Spencer is totally going to start crying like a little baby! Crybaby, crybaby!" he called out, getting the bus to join in. "Crybaby! Crybaby!" Soon the entire bus was shouting at Max like they were back in elementary school. At the next stop Max bolted from his seat, squeezing past Ricky and making for the door.

The chants continued as the bus began to pull away. Max looked up to see the myriad faces pressed against the windows. He knew he shouldn't have looked, just like he knew to keep his glasses off in the gym. But this time he did, and the laughing, mocking expressions stung even more as the bus drove by. And then there was Dirk, who simply mouthed, *Dude, that's not your stop!*

When Max glanced at the clock, it read 12:15 a.m. He was supposed to be in bed by ten thirty, but the online campaign had gone longer than anyone had expected. Max just wasn't feeling it, however, so he excused himself and hurried and logged out. He was sure there'd be some angry complaints from the others, but he didn't care. His eyes drifted to the newspaper article pinned next to the monitor. MISSING STUDENTS FOUND, the headline proclaimed. There was a picture of him, Dirk, and Sarah, standing arm in arm in front of the school. Somehow they had to explain their disappearance last year, so Dirk had come up with the story. They told everyone they had been walking home when there was a sudden bright light—and the next thing they knew a number of days had passed. Max thought it was the worst story imaginable, but Sarah said the simplest explanation would work best, no matter how crazy it sounded. So they all agreed to tell a small white lie rather than explain the truth: that Max was the long-lost relative of a great sorcerer and had accidentally used his spell book to cast them into the future. And that once there, they'd had to fight against Robo-Princess, a decidedly evil unicorn who had been hunting them. Then they'd made a promise to a great dragon king, who sent them back in time to the Magrus (the magical kingdom). There they had to take the *Codex of Infinite Knowability* to the place it was created—which happened to be the Wizard's Tower, where a powerful sorcerer had been after Max and his friends all along. They defeated Rezormoor Dreadbringer and his minions and were taken back to the Techrus (the human realm) by means of a magical coach. When they arrived in Madison, they had effectively doubled back in time, so it had only been a few days since their mysterious disappearance.

So bright light and time loss it was. Ricky knew the truth because he had ended up in the Magrus somehow— Max wasn't sure *how* that had happened exactly. That left Dwight as the only other person who knew the truth. Dwight was the owner of the Dragon's Den, the game and comic shop on Main Street. They had always thought of him as a little person, but it turned out Dwight was an actual dwarf. Dwight had been on the whole adventure as well, taking them all the way to his ancestral home of Jiilk. There, Max had earned the respect of the dwarf king and stood between two armies ready to go to war. That seemed a strange memory now that he had to put up with the daily humiliation of being plain old Max Spencer. It didn't seem fair, and Max had started to wonder if coming home had been a mistake.

He rose from his chair with a sigh and plopped on the bed, bouncing Moki from his sleeping position on Max's pillow. Moki was a fire kitten and had come with Max all the way from the Magrus. In fact, the little fire kitten had saved Max and his friends more than once. He'd originally gone home with Sarah, but apparently her mom was allergic to fire kittens. Max had taken him in happily, and he now stroked Moki's head as the fire kitten purred with contentment. Fire kittens could also talk, and he and Max had to be careful—a few close calls with his mom had nearly unraveled everything. A talking cat was the kind of thing a parent would blow out of proportion.

"Do you miss the Magrus?" Max asked. Moki stretched as he contemplated his answer.

"I like it here," Moki replied. "TV is great." Max smiled—Moki pretty much thought everything was great.

"Sometimes I miss it," Max admitted. "I had power in the Magrus. People respected me."

"You are a great wizard."

"But not like before—magic doesn't work the same here." Max opened his nightstand and pulled out the *Codex of Infinite Knowability*. Moki frowned when Max's scratching hand left to become a page-turning one. "I'm the only person in the three realms who can use this," Max continued, "and it pretty much just sits in my drawer collecting dust." He flipped through the ancient book, the handwritten pages and elaborate drawings part of the encyclopedic knowledge the *Codex* had of just about everyone and everything. And as far as Max could tell, the *Codex* also had a mind of its own—its pages would change and the book would communicate what *it* wanted, regardless of what the reader was interested in. Because the *Codex* had been created by the greatest arch-sorcerer who had ever lived, it also contained the Fifteen Prime Spells—the most powerful magic in all of existence, and the foundation of all other magic in the universe. The fact that the arch-sorcerer had turned out to be Max's father was still too new a revelation for Max to completely appreciate. But maybe that was why he felt the pull of the place—he was born there. The Magrus was his real home.

Max stood with the book in his hand. He reached out with his mind and found the strange sensation that was the *Codex*. In the human realm, magic was slippery and hard to hold on to. Still, he found the tide of power that flowed through the book and pulled it back. It engulfed him like a warm ocean current. He closed his eyes and reveled in the feeling, not aware of the books, papers, and other items that lifted into the air and began to float around the room. Moki slid along the bed as well, finally grabbing hold of the bedpost with his claws. The power swelled in Max, and he smiled at its warm and comforting embrace. *This is who I am,* he said to himself.

Outside Max's house the trees in the yard bent as if caught in an invisible wind. Then the old water hose began to move across the yard like a snake until it lifted into the air. The hose was joined by several newspapers and a number of long-lost toys hiding under bushes or in rain gutters. Several dogs started barking, and suddenly one of the neighbors' cars lurched forward.

All around Max's house items took flight, carried on the invisible current of magic. Then the neighbor's car began to slowly lift from the ground, triggering the security alarm. Max's eyes shot open as he became aware of what he'd been doing. The magic slipped away and everything fell down, including a grateful Moki, who had been losing his grip on the bed. The car outside bounced as the front end fell to the driveway, blasting the horn on impact. Max looked out the window in time to see his neighbor run outside, nearly getting struck by a falling garden gnome. He drew the blinds and pressed himself against the wall, keeping out of sight, then waited a minute before chancing another look. His neighbor was standing by his car, gnome in hand, scratching his head.

Max put the *Codex* away and closed the nightstand drawer. It was far too dangerous to use magic in the Techrus—no matter how good it made him feel.

CHAPTER TWO

RUMBLE IN THE PIT

MAX SHOULD HAVE SEEN IT COMING. SINCE WHEN DID COACH MATTSON ask to see him during lunch? And why would he want to meet him in the wrestling pit (a small, smelly room in the basement where the wrestlers practiced) instead of his office? If Max had been thinking right, he would have realized something was wrong, but he'd been walking around in zombie mode after his magical episode the night before. When Sarah saw him, she asked if he was sick, so Max figured he probably looked as bad as he felt. But now things were about to get much, much worse.

He stood at the bottom of the long, narrow flight of stairs that led to the pit. There were people waiting for him, but none of them happened to be Coach Mattson. Instead, Ricky Reynolds and a few of his wrestling buddies were eyeing him like a rabbit in a lion's den. Max heard the door at the top of the stairs slam shut, trapping him inside.

"Hey, look who's here!" Ricky announced, a gleam in his eye. "I told you he'd come."

"Not too bright," another wrestler said as he cracked his knuckles.

"Okay, very funny," Max said, putting his hands up. "You got me."

Ricky approached Max and grabbed him by the shirt, pulling him into the room. "I don't think Max has ever been Captain Hooked. Have you, Max?" Max cast a worried look at the row of hooks on the brown brick wall. He'd never been Captain Hooked before, but he'd heard stories—the wrestlers would lift some poor kid up and catch his underwear on the wall hook. Then they'd just leave him there, hanging by his underwear and getting the world's worst wedgie. It was more than painful, and once you were Captain Hooked you couldn't do anything about it. And if Max knew Ricky and his friends, they'd leave him like that until somebody wandered down after school. The thought of it made Max's heart race as he tried to pull away.

"No!" he cried out. "Please don't!"

The half dozen or so other wrestlers surrounded Max, taking control of his arms and legs and easily dragging him toward the line of hooks.

"You ready?" Ricky mocked. "You can cry all you want down here 'cause nobody's gonna hear you."

"Please, just let me go," Max pleaded. Despite his panic he had to resist the urge to use magic. It was too powerful and too unpredictable, and somebody could really get hurt. All he could do was struggle against the stronger kids and try to delay the pain and humiliation as long as possible. He was quickly losing the battle, however, when a new voice filled the room.

"Put him down."

All eyes turned to see a boy standing at the bottom of the stairs. Max didn't recognize him, and he definitely wasn't the sort you'd soon forget. He was big—the biggest kid Max had ever seen—with massive arms and a broad chest and shoulders. But he didn't look like the guys who spent all their free time in the gym getting pumped up. The kid just looked strong, like he'd spent every waking hour on some farm throwing bales of hay around—or possibly cows. It was enough for everyone to stop what they were doing and take in the sight of the stranger filling the doorway.

"Who are you?" Ricky demanded. Ricky wasn't the kind of person to be intimidated by anyone.

"I'm the one who told you to put him down," the kid replied.

"This is none of your business," Ricky answered.

In response the big kid walked toward the group, stopping in front of Ricky so he was chest to chest and staring down at him. "It is. So put him down before I have to make you."

The other wrestlers obeyed, their survival instincts kicking in at the sight of the hulking boy. As soon as Max's feet hit the floor, he spun away and ran to the far wall.

"What's your name?" Ricky pressed. "You don't go to school here."

"I'm Wayne. Today's my first day."

"Okay, Wayne, maybe you don't know how things work around here," Ricky replied, standing his ground. "You're new, so I'll tell you. I'm the captain of the wrestling team, and what I say goes. In the pit, and anywhere else I happen to be. And right now I say we're going to Captain Hook this dweeb. Understand?"

Wayne turned to Max, ignoring Ricky. "Are you Max Spencer?" he asked.

"Yeah," Max managed to get out, his heart still racing. "Do I know you?"

"No. But your friend Dirk told me where I could find you," Wayne answered. Max should have figured if anyone was going to find the biggest kid in the world and send him to the rescue, it would be Dirk. He owed his best friend big time. Wayne returned his attention to Ricky and said, "We're leaving now."

"I don't think so," Ricky grunted, raising his hands and pushing the bigger kid in the chest. But Wayne hardly moved, and Ricky stumbled backward, his eyes wide in surprise. Then Wayne grabbed Ricky with as much effort as lifting a bag of potato chips (that was the first thing that came to Max's mind) and tossed him halfway across the room. Ricky landed on the mat with a heavy thud and managed an awkward roll as he tried to get back on his feet. The other wrestlers took a collective step backward, wanting nothing to do with it.

Wayne turned and pointed a massive hand at Ricky. "Stay down," he commanded. It was probably the hardest thing in the world for Ricky to do, and mixed in with the confusion that played across the Kraken's face there was a new emotion—fear. Ricky turned his head, remaining on his hands and knees.

"Come on," Max said to Wayne. Wayne turned and followed Max across the mat and out of the pit. They emerged into the gym and Max extended his hand. He wasn't sure how you thanked somebody for saving his life, but he figured a handshake was probably a good start.

"Thanks. You totally saved me down there," Max said. The big kid looked puzzled, but slowly reached out and clasped hands. Max could feel the power behind the big kid's grip.

"Max!" Sarah called out. She was with Dirk, and the two of them hurried over to where he and Wayne were standing. "Dirk told me about the note," she said, sounding relieved.

"Yeah," Dirk said. "You're lucky I found it. How did you not know that was a trap?"

"I guess it was pretty obvious," Max admitted. "I just haven't been myself lately."

Sarah turned to Wayne. "Hi, I don't think we've met. I'm Sarah."

If there was anyone in the world that Max looked

up to, it was Sarah. Not only was she way too smart and too pretty to be hanging around with a pair like him and Dirk, but she was tougher than both of them put together. And where Max was pudgy with glasses and a thick mop of black hair, and Dirk lean (okay, more like scrawny) with a short military-style haircut, Sarah was tall with auburn hair and dark, expressive eyes. Max had seen her both as the quiet smart girl sitting in the front of math class and the fearless warrior who used her judo to bring grown men to the ground. In short, Max was in awe of her, and counted himself lucky to be her friend.

"That's Wayne," Dirk said, confirming the fact that he'd had something to do with the big kid's appearance in the wrestling pit.

"Good to meet you," Wayne replied.

"I guess you got to Max in time," Dirk said, looking his friend over. "No damage done?"

"Just my pride."

"Yeah, I bet." Dirk added. "Good thing I saw Wayne. I figured, here's the biggest kid I've ever seen—I'm going to be his friend. And then my new friend will rescue my old friend. That's what having high charisma does for you."

Sarah rolled her eyes in response. "So what's your story, Wayne? Where did you move here from?"

"Oh, well I just moved from that small room to here," he answered. There was a pause, and then Max and his friends starting laughing.

"Yep, you're going to fit in just right," Dirk added. "Hey, you should come to lunch with us."

"I am hungry," Wayne admitted.

"Then lunch is on me," Max said. "My way of saying thanks."

Max and his friends watched as Wayne not only ate a lunch tray full of food but finished Sarah's leftovers as well. "So, you never said where you were from," Sarah remarked, watching as Wayne dunked the fries in ketchup and wolfed them down.

"You gotta respect a man who can eat like that," Dirk said. "Unlike Max—he's dainty."

"Very funny," Max shot back. "How many times have I saved your skinny hide now?"

"A few," Dirk said with a nod, settling into his chair. Wayne swallowed before answering Sarah.

"Where I'm from? Well, it's a little complicated, and

I wanted to make sure you were the right people before I said anything. But you are, aren't you? You're the three who brought down the Wizard's Tower."

Max shared a surprised look with his friends—how could he possibly know *that*?

"It's okay," Wayne continued, mopping up the last of the ketchup. "I know it's something that isn't talked about here. I mean, everyone in the Magrus knows about the Techrus. But for some reason people here don't know about us."

"Or the Shadrus," Dirk added. They had all spent time in the magical Magrus, but the Shadow realm was largely a mystery.

"Dirk," Sarah cautioned, "I'm not sure we should be talking about this."

Wayne continued, "They say you left before all the uproar that followed the defeat of Rezormoor Dreadbringer."

"We did," Dirk confirmed. "Although I thought we should hang around and bask in our hero-ness for a while. Pose for statues and such."

"What happened?" Max asked. "After."

"The wizards were suddenly without a leader, and the

Tower was in ruins," Wayne continued. "Word spread quickly about the boy who could read the book and his companions. The rulers of the Seven Kingdoms were more than a little nervous, of course. They met in a great council where the dwarf king and the king of Mor Luin shared their stories about meeting you."

Max glanced around the lunchroom, but nobody seemed particularly interested in what they were talking about. If anything, it probably sounded like they were discussing an online game or something. "How did you find us?" he asked.

"You have many friends in the Magrus," Wayne continued. "Unicorns, dragons, and an elf who drives a magical coach."

"Sumyl," Dirk said with a smile. "She's cool."

Wayne nodded. "I was sent by those who seek your return. All the realm knows what you've done for us." He put his food down and turned to Max. "You're the keeper of the *Codex of Infinite Knowability*. We believe that you and the *Codex* belong in the Magrus. The Tower would come together if you were to return and rebuild it. And the kings of the Seven Kingdoms desire to have you as an ally."

"So you've come to take us back?" Dirk asked.

"Only if you want to," Wayne replied. "I'm here to watch over Max and invite him and his friends to return." Wayne turned to Dirk. "When you asked me to help, I knew it was more than a coincidence."

"Dude!" Dirk exclaimed to Max. "You have your own *tank* now. That's awesome! He's like your bodyguard and stuff."

"But you're only a kid," Sarah said to Wayne. "No offense, but why send you?"

"We know very little about you," Wayne replied. "The council thought it made sense to send one boy to talk to another. We're basically the same age."

Dirk laughed. "Maybe, but look at your arms. I wish I had guns like those."

Wayne looked at his arms. "Guns?"

"He didn't mean that literally," Sarah clarified.

Wayne nodded as if he understood. "I've always been big."

"So, to be clear, you're telling us to leave our homes and travel all the way back to the Magrus?" Sarah asked.

"I carry something that can open a doorway between the two realms," Wayne replied. "It's called the Shadric

Portal, and it was crafted by the Wizard's Tower long ago. In fact, it was created by Maximilian Sporazo. There is no need for a long journey—if you choose to return, Max will be able to open the portal and simply walk through."

"Awesome," Dirk said, to nobody's surprise.

"Dwight the dwarf is here as well, is that right?" Wayne added.

Max nodded. "Yeah."

"Ask him about the Shadric Portal and what's required to carry it," Wayne said. "I think it will mean more coming from him." He pushed himself up from the table. "Now I'm supposed to meet a man about something called *football*."

"Yeah, I bet the coach is anxious to talk to you," Max replied. "Thanks, Wayne. I guess you've given us a lot to think about."

"Anytime," Wayne replied with a nod. He turned and walked out of the lunchroom, getting more than a few looks from the other students.

"Okay," Max said after a moment. "Didn't see that one coming."

"We're all like heroes and junk," Dirk said. "I bet someone's carving a statue of me right now."

"In your dreams," Sarah replied. "So what do you guys think?"

"Being in the Magrus was awesome," Dirk said. "But if comics have taught me anything, it's that heroes just don't get up and go where they want."

"Life isn't a comic book," Max replied. "If it was, Ricky wouldn't still be bullying me—not after everything we've been through." Max had hoped that Ricky had changed after their battle in the Tower. And for a while it seemed as if he had—but once they were home he returned to his old ways.

"Maybe," Dirk answered. "But then he'd just find somebody else."

"So what about this Shadric Portal thing?" Sarah asked. "Do you think we should talk to Dwight about it?"

"Yeah, at the very least," Max answered. Dwight was the resident expert on all things otherworldly.

Sarah gathered her lunch tray as the class bell began to ring. "This is the second invitation you've gotten today, Max," she said. "The wrestling pit, and now the Magrus. Maybe you should remember what happens when you go somewhere without thinking it through."

"Not everything's a trap," Dirk answered. "I, for one, like surprises."

Sarah punched him in the shoulder. "Surprise," she said with a grin. "Happy now?"

Dirk frowned, rubbing his shoulder. "No."

But Max's thoughts remained on Dwight. He was anxious for school to end so he could head to the Dragon's Den and find out more about the so-called Shadric Portal. Then he realized that for the first time in a long time, he actually felt hopeful. He wondered if that was a good sign or not.

ON PORTAL POTTIES

⁜

VISITORS TO THE MAGRUS SHOULD BE aware of the various customs and options available when needing to use bathroom facilities. For example, while learning a local dialect can be fun, never ask an ogre where the bathroom is in their native tongue (it's only slightly different from a marriage proposal, and getting the two mixed up can lead to unwanted consequences). The best option is to find one of the Portal Potties, spread throughout the kingdom and voted "Invention of the Year" in 214. Unlike the porta-potties found in the Techrus, Portal Potties are imbued with magic so that their contents are whisked away to another realm without fuss or bother. Exactly where said contents are transported to is not known (some suggest Idaho).

✛✛✛

CHAPTER THREE

THE DRAGON'S DEN

EVERY SMALL TOWN NEEDS A SHOP LIKE THE DRAGON'S DEN. FILLED WITH comic books, games, paintable miniatures, dice, and used sci-fi and fantasy paperbacks, it was a refuge for those who didn't skateboard or play sports or who just thought the ordinary world could do with some spicing up. It was also holy ground for the not-so-popular kids—a sanctuary against jocks, bullies, the mean-spirited, and those with more brawn than brain. Nobody judged you at the Dragon's Den.

The building that housed the Dragon's Den was part of "historic" downtown, which Max had never understood because there wasn't a newer downtown to really compare it to. It was made of red brick, with white columns out front and a metal overhang that served to keep the sidewalk dry when it rained. The shop was part of a string of old buildings that ran along Main Street, nestled between the Hot Buns bakery and the Madison Pharmacy (which was a good next stop if loading up on hot buns). The Dragon's Den had been remodeled recently, given a fresh coat of paint as well as a new door that actually acted as if it wanted to be opened. Pristine panes of glass had replaced the previous ones (more than one of which had had duct tape covering long cracks), and the faded sign had been updated with one that lit up. The place actually looked respectable now—the kind of shop a mom might drop her kids off at without worrying about roving bands of hooligans or insect infestations.

Max pushed his way past the front door with Dirk and Sarah in tow. He had a sudden flashback to the rainy afternoon when the three of them had brought the *Codex* in for the very first time.

"I'm having déjà vu," Sarah said as they entered the shop, thinking similar thoughts to Max's.

Dirk smiled. "Yeah, that was awesome."

Sarah shook her head. "What *don't* you think is awesome?"

"Homework."

Max ignored his friends and walked to the counter, where Dwight was sitting on his stool and reading a magazine. He'd gone back to wearing his beard nicely trimmed (black like his hair) and was dressed in a white button-up shirt and red suspenders.

"Dude, you look like an elf!" Dirk exclaimed. Dwight glowered and put the magazine down.

"Whatever you want, just turn around," Dwight said, motioning toward the door. "I see the three of you together and I know there's trouble." Dwight was mostly looking at Sarah when he spoke—she might have been friends with Dirk and Max, but she definitely wasn't the type of person who showed up at the Dragon's Den looking for new twenty-sided die.

"Pleasant as ever," Sarah replied sarcastically.

"Hey, Dwight," Max said as they reached the counter.

"Hello there, Mr. Spencer," Dwight replied. "Or should I say Mr. Sporazo?" Max still wasn't exactly comfortable with the idea that he was Maximilian Sporazo's son, which was probably the reason Dwight brought it up. "So if I can't persuade you to leave, just how can I help you?"

"We had a very interesting encounter at school," Sarah replied.

Dwight raised an eyebrow.

"We met a kid named Wayne," Dirk jumped in, "and he's from the Magrus."

"Really . . . and how do you know that?"

"That's what he told us," Max replied. He went on to recount the events of the day.

Dwight shook his head as he took it all in. "I assumed someone might approach you at some point," he said. "We defeated Rezormoor Dreadbringer after all. That's going to leave an impression. Plus, the real danger is still out there."

"The Maelshadow," Dirk said, turning to Max. "Weird to think that there's this ultrapowerful dark lord still after you."

"Yeah, thanks for reminding me."

"Maybe we were naive to think that once we made it home, everything would be fine," Sarah said. She had always been the logical one, and the idea of magic and monsters wasn't easy for her to wrap her brain around. But she wasn't afraid to follow the facts, no matter where they led. And if that meant that otherworldly monsters were hunting them, she'd be the first to admit it.

"He mentioned you, too," Max said to Dwight. "He said we should ask you about the Shadric Portal."

Dwight blinked several times before responding. "He said what? The Shadric Portal? Are you sure?"

Dirk tapped the side of his head. "Yep. I stored the name away as possible booty."

Dwight slid off his stool and walked toward his back room. "Stay there. I need to find something."

Just then the bell jingled and a small group entered the Dragon's Den. Max recognized Melvin Jenkins at once, followed by Megan and Sydney, two sisters who were part of Melvin's LARPing club. Megan was in Max's grade, big-boned with dark hair and glasses. She was also one of the few people who could compete with Sarah for school valedictorian. Sydney was a year younger and a grade below, with blond hair framing a perpetual smile.

"Hi, Max!" Sydney exclaimed. She practically pulled her sister across the room until they reached Max and his friends.

"Oh, uh, hi, Sydney," Max replied with a cough. He pushed his glasses up and looked away awkwardly. Dirk and Sarah shared a glance.

"Are you going to go LARPing with us?" Sydney continued, beaming. "Oh, that would be so much fun! You totally could if you wanted to."

"It takes a certain amount of commitment," Melvin added. "It's not really for *casual* gamers."

"Who you calling a casual gamer?" Dirk shot back.

"He didn't mean it like that," Megan said, ever the peacemaker. When she played the live campaigns, she was always a priestess healer. "There's just a lot of preparation required, like building weapons and armor."

Sarah frowned, confused.

"I know you—you're Sarah Jepson," Melvin said with a bow. He was thin with dishwater-brown hair and a haircut that looked like his mom owned a set of clippers she hadn't quite mastered yet. And while he wasn't as tall or as fast as Dirk, he was head of the chess club, played in band, and would pick dressing up as an elf and shooting plastic arrows over online gaming any day of the week. "You're the girl who wasted the Kraken last year."

Sarah offered a forced smile—no matter what she did, she'd never get to live that one down. "So you guys dress up and stuff?"

"Totally," Sydney replied. "It's way super awesome."

Melvin leaned on the counter and did his best cool-kid impression. "It's hard to describe the rush, especially if you've never felt the thrill of battle before."

Max slapped his hand over Dirk's mouth before he could answer. They'd all seen their share of real battles. "We mostly play online," he said.

"What's your character's name?" Sydney asked. "You could friend me and then we could campaign together. I mean, I'd have to get the game and get permission from my parents to go online and learn how to play it and everything, but I totally would."

"Uh . . . ," Max said, loosening his shirt from around his neck—suddenly it felt awfully tight.

"Anyway, we really don't have time for idle chitchat," Melvin said. "We just stopped by on our way to the park. We're going to be fighting a troll war party."

"Trolls?" Sarah asked.

"Part of the fun of LARPing is dressing up like monsters," Megan answered. "Today a band of humans and elves will fight a bridge battle against a gang of trolls."

"Are you sure you don't want to come, Max?"

Sydney asked. "You could even be a troll if you wanted."

Max could feel everyone's eyes on him. "Thanks, Sydney. Maybe another time."

"No problem," she said, her enthusiasm unfazed.

Dwight reappeared with a large leather-bound book in his hand.

"Hey, Dwight," Melvin called out. "We just stopped by to check on those boots I ordered."

"Fairy boots?" Dirk asked. "With bells and stuff?"

Melvin frowned. "Elf boots."

"Haven't seen 'em yet," Dwight replied, dropping the book on the counter. "Probably be here Monday if you want to try then."

"Sounds good," Melvin said, leading the two sisters away. He paused at the door and turned to Sarah. "You have an invitation to play with us anytime, Sarah. I would put you under my personal protection."

"Oh, okay. Thanks," Sarah replied, not sure how to respond to the offer.

Dwight gave them a wave as they left.

"I don't remember you ever waving at us like that," Dirk said.

Dwight climbed on his stool. "Yeah, well, they

actually spend money once in a while." He began flip-ping through the pages and the group leaned in to get a closer look—the book was written in a language they didn't recognize.

"That's not from the Techrus, is it?" Max asked.

Dwight kept turning pages. "Nope. It's the *Dwarven Book of Lore.*"

"Sweet," Dirk exclaimed. "I mean, probably."

"Okay, let's see here," Dwight said, turning a final page and moving down the text with his finger. "There's the Sandals of Stink—that's a cursed item—the serpent's escutcheon—been there and done that—the Seer Stone of Olfaction—you see and *smell* your future—oh, here we go . . . the Shadric Portal. Says here it was constructed by Maximilian Sporazo after he became the regent of the Tower. He used it as a way of slipping out of bor-ing meetings. Later, he discovered that it could also be used to open a doorway between realms by way of the umbraverse."

"Umbraverse?" Sarah asked.

"Yeah," Dwight answered, "there's the universe and the umbraverse. The umbraverse is a place where wizards and other fools go because the rules that should apply to things don't apply there. Obsikar drew on it to send us back in time."

"Using something like that seems risky," Sarah continued.

Dwight returned to the book. "Yep. And it goes on to say that Sporazo used Shadric magic to make it work—definitely a mixed bag with that—and decided to wrap it in two protective spells to keep it from falling into the wrong hands."

"Like a curse?" Dirk asked.

"Kind of. The first spell makes it so that only one of his blood can remove it from the Tower." Dwight looked up at Max. "How do you suppose this kid ended up with it?"

Max shrugged. "Don't ask me, I never touched any portals."

"Maybe you did accidentally?" Dirk suggested. "You didn't use any Portal Potties, did you?"

"I don't think so."

"If Max didn't remove the portal from the Tower, who did?" Sarah asked.

Dwight frowned. "Good question." He turned his attention back to the book. "The other protective spell is kind of interesting . . . it says only one who is *mostly good* can handle it."

"So that means Wayne's a good guy," Dirk announced.

"Just because you have good intentions doesn't mean things can't go wrong," Sarah noted.

"Yeah, just take a look at the bard character class," Dirk agreed. "Sure, they were supposed to be all versed in lore and even have special arcane powers and stuff, but having to sing songs while the rest of the party fights is lame, no matter how you slice it."

"You said only one who is good could handle it," Max said, wanting to get the conversation back on track. "Does that mean use it too?"

Dwight glowered. "I don't know. Portals are like doors—they're often much harder to open than to close. My guess is it takes a good deal of magic to get something like the Shadric Portal open."

"And not just that," Dirk added, "but from a wizard who was good—otherwise they couldn't even touch it."

"It does seem like an effective series of locks," Sarah said.

Max thought it over. "So what does it all mean?"

Dwight closed the book. "It means we need to be very careful."

"I'm not sure this is a group that knows *how* to be careful," a familiar voice called out. Puff the fluff dragon entered the room with a yawn. He'd taken a job as "the world's ugliest watchdog" and had moved in with Dwight some months ago. Max was actually glad to see the dwarf and former dragon getting along, since the two races had a long history of enmity between them.

"Hey, Puff!" Sarah exclaimed. "You look good."

"Thanks," Puff said. Dwight had hired a dog groomer to weave all of his fluff into dreadlocks, passing him off as a puli. Max had had to look the breed up on the Internet, and he was surprised at how well Puff managed to pull it off.

"Just having the Shadric Portal around you is dangerous," Puff continued. As a former dragon he was well versed in things of a magical nature. "It's honed to your blood. It's possible the Maelshadow is using it to find you."

"I think you should tell Wayne to return to the Magrus," Sarah said. "It's not like we're going to consider his offer to go back." Max wasn't so sure about that, however. He'd been spending a lot of time thinking about the Magrus lately.

Puff nodded. "You should find this Wayne and convince him to go home—the sooner the better."

"He mentioned something about football," Max said. "I bet he's meeting with the coach or practicing with the team or something."

"Sarah's right," Dwight said. "Decline his offer and have him return to the Magrus. We all know how your blood gets us into trouble, and I don't like the thought of a Shadric artifact so close."

"If you do that, we can't go back," Dirk protested. "I'll never get to see my statue."

Sarah lifted a brow, very curious about the statue Dirk was imagining.

"There's always the long way back," Dwight replied. "If there's a need to ever return to the Magrus, we can."

"Fine," Dirk sighed, giving in. "Let's go find him, then—"

"No!" Max interrupted, the word flying from his mouth before he had time to think. Sarah gave him an inquisitive look.

"You okay?" she asked.

"Yeah, sorry. Just sort of a stressful day." An idea had taken root, but Max couldn't share it with the others. "Look, I'm going to talk to Wayne, only by myself. I owe him that much."

Dirk didn't look too happy about it, but he nodded. "Okay, Max."

"I'll see you online later," Max added. "Really, don't worry." He grabbed his things and headed out the door.

"That was weird," Sarah said after he'd left.

"Yeah, tell me about it," Dirk agreed.

Max crossed Main Street and headed back to school, noticing storm clouds building on the horizon. They seemed to reflect the chaotic feelings stirring inside him. *What do you do when home doesn't feel like home anymore? What does family mean when you find out you're not really who you thought you were? And what if what you want means leaving all your friends behind?* Max kept thinking about the portal and the knowledge that Sporazo—no, his father—had created it. It was part of his inheritance, left to him over the ages. Max somehow knew that he'd be able to open the portal and get away from Madison.

But leaving without saying good-bye . . . could he even do it?

Yes. Because saying good-bye is too hard.

Max rounded the corner and Parkside Middle School came into view. By the time he'd reached the front doors, he'd made up his mind.

CHAPTER FOUR

STORM DOORS

WAYNE WAS IN THE LOCKER ROOM LOOKING FOR SHOULDER PADS BIG enough to fit him (the coach had said he'd find him a pair even if he had to go to the NFL). If the big kid was surprised to see Max, he didn't show it.

"Can we talk?" Max asked, wanting to get right to the point.

Wayne nodded as he put the undersized shoulder pads down. The sound of muffled voices and a locker closing could be heard nearby. "Somewhere more private?" Wayne suggested.

"Yeah, good idea."

Wayne grabbed a leather satchel and he and Max left the locker room (besides being noisy it smelled like wet feet). They eventually found a quiet spot on the gym bleachers. Max couldn't help but notice the rope stretching down from the ceiling—even just hanging there it seemed to be mocking him.

"Is this about my offer?" Wayne asked.

"Yeah. It's practically all I've been thinking about."

"Did your dwarf friend help?"

"He told us about the Shadric Portal and the fact that you had to be good to handle it."

Wayne reached into his shirt and removed an amulet that hung around his neck. It was silver and had a diamond-shaped stone that was misty gray in color. "The Amulet of Alignment," he said, holding it up for Max to see. "It turns color based on your deeds: white for good and black for evil."

Max squinted at the small stone set in silver. "It's kind of grayish."

"Most people aren't black or white," Wayne said with a shrug. "I try to do the right thing. Anyway, this was a gift to help remind me of that."

"Cool," Max said, watching as Wayne slipped the amulet back under his shirt. He looked at the rope, remembering his humiliation from earlier—it represented everything that was wrong in his world. Here he was a loser. In the Magrus he was something special.

Overhead, the patter of rain began to hit the old school's roof.

"If I go, can I come back?" Max asked after a moment.

"Of course."

"I can just step back and forth anytime I want?"

"I don't see why not."

Max scratched his head. "And they really want me to come back? To rebuild the Tower?"

"They do," Wayne answered. "You're an important and powerful person."

Max hesitated—it was one thing to think he'd made up his mind, but another to actually say it out loud. He took a breath. "Yes—I want to go back."

"Aha!" came Dirk's voice from behind the bleachers. He stepped out to face them, pointing at Max with an accusatory finger. "Send me away while you go and find Wayne by yourself, huh? And you really thought I was going to fall for that? I knew you were up to something."

"You *followed* me?" Max did his best to sound outraged even though he knew Dirk was right.

"We both did," Sarah announced, stepping out to join Dirk.

Max suddenly had a lump in his throat that felt as big as a grapefruit. "Look, I didn't want to hurt anyone's feelings. I just didn't want to say anything."

"Yeah, well, obviously," Dirk replied, his hands on his hips.

"It's just that everything's different now," Max continued. "You don't know how it feels to have the kind of power I had in the Magrus. I stood before kings and their armies, and they listened to me. And then I come home and have to put up with people like Ricky Reynolds. They just won't leave me alone, even though I know I could reach out to the *Codex* and stop them. Even here in the Techrus where magic doesn't work right, I could do enough to make sure they never laid a hand on me or anyone like me again. But I . . . can't. And so I'm just tired of being the victim."

Sarah's expression softened. "Max, I'm so sorry."

"It used to be that I was a kid pretending to be a wizard," Max continued. "But now I'm a wizard pretending to be a kid. I was born in the Magrus; my father was the greatest arch-sorcerer who ever lived. Whatever I'm supposed to do with my life, it's going to be there— not here."

"What about us?" Dirk asked, his voice growing quiet. "You know, your friends?"

"Guys, it's not like I'm going and will never come back. I'll have the Shadric Portal, remember?" Max turned to Wayne, realizing he wasn't 100 percent sure on that point.

"It belongs to you," Wayne said. "Who else could even use it?"

"See?" Max continued. "I can step between the realms whenever I want. You guys can come and visit me whenever *you* want."

"What about school?" Sarah asked. "You can't just drop out."

"He can continue his studies at the Wizard's Tower," Wayne interjected. "I'm sure there's still a lot for him to learn."

Max nodded. "So when you think about it, it's not like I'm quitting school—I'm just switching schools. Don't you guys see? This is what I'm supposed to do."

"Even if it is," Sarah said, choosing her words carefully, "there are ways back to the Magrus that don't involve black magic. Messing around with something like the Shadric Portal shouldn't be taken lightly—you of all people should know that."

"Yeah," Dirk jumped in, "Send Wayne back to find Sumyl and her magic carriage. But for now, you need to listen to Sarah." Hearing Dirk argue that he should stop and think things over was like the Pillsbury Doughboy swearing off bread. But they did have a point. Then again, Max's own father had made the artifact, just like the *Codex of Infinite Knowability* resting in his backpack. Something had made Max take it from his nightstand— as if the magical book *knew* what was going to happen. Whether that was a good thing or not, Max wasn't sure.

"I'm sorry," Max said, rising from his seat. "I've actually been thinking about this for a long time—long before Wayne got here. This isn't my home anymore."

Sarah stepped up to him and put her hand on his arm. "Max, I'm asking you not to do this. I know things have been hard, but taking the easy way out—especially when it involves Shadric magic—isn't the answer. This is how people lose track of themselves—they take shortcuts. They forget that when it comes to the easy way, there's always a cost."

Wayne rose and pulled a black object out of his satchel. It was about the size of a small laptop computer and was shaped like an oval. It reminded Max of an empty picture frame, only it was a shimmering black and adorned with intricately carved skulls. The skulls made a design so that they were bound together by a twisted, thorny vine. Four blue gems were inlaid along the surface, and at the top a rune-covered door peeked through the twisting mass of skulls and vines. "This is what the arch-sorcerer Sporazo created," Wayne said, holding it in front of Max. "This is the Shadric Portal."

"Please, don't . . . ," Sarah warned, but Max wasn't listening. He took the ancient artifact in his hand and the blue stones immediately began to glow.

"Dude, skulls are not good!" Dirk warned. "But at least they're not *red*."

Suddenly the stones turned red, casting a crimson light over the portal's surface.

"It knows you," Wayne said.

Max rose and slowly walked to the center of the gym floor, the Shadric Portal humming in his hand. The others trailed behind him.

"Seriously, just put it down," Dirk said, his voice growing tense. "When have glowing red skulls ever been a good thing?"

"Max, listen to us," Sarah urged. "Don't open the portal."

But Max could feel the magic crawling up his arms like he was reaching into a warm bath. The humming sensation increased, filling his ears and drowning out the voices of his friends. The artifact grew even warmer, and the strange metallic frame started to soften and stretch. Max knew that magic was being employed, but it was as foreign a feeling as it was familiar. Whatever the Portal was, it was a part of him. And yet it was also alien and unknown.

Max began to pull the sides of the Shadric Portal apart, watching as the frame expanded, growing impossibly as it did so. He stretched his hands as far as he could, widening the portal to the size of a small door. Through it, reality seemed to bubble and grow dark. Max let go, somehow knowing that the portal wouldn't fall. He stepped back and watched as it hovered in the air. On the other side a strange world came into focus: The ground floated like great islands of ice over a swirling, chaotic storm. In the distance a structure rose, like an ancient temple thrust together when the world was new. Then the voice rolled through the door and exploded around them. It was deep and moved with the impending finality of an iceberg calving into the ocean. "It is done!" the voice roared, and there was no doubt who it belonged to.

"The Maelshadow!" Max cried out, letting go of the portal.

"Hurry, close it!" Sarah exclaimed. "Max! Do something!"

Max grabbed hold of the artifact again, this time pushing on it with all his might. The stones flickered, but grew a darker shade of red. The frame refused to budge.

"It's not working!" Max cried, not knowing what else to do. Suddenly a black fog poured from the open portal, reaching with handlike fingers as it crawled along the floor.

"Don't let it touch you!" Wayne shouted, stepping away.

The sound of thunder exploded around them as a lightning bolt tore through the ceiling of the old gymnasium. The blast sent Max and his friends tumbling as bits of tile and insulation fell with the rain. They scrambled to their feet, standing knee-deep in the sable fog flowing like a river from the mouth of the portal.

"It touched us," Dirk said, looking from the black fog back to Wayne. "It's not going to be good, is it?"

"No," Wayne answered.

Above them the storm raged as black and gray clouds bubbled to life; lightning danced between them, followed by a shrill screech as if the very sky was being torn apart. The wind and rain broke more pieces of the ceiling off, but this time the chunks of roof flew upward, joining a cyclone of flying debris. Max looked up through the rain and wind and saw, to his horror, a twisting tornado taking shape.

"Run!" Sarah yelled, pulling Max and dragging him toward the exit. Dirk quickly followed, and the three scrambled toward the door. Wayne hesitated, however, looking at the portal and then back at Max.

"Hurry, Wayne!" Max cried back to him. Wayne considered the mass of black swirling around him, then turned and ran after the others. The group sprinted down the stairwell, up to their waists now in the fog, before darting down a side hallway and to a set of double doors that led outside. They flew through, but were nearly swept off their feet by a gust of wind that hit with the force of a boxer's punch.

"Look!" Dirk cried. Above them the storm continued to rage, the clouds not only stretching *across* the sky, but also *down*. Madison was being walled in.

A shudder traveled down Max's spine as a nearby wall exploded. He felt chunks of brick pelt him along his back and side. As one, the group took off across the schoolyard, dodging debris and rain that moved like bullets in the ferocious winds. But there was something else going on—something more terrible than the storm. Max turned around in time to see the school *grow*. The rows of neatly packed red bricks broke apart as large gray stones erupted into place around them. Then the whole structure rose from the ground, the stones coming to the surface like the roots of an obnoxious weed pulled from the earth. The building twisted on itself, rising like a tower—and at its top, a tornado whipped about and stretched to connect with the dark clouds above.

The humming in Max's ears returned, and with it a new pain exploded in his head, causing him to stumble forward. The others stopped to help him as the black fog spilled from the former school's misshapen windows, pouring to the ground and surging like a wave. There was something in the fog—something that was dark and menacing and surged with the power of dark magic. Max could actually feel it. He looked at his friends, and they stared back at him, their faces flushed and eyes growing distant. The magic was affecting them—it was *changing* them!

Max reached out with his mind and found the *Codex* in his backpack. He'd long since committed the names of the Prime Spells to memory—spells so powerful that all other magic was drawn from them. He felt his own mind begin to drift, the spell slipping away. He was beginning to change too.

"Panoply!" he shouted, and the Prime Spell came roaring to him. It flowed through Max and his friends, pushing the black magic away and surrounding them in a kind of bubble. *Panoply—to cover and protect.* But using the *Codex* in the human realm took nearly all the strength Max had. He collapsed, barely able to hold the spell together. Wayne reached down and scooped him up in his arms.

"What's happening?" Sarah exclaimed. "Something was *inside* of me."

"Hurry, get us inside," Max said, his voice barely audible over the storm. "It's going to change things. It's going to change everything."

They put Max down in the back room of the Dragon's Den, where Dwight kept an extra cot. Max fought to keep hold of the spell he'd cast, pushing it outward as far as he could. He thought the protective bubble encircled the Dragon's Den, but it was hard to tell. He could feel it weaken the farther he stretched it. He concentrated on the building, willing the spell to leave his control and attach itself to the brick and mortar outside. He could feel the connection between the Prime Spell and the *Codex*— the magic would have to sustain itself. "Don't leave the building, no matter what," Max whispered. The Prime Spell had taken everything from him, and he felt his body shutting down. The others were gathered around him, watching with worried expressions, the sound of the storm muffled by the magic Max had put into place.

"Dude, what did you do?" Dirk asked.

"I opened the door," Max admitted. "He was waiting on the other side."

CHAPTER FIVE

A NEW WORLD

MAX WALKED INTO THE MAIN ROOM OF THE DRAGON'S DEN, RUBBING HIS eyes and trying to ignore the pounding in his head. He found Dwight standing by the counter and asked, "Do you have an aspirin or something?"

His friends had been pressed against the windows, and they turned at the sound of his voice. He'd lost track of time, and outside a kind of gray light pushed through the windows. He caught sight of the storm clouds in the distance, gripping the sky like a vise.

"Max, you're awake," Sarah said, her voice tight.

Dwight wandered off to find something for Max's headache as Puff padded to his side. "I'm glad you're okay," the fluff dragon said, looking up at him. "Whatever magic you used to protect us worked."

For the briefest of moments Max had hoped it had all been a bad dream. He knew better, of course. His nightmares usually involved being chased by vegetables. "Is everyone okay?" he managed to ask.

"Dude," Dirk replied, but then his voice trailed off. Max frowned—his friend wasn't usually at a loss for words. He walked toward the window as the memories from the day before fell into place: getting the portal from Wayne . . . opening the doorway to another world . . . the black fog . . . fighting against the magic that had tried to change him.

Max reached the window and stared outside in silence. Madison's Main Street was gone, and in its place a dirt path wound through brown weeds and dead grass. There were a number of tall black trees, with long branches that drooped to the ground and ran in tangles before rising again and growing into the next. Everywhere a gray haze hung in the air, and Max could barely make out the building where the town library used to stand. And beyond that were the beginnings of some kind of footbridge. He could hear the wind blowing through the window, carrying with it a kind of gurgling sound. Water, maybe . . . although it sounded more like hot cereal bubbling on a stovetop. Overhead the dark storm blanketed the sky, slowly churning as flashes of lightning danced across its surface. Everything had changed, and Madison looked more like an online game would than the town he'd grown up in.

Dwight brought Max a couple of pills and a glass of water, and he threw them back and drained the glass, not realizing how thirsty he'd been. "Thanks," Max said, handing the glass back to the dwarf. Dwight nodded and then motioned outside.

"The storm's messing with everything—no TV or Internet, and all the phones are down. Not even the blasted radio is getting through. Whole town's been cut off."

"What town?" Sarah asked, an uncharacteristic chill in her voice. "That's not Madison out there. Not anymore." Her words stung, and Max felt a sudden pang of guilt. It was his fault—all of it. And not in the way their first adventure had started—that had been an accident. *This* he'd done on purpose. It didn't matter that he'd had good intentions; he'd ignored his friends and opened the portal despite their warnings.

It took a second before Max realized something else

had changed. He rubbed his eyes and stared at Sarah—
she was dressed in leather armor. He'd seen her like that
before, but never in the Techrus. This time her armor
was black with gold trim, and had a leaflike pattern on
the front and shoulders. Beneath it she wore a mesh of
tiny woven rings, with a floor-length white cloak draped
around her shoulders. It nearly covered the sword hanging from the leather belt around her hips.

"Er," he began, "Why are you dressed like that?"

"Good of you to notice. We were kind of waiting for
you to tell us."

"Us . . . ?" Max began, then turned and saw the others.

"Yeah," Dirk said, stepping forward with a frown.
He wore a colorful tunic with large, quarter-sized
buttons. The tunic's sleeves were of the puffy might-
have-belonged-to-a-pirate variety, cut high so the
cuffs of an even puffier might-have-belonged-to-
a-pirate-masquerading-as-a-clown undershirt poked
out from the bottom. Purple tights—Max had to blink
several times to confirm—yes, Dirk was also wearing
purple tights that disappeared into knee-high and entirely
far too pointy boots. A thin belt was tied high around
Dirk's waist, and a red satchel hung from his shoulder.

And if that wasn't enough, he was also carrying a lute.

"Wow," Max said. He'd seen Dirk dressed as an elf, but this was something else entirely. "Did you know you're carrying a lute?"

"Duh," the lute replied, and Max recognized the voice.

"Glenn?"

"How many other talking objects do you know?"

Max scratched his head—it *sounded* like Glenn, the Legendary Dagger of Motivation, but the Glenn he knew probably didn't have banjos as relatives.

"Yeah, tell me about it," Dirk said with a frown. "Glenn is now this stupid musical instrument thing."

"A lute," Sarah said.

"Yeah, a *lute*," Dirk repeated, not liking the sound of the word in his mouth.

"Well, at least I'm not dressed like a walking parrot," the lute replied. Max frowned—Glenn was usually more encouraging.

"What's going on exactly?" Max asked.

"Dude, I'll tell you what's going on: I'm a stinking *bard*!" And now that Dirk said it, Max could see that his best friend did look very much like the musical minstrels they'd seen (but never ever played) as online charac-ters. "I keep wanting to sing—seriously, it's driving me crazy."

Max looked at Dwight—he seemed his same old self. The dwarf shrugged. "What can I say, still handsome as ever."

"And I haven't changed either," Puff said from his spot near the counter.

"Best guess is that it has something to do with that black fog," Sarah announced. "I think it's the reason the town has been transformed."

"Yeah, look at me," Dirk complained. "I'm wearing *tights*. Do you know how long it takes to undress just so I can go to the bathroom?"

"But I still feel the same," Max said.

"I don't think you've looked close enough," Glenn replied.

Max glowered, looking down at his clothes. Unless he'd somehow slipped into someone's nightshirt, things had gone horribly wrong. He ran over to the mirror on the far wall as the others trailed behind him. Max saw his reflection staring back at him; he was dressed in a long blue robe with a sparkling sash tied around his waist. *A sash? Real men don't wear sashes!* Slung over Max's shoulder was a white leather satchel, and he could feel the weight of the *Codex of Infinite Knowability* inside. But what really shocked him was his hair—usually a thick mop of brown, it had turned nearly white and grown to reach his shoulders. "I'm old! And a hippie!"

"Wizards don't age like normal people," Dirk announced, walking over and joining Max's reflection in the mirror. They looked like two characters out of their role-playing games.

"Is it Halloween already?" Glenn asked. "Let me guess your costumes: nursing-home grandpa and deranged clown. You two will be getting lots of candy for sure."

"Dirk says I'm a paladin," Sarah added, ignoring Glenn. "Whatever that is."

Dirk nodded in agreement. "Only paladins can pull off wearing white cloaks."

"But how?" Max asked. "And why?"

"We were in the fog," Sarah answered. "We all felt it doing something to us, but then you stopped it."

Max moved away from the mirror, not liking the whole white-hair-and-blue-robes look. "I felt something magical start to take hold. It felt dark and old. And powerful. The only thing I could think of was to grab a Prime Spell. I guess it was strong enough to work."

"And good thing you did," Puff said. "I've heard of such magic before. It would have changed you into something monstrous. Now it's just changed you into something . . . *else*. Although Dirk could still be considered monstrous, I suppose."

"Wait, where's Wayne?" Max asked, suddenly remembering him.

"He's upstairs sleeping," Dwight said, "with the others."

"Others . . . ?"

"Melvin, Megan, and Sydney," Sarah answered. "They came back after the storm started."

"Then they came under the protection of the spell," Max said. "Before I passed out, I was able to attach it to the building."

"I think I know what's going on," Dwight said. He retrieved his *Dwarven Book of Lore* from under the counter and dropped it with a thud. After climbing onto his stool, he began flipping the pages. The others gathered around. "Here it is—the Cataclysm."

"Things that start with 'cat' are not to be trusted,"

Dirk informed them. "Cataracts, catapults, catsup, catalogs—"

"Finished?" Dwight asked. "Or do you have more prattling to do?"

Dirk frowned but remained quiet.

"The Cataclysm is what happens when a realm is touched by the umbraverse," Dwight continued. "It has the power to change everything in its path, drawing upon whatever magic caused the doorway to open."

"And that would be the Shadric Portal," Sarah said, doing her best not to look at Max. "Black magic."

Max scratched his head. "So you're saying that the black fog was the umbraverse taking over our world?"

"Not so much taking over but transforming. Turning the Techrus into a shadow realm, like the Shadrus."

"If this is indeed a Cataclysm, the storm outside will continue to grow," Puff warned. "It will slowly build until it has the strength to surge outward again, transforming more of the Techrus each time. Eventually it will grow large enough to encircle the world."

Dwight scratched at his beard. "This is the doing of the Maelshadow, I'm sure of it."

"What does that mean for the rest of the town?" Sarah asked. "What about our families?"

"The Cataclysm will change them, too," Dwight answered. "If not for Max's spell you would have suffered the same fate. And Puff is right—the transformation still happened, only it was robbed of its dark magic."

"So we became what . . . ? Characters?" Sarah asked. "I don't get it."

"Me either," Dwight admitted. "Maybe you became what the *Codex* wanted you to become. Or maybe you became whatever it was that Max was dreaming about while he slept. Magic is tricky business."

"Dude!" Dirk exclaimed, swatting Max on the back of the head. "Why are you dreaming about me being a bard?"

"I didn't!" Max said. "Did I?"

"Guys, we have to figure out what happened to our families," Sarah said, trying to get them back on track. She turned to Max. "And Max, you have to find a way to fix all of this." She didn't need to say *because it's your fault.* He had no idea how to stop a Cataclysm or what it meant to deal with Shadric magic, the umbraverse, or the Maelshadow. He just knew he had to do something about it.

"Sarah, everyone, look . . . I'm sorry," Max said. "I didn't listen to you, and I should have." No one said anything, but Max knew his friends would forgive him eventually. Unless something terrible had happened to their families— he knew Sarah would never get over it, and it would be the end of their friendship. The thought of *that* was almost too much to bear. "Is there anything else we know about this Cataclysm?" Max asked, his voice wavering a little.

"I'll see what I can find out," Dwight said. "I have a few more books in the back."

"I remember something, actually," Puff said, searching his dragon-aged memories. "First the Cataclysm changes the *substance* of a thing. Later it changes its *essence*. Remember the one is not necessarily the other."

Dirk scratched his head. "Huh?"

Sarah stepped in. "I think Puff is suggesting the changes aren't permanent—at least not yet. Actually it's a notion that goes back to Aristotle."

"Yeah, I was just going to say that," Dirk said.

"You wouldn't know Aristotle if the Lyceum fell on your head," Glenn replied.

Dirk frowned. "That's not true—it's like my favorite band."

"Maybe we should be getting ready to leave?" Max interjected.

"Good idea," Dirk replied, reaching for Glenn. "And I think a packing-stuff-up montage song would do nicely here—"

"No!" everyone shouted at once.

It wasn't long before the others woke. Like Max and his friends, they'd been changed by the storm, but Max's spell had altered the course of their transformation. Megan had become a priestess healer in a long white robe, while Sydney was a pixie about the size of Dwight, and with wings! Melvin had become an elf with a quiver of arrows and a longbow (Dirk immediately felt a wave of elf envy at the sight of him). Wayne had appeared dressed in chain mail and carrying a heavy shield and axe.

They gathered at the front of the store and Max explained everything that had happened, which included going into his own history as well. They listened as he talked about the robot-fueled future that featured tele-vised hunts and arena-style combat, the meeting with the dragon king Obsikar, and the perilous journey back in time to the Magrus to return the *Codex* to the Wizard's

Tower and defeat Rezormoor Dreadbringer. Dirk interjected his own commentary along the way, including his bringing an online character to life and the fact that Princess the Unicorn and her wizard had decided to stay in Madison (and she totally had a crush on him). The others took it all in without any real problems, which must have come from years of LARP training.

"All our adventures were simply preparations for this day," Melvin announced. "It will be my honor to lead us into battle to defeat the one you call the Maelshadow."

"Hold on there," Dirk exclaimed. "Nobody is leading anybody around here but Max."

"Well, I think we should put it to a vote," Melvin suggested.

"I vote for Max!" Sydney exclaimed. She continued to hold her hand in the air as if to remove any doubt. The mood grew tense as the others were unsure what to do.

"If I may, this is a battle of *magic*," Megan said, turning to Melvin. "I believe it's best if our wizard leads the party." Max took note of how Megan made it about magic and not about who was actually the best leader. Healers were full of wisdom, he supposed.

"Yay!" Sydney said, clapping her hands together so

fast that her wings jiggled above her head. "Max is our leader!"

Sarah had to force herself not to roll her eyes.

"So here's what I know," Max said. "I think the Maelshadow was waiting for me and didn't want the portal closed."

"Then we should do the opposite," Melvin added. "We should definitely close the portal."

"You think?" Dirk replied. "We tried that already and it didn't work."

"True," Max admitted. "But we still have the *Codex* and time to put a plan together. We were caught by surprise, and that's not going to happen again."

"Then what are our side quests?" Melvin asked. "Should we explore what remains of the town? I have a spiral notebook full of graph paper—I could draw a map."

"What's important here," Sarah said, jumping in, "is that our families were likely caught in the storm. We need to find them and figure out a way to reverse what happened."

Max nodded. "The portal opened at the school, but it's not really a school anymore. It's kind of something else."

"And we're going with you," Dwight announced, motioning to Puff. "I've got more adventuring experience than the lot of you put together."

"And me," Wayne added. "Just tell me what you want me to do."

"You're our tank," Dirk replied. "You keep the bad things off of us by being so intimidating they naturally flock to you."

"Wait, how does *that* work?" Sarah asked. "You think monsters *want* to run toward the biggest and scariest-looking warrior in the party? If I was a monster I wouldn't do that at all."

Dirk shook his head. "It's game logic—it's how these things work."

Wayne folded his massive arms in front of him, not really understanding the game logic business. "I'll do my best to protect you," he announced.

"Then let's do a last check and get going," Megan suggested. The group moved off to make their final preparations (which included a long bathroom run for Dirk as he fought with his tights).

Max gave Puff a friendly pat (only he was allowed to do that) and walked back to the window. The wind had died down significantly, but in the distance the storm continued to rage. He could make out a single black tower rising in the distance. From its rooftop a tornado twisted and turned, reaching upward until it connected with the storm clouds above. Strange blue lightning coiled around the tornado, and even at such a distance Max could feel the distinctive chill of magic. But where most magic was warm, this felt cold. He wondered at the kind of creature that could summon such power. He'd managed to defeat an evil sorcerer once before, but that was in the Magrus, where the *Codex* was stronger. Things would be much harder here.

"Ready?" Sarah asked a few moments later. The others had lined up behind her, looking very much like an adventuring party from one of their games. Dwight had donned his armor and Dirk had found one of those spiked dog collars worn by junkyard guard dogs and fastened it around Puff's neck. Nobody had the heart to tell the fluff dragon it made him look like a punk rocker poodle.

"Ready," Max answered Sarah, trying to sound braver than he felt. The others nodded in silence. Max swallowed and opened the door.

CHAPTER SIX

ALL HAIL THE BARD

THEY WALKED OUT TO WHERE THE MIDDLE OF MAIN STREET USED TO BE and looked back at the Dragon's Den. It was the only original building standing from the row of shops. Where the bakery had been there was now a large fire pit filled with charred bones, and the pharmacy had become a kind of dilapidated old windmill.

"I can't believe it," Sarah said, looking around. She had experienced being transported to the far future and had seen her town in ruins before. But this was different.

Melvin strode up to her, his face stern as he clutched his elf bow. "It is a dark evil that has transformed our once-proud hamlet," he announced as if reading from the start of one of his role-playing campaigns. "But take heart, fair maiden, for the light shall win the day."

"Yuck," Dirk said in response, his lute in his hand. "You're not going to talk like that the whole time, are you?"

"Mayhaps," Melvin replied.

Dirk frowned, then motioned to the tall, misshapen tower in the distance. "Everyone see the tornado tower over there? That's a message—when you can put a tornado on your roof, you're letting the world know that you're not someone to be messed with."

Puff shuddered. "I feel the influence of the Shadrus all around us."

Dwight suddenly let out a deep breath. He looked himself over, then seemed to relax. "I was afraid the magic might transform me."

"I think that part has passed," Max said, looking at the solid wall of clouds in the distance. "It's the storm that's doing the changing now."

"And it's expanding," Puff said. "Inch by inch, until the world is consumed."

"Then we must do no less than to save the world," Melvin announced.

Dirk cleared his throat. "You mean, save the world *again*. Oh wait, you weren't with us when we did all that.

My mistake. I don't want to take away any of your noob excitement." Melvin shot him an annoyed look.

"Let's head toward my house," Max said. "It's close and we can see what's happened to everyone." In addition to his mom, Max wondered about Princess and Magar. Princess had decided Madison High School was to her liking and had stayed. Magar had tagged along and been hired as a chemistry teacher. If anything was powerful enough to fight off the storm, it was Princess and her wizard. But then again, if the storm had changed her into something else . . .

"A quick detour to your house and then to what's left of the school," Dwight said. "That's where we'll find the portal."

The group agreed and they began walking in the direction of Max's old neighborhood, passing the remains of the strange black trees that reminded Max of power lines. Not long after they found themselves at a bridge— but instead of water, the river beneath was a black liquid with white specks. It bubbled in places and spewed foul-smelling steam into the air.

"That's a messed-up river," Dirk announced.

"It's evil," Megan pronounced. Her long white robe

contrasted with the black of the river, and she was holding a large, ornate staff that doubled as a walking stick. "I don't like how it makes me feel." Max wondered how far their transformations had actually gone. Could Megan really be a priestess healer and Melvin an archer? There was no doubting Sydney was some kind of pixie with her new wings and all, but what could any of them really do?

"We're not on some field trip here," Dwight grumbled. "Stay focused."

"I don't recommend anyone touch the water—or whatever it is," Sarah added. Nobody looked inclined to disagree with her.

"Never thought I'd see a river running through the middle of town," Sydney added. Her voice had gone up in pitch with her diminished size.

"Let's keep going," Dirk pressed. "We're not getting experience points for just looking at stuff."

Wayne stepped forward. "I'll scout the way ahead. A bridge makes for an easy ambush."

"The warrior has spoken true," Melvin added. "I think my elf senses are tingling with danger."

"More like hay fever," Dirk added.

"Wayne's idea isn't a bad one," Puff added. "We don't

know what's out there, and being stuck on a bridge *is* a tactical disadvantage."

Max nodded. "Okay, Wayne, just be careful."

The big kid took off, carefully crossing the bridge. Max kept expecting a barrage of arrows and spears or something, but it never came. Sarah grabbed Max and gently led him away from the others. She spoke, keeping her voice low. "I've been meaning to ask you about Wayne. Have you considered the possibility that he was in on this from the beginning?"

"I . . . ," Max began, but he realized he'd been avoiding thinking about it. "I guess I don't know."

"I'm just saying we don't really know what's going on, except everything happened after Wayne's arrival."

"Well, if Wayne was involved, it doesn't seem like he had a very good plan. Isn't he stuck here like the rest of us?"

Sarah thought it over. "Maybe. We don't have enough facts yet. But we need to be careful."

Dirk noticed the two of them talking and hurried over. "What are you guys whispering about?" He looked over his shoulder to see Melvin practicing pulling his bow while Sydney clapped gleefully with each successful draw.

"Wayne," Max answered.

"I was just saying that we don't really know him, so we should be careful," Sarah said.

"But he's got that amulet," Dirk replied. "Dwight said Wayne couldn't carry the portal unless he was good."

"Mostly good," Sarah corrected.

"Still, purposefully dooming a world is pretty messed up."

"It is," Sarah agreed. She looked up to see Puff and Dwight moving to meet Wayne as he made his way back. "I'm not accusing him. Just keep an open mind."

"My mind is like a steel trap," Dirk said. "It doesn't open unless you really push on it."

They rejoined the others as Wayne stepped off the narrow suspension bridge. "It's clear," he announced. "On the other side there's a path that winds into some hills. Plenty of places for an ambush, but I didn't see anyone."

"I say we advance, but keep our weapons at the ready," Melvin suggested. "I will also call upon my elf ancestors to bless us with a magical buff."

"Buff . . . ?" Sarah asked. She vaguely remembered Dirk using the term before.

"It's like a magical spell that helps you out," Dirk

answered. "I bet our priestess could do it." All eyes turned to Megan.

"What we *don't* need is a bunch of amateurs experimenting with magic," Dwight interjected. "Let's just keep things simple, okay?"

Melvin looked disappointed. "I will assume our dwarf's wisdom is as long and deep as his ancestors' mines," he announced.

"Or their toilet trenches," Glenn added.

"Come on, we're wasting time," Max said, motioning toward the bridge. They crossed in twos: Max and Wayne in the lead, followed by Sarah and Dirk, Puff and Dwight, Megan and Sydney, and finally Melvin. As Max walked, he felt the weight of the *Codex of Infinite Knowability* hanging from his shoulder. And while he didn't particularly enjoy the swishing of the blue robe he was wearing (it reminded him of one of his mother's dresses), he was glad to have the *Codex* close.

"I think we should call ourselves 'the Nine,'" Melvin announced from the back. "I might start working on a poem with that as the title."

"Just do it in your head," Dwight called back. "Or I'll be changing it to 'the Eight.'"

On the other side of the river they found the trail. There had been pine-covered foothills outside Madison before, but nothing like the sudden eruption of giant slabs of rock and earth that rose ahead of them. They paused for a moment to take it in before continuing in rows of two down the winding path. They had traveled a half mile or so when the trail opened into a small clearing and Max came to an abrupt stop. Ahead of him a squirrel stood in the middle of the trail (not that a squirrel standing on its hind legs was a stop-worthy event, but one wearing a sword and armor was).

"Ha!" Dirk exclaimed, pointing at it. "Look at that squirrel. It thinks it's people."

"None shall pass!" the squirrel knight squeaked ominously. The squirrel held a shield adorned with a purple-and-red sigil with a gold acorn, and on its side was strapped a miniature sword. Behind the rodent knight was a large field that led to scattered dwellings in the distance. Max could see the distinctive shape of the distinctive mermaid weather vane that had belonged to Old Man Peterson. The weather vane had been an irritant and source of embarrassment to the neighborhood for years.

"I'll handle this," Melvin announced, hurrying to

the front of the group. He faced the squirrel, bowing. "Woodland creature, I am of that royal lineage known as elf." He rose and motioned with his hand. "We are bound together by our respect for the harmony of nature. Do not be afraid; we come in—"

Boink!

Something brown had whizzed through the air and smacked Melvin in the head. He stumbled backward, nearly stepping on the acorn that had hit him. "Ouch!" Melvin exclaimed, rubbing his head and dropping his bow. "Someone threw a nut!"

The squirrel drew its sword.

"What's the matter," Dirk mocked, pointing at Melvin, "never LARPed with a squirrel before?"

There was a definite welt forming on Melvin's forehead, and Megan hurried over to take a closer look.

"Turn around, *humans*," the squirrel demanded, saying the last word with as much enthusiasm as if chewing on cat litter.

"You mean to tell me that when a portal between the worlds opens, the best the Shadrus can do is this?" Dwight laughed, pointing at the squirrel. "All the hamsters must be terrified."

"Uh, I'm not sure mocking him is such a good idea," Puff suggested.

"Do not press me further," the squirrel knight continued, his face furrowed into a frown. "You have been warned."

"Look, we don't want any trouble," Sarah jumped in. "We just need to get past and we'll be on our way."

"We're looking for other people like us," Sydney added, trying to be helpful. "You know . . . humans. So, I guess not so much like me right now, but how I used to be. Not that you'd know that, silly me. I wish I had some peanut butter to give you and maybe we could be friends."

The armored squirrel shook its head and took a step forward. "There are no other humans here, so be gone."

Max didn't like the sound of that.

"I think we should turn around," Wayne suggested.

Melvin picked up his bow and began yelling at the squirrel. "By all rights you've drawn first blood! I tried to honor you with my elf customs and you attacked me!"

It took a moment for the others to notice that Melvin now had a Hello Kitty Band-Aid on his forehead.

Megan shrugged. "It's all I could find."

"Enough!" the squirrel knight squeaked. "You have been warned. To arms!" Suddenly dozens of armored squirrels sprang from hiding places in the rocks and formed into ranks. But more worrying to Max was the movement in the distance. Even through the grass he could see thousands of tiny reflections like the ocean at sunset. Tens of thousands of armored squirrels marched in the field! And they were rolling hundreds of tiny trebuchets into position, no doubt loaded with nuts.

Max slipped his hand inside his satchel and found the *Codex of Infinite Knowability.*

"Don't even think about it, wizard!" the lead squirrel threatened, pointing at Max with his drawn sword. Max wondered how the squirrel knew him, then realized what he was wearing. "We'll swarm and cut you to pieces before you get to whatever magic you keep in your bag."

Max could feel Wayne growing tense next to him. Things were quickly getting out of hand. He remembered reading something in the *Codex* about squirrels taking over the world . . . was this how it happened? Had he inadvertently started the squirrelpocalypse?

"Easy, everyone," Sarah said in a low voice. "There's too many of them."

"Maybe we should make a slow retreat," Puff suggested. "Nice and easy, like."

"I think that's a good idea," Dwight confirmed. "Although if my kin ever hear I retreated from a squirrel . . ."

"There will be no going back!" the squirrel knight exclaimed. Behind them the trail filled up with more of the tiny knights. "You are surrounded."

"Max . . . ?" Sarah urged. Max knew what she was suggesting—he could use the *Codex* without reading it. He let his mind drift to the magical book at his side. He reached for a Prime Spell. As he saw it, the problem wasn't about coming up with a way to defeat an entire army of squirrels so much as it was about making an escape. He could feel the sweat break out on his forehead as he pushed into the *Codex*, sensing the surge of the spells as they began to fill his mind.

Suddenly a musical chord filled the air.

Max lost his concentration and the Prime Spells retreated. All eyes turned to Dirk as he repositioned his lute.

"Uh, Dirk . . . ?" Sarah asked.

The squirrels advanced, moving with a perfectly

timed step that made thousands of tiny boots sound like the advance of a single, armored giant. And then, to everyone's surprise, Dirk strummed another chord and began singing.

> *Come gather ye heroes*
> *And I'll sing you a tale,*
> *'Bout an adventuring elf*
> *Named Melvin the Frail . . .*

"Hey!" Melvin shouted, not liking where this was going. But Dirk ignored him and began singing and playing even louder. The squirrels stopped—thousands of rodent eyes turned their attention to the strange musical human.

> *He crossed paths with a squirrel*
> *Who told him what's what,*
> *But Melvin was bested*
> *By a tiny walnut!*

Then Dirk began to dance as Glenn joined in and the two of them belted out the chorus together:

A tiny walnut! A tiny walnut!
The elf had a lump
From a tiny walnut!

"Hey, that's not exactly true!" Melvin cried out, his hand drifting unconsciously to his Band-Aided forehead.

"Dirk!" Sarah shouted, and the music stopped at once. "Seriously?"

"I couldn't help it," Dirk replied.

"I should save the entire elf army the trouble and cut you down myself," Dwight threatened Dirk, shifting his axe from one shoulder to the next. But before Dirk could respond back, the ranks of squirrels began singing.

He crossed paths with a squirrel
Who told him what's what,
But Melvin was bested
By a tiny walnut!

Dirk broke into a grin and strummed his lute loudly, joining in:

A tiny walnut! A tiny walnut!
The elf had a lump
From a tiny walnut!

This continued for several more rounds, each chorus growing louder and more raucous. When it was finally over (to Melvin's great relief), the lead squirrel approached Dirk and removed its helmet. "You have immortalized us in song," the squirrel announced. "You have honored us, great minstrel."

Dirk nodded and leaned against the rock wall. "Yeah, it's what I do."

"What's happening?" Wayne asked, looking confused.

"I honestly don't know," Sarah replied.

"Now and forever," the squirrel continued, "we shall gather and sing of the besting of Melvin the Frail."

"Great," Melvin sighed.

The squirrel continued. "For this Melvin will represent all whom we defeat, and his song will be sung by our children and our children's children. You may pass now, humans. And you shall sing this song wherever you go."

"Done and done," Dirk agreed.

"I don't get it?" Sydney asked Puff, who was standing next to her.

"You can only win a battle once," Puff answered. "But immortalize it in a song, and the battle is won a hundred times over."

"Neat," she responded.

"Yeah, terrific," Melvin said. "Can we get out of here now?"

The sea of squirrels parted.

"What happened to the humans?" Max asked as they prepared to leave. The squirrel knight motioned to the tower in the distance.

"They have been undone by the Malaspire."

"You mean our school?" Melvin asked.

"It is the Malaspire now."

"I thought it was creepy when it was just called middle school," Dirk added.

Sarah, however, had other things on her mind. "What do you mean by 'undone'?"

The squirrel shrugged. "I do not know the words to describe it."

"Do you mean dead?" Megan asked, a lump catching in her throat as she got the words out.

The squirrel shook its head. "No, not that. Not yet."

"Can we save them?" Sarah pressed.

"I do not know," the squirrel confessed. "We have our own affairs to see to. But if there are answers to your questions, you will find them in the Malaspire."

"Come on, then," Dwight urged. "Let's get going."

Puff came up to Sarah and rubbed against her leg. "Don't give up hope," he told her. "In all that I have read about the Cataclysm, there is time to reverse its effects."

Sarah reached down and absentmindedly patted Puff on the head. "Thanks." Puff only recoiled a little at the unauthorized petting.

The group made their way through the ranks of the squirrel army. They were followed by thousands of eyes largely hidden in the shadows of their tiny helmets. "They're just so cute!" Sydney said. "Can I keep one?"

"Not if your life depended on it," Dwight answered. "And it probably does."

Dirk smiled as they passed the last of the rodent ranks. "Score one for the bard."

"First time anyone's said *that* in an adventure," Melvin muttered. "Ever."

CHAPTER SEVEN

MEET THE NEIGHBORS

THEY RESTED BENEATH THE MERMAID WEATHER VANE AND THE REMAINS of Old Man Peterson's house. At first it looked as if the place had survived the severe transformation of the Cataclysm, but as they drew near, they saw that the entire house had been sheared in half: The earth having dropped away to expose a sudden, unexpected cliff. Several other houses were likewise ripped apart, and whatever was left of Max's neighborhood had disappeared into the thick forest hundreds of feet below. Max found a spot and took a seat, looking through the *Codex* for anything useful, while Sarah and Melvin picked their way through the house's remains. The others watched the great storm slowly churn in the distance.

"This is strange," Sarah announced as she stepped

over the rubble from a collapsed wall. "There're no electronics left: no televisions or appliances or anything like that. Not even an old clock."

"It's part of the Cataclysm," Wayne replied. He was sitting in his chain mail, his shield at his side and his axe across his knees. He wore a dark expression that seemed to mirror the storm. "Those things unique to the Techrus will not survive."

"Dude!" Dirk exclaimed, jumping up. "He's talking about game consoles! And satellite TV!"

"None of that matters," Megan added. "It's the people who used to live here—that's what we need to be worried about."

"Hey, Dwight," Dirk called out, "how you going to order those old-timey Sears Toughskins if there's no Internet?"

Dwight grunted. "I told you not to talk about my special pants."

"Guys, let's try and stay focused here," Max suggested.

"Sure thing, Gramps," Dirk added. Sydney giggled before clapping her hands over her mouth and looking horrified that Max might have heard her. Max scowled—it was hard enough walking around in a dress, but the whole white-hair thing was starting to bug him.

"Listen here," Max said, turning to the *Codex* and reading:

ON THE UMBRAVERSE

⁜

EVERY PLACE OF SIGNIFICANCE WILL have a part of town worth avoiding. In Wallan, it's the Inflatable Pigpens of Zerhem; in the Mesoshire, it's Spenderwick's "One Day from Retirement" Café; and in the Techrus, it's Arby's. Slightly worse than those, however, is the umbraverse—a mysterious nether plane where the well-established rules governing decorum and good taste don't apply (see also "New Jersey"). Because of the umbraverse's habit of bending time and space, many time travel enthusiasts do their best to get there. Such interdimensional pursuits have generally been disastrous, albeit a financial windfall for the warlocks who sent them there (all fees are due prior to departure).

As a result, the Wizard's Tower declared such expeditions criminal and possibly world-ending, theorizing that should the barrier between the umbraverse and the three realms be broken, the umbraverse (being older and more dense) would seep into the other realms with disastrous results.

In the unlikely event that Shadrus magic is used to penetrate the barrier between the umbraverse, a truly horrific event called the Cataclysm may ensue. If you're reading this because you're facing said Cataclysm, best to close the book and give it as an offering to whatever shadow-based overlord is set to rule. You may spend the rest of your days as a slave, but better that than a long and torture-filled death.

"Well, that wasn't very helpful," Melvin said, watching as Max put the *Codex* away.

"Yeah, tell us something we don't know," Dirk replied, motioning toward the old book. "It's a mystery, wrapped in an enigma, then covered in old newspapers and buried under a broken garden gnome in my neighbor's backyard."

"That's awfully . . . specific," Megan said.

"Guys, I think we have other problems," Sarah announced. She had moved to a section of the wall where five long gouges ran for several feet. They tore across the drywall before ending in a mangled pile of wood where a door used to be. The others moved in for a closer look, but it wasn't until Dirk put his hand against them that Max realized what they were.

"Oh . . . ," Megan said, catching her breath. "A *hand* did that?"

"Something shaped like a hand, only bigger. And sharp enough to cut through drywall like it was paper," Sarah said.

"I thought you were going to say 'butter,'" Max admitted.

"Max always appreciates a good butter reference," Dirk added.

Melvin took a closer look at the shattered frame. "More than just sharp—strong, too."

"This doesn't make sense. Old Man Peterson was a frail old guy who used to yell at me when I rode my bike across his lawn," Dirk said, looking over the damaged wall.

"Not anymore," Wayne announced from behind them. They turned to see the giant of a boy staring at the marks. "Near the village where I grew up, there was a cave called Night's Throat, and it ran deep into the earth. So deep, in fact, that many believed it touched the Shadrus itself. On the shortest days, when night ruled

the winter sky, we could sometimes hear sounds coming from inside. We called those who made such sounds
'howlers,' and when we heard their screaming, the elders
gathered us together in the main hall to wait out the
night—our warriors at the ready. The next day we found
our livestock slaughtered and missing. And all around
were marks like these."

As if on cue, a great wailing rang out. Wayne lifted
his axe.

"I have a bad feeling—" Dirk started to say, but Sarah
slugged him in the shoulder.

"Don't say it," she warned.

"But it's tradition!"

"Hurry, outside!" Wayne shouted. They followed
him through the ruined house, the links of his chain
mail flowing around his large frame as he picked his way
through the debris, carefully scanning for any signs of
movement. Max retrieved the *Codex* and flipped it open
to a fireball spell. It was one he pretty much had memorized, and he began uttering the incantation under his
breath, joining the others as they formed together in a
circle.

"My staff . . . ," Megan said, looking up. "It's glowing."

The end of her staff was pulsing in waves of light blue.

"Probably a healing staff," Dirk announced as he looked it over. "But on second thought, better not point it at anyone until you're sure."

"It's pretty, though," Sydney added, her wings fluttering behind her.

Sarah drew her sword while Dwight hefted his axe from one hand to the other and squinted through his helmet.

Puff regarded Wayne. "I've never heard of a human encampment near Night's Throat. Where did you say you were from again?"

"I didn't," Wayne grunted, dismissing the fluff dragon as he continued to scan the area. The howling came again, this time joined by a chorus of others.

Max didn't like the panic he was starting to hear in Wayne's voice. When you were as big as Wayne, you weren't supposed to be afraid of things. It didn't seem like a particularly good sign.

The cries of the howlers crashed over them again; this time it was as if the creatures were right on top of them. Sydney screamed and Megan pulled her sister to her.

"Are they invisible or something?" Dirk shouted. But

it was Puff who worked it out first. He spun around, looking back in the direction of the ruined house and the cliff beyond. He saw the first deformed hand, outstretched and sprouting long talons, reaching over the edge.

"They're climbing the cliff!" he shouted.

They whirled as one, weapons at the ready and hearts pounding. The first of the creatures bounded over the edge of the cliff and landed in the remains of Old Man Peterson's living room. It had long limbs with oversized feet and hands, and was covered in grayish skin. The head held extra teeth along its elongated jaw and it wore a pair of overalls. The creature regarded the group with cold, black eyes.

"I think that might be Mr. Peterson," Dirk said, recognizing the clothing.

In response, it lifted its hand and pointed at Dirk, crying out in a voice that hissed like air through a punctured hose, "Get off my lawn, Dirk!"

"Yep, that's him all right."

Thwuump! The sound cut through the air as Melvin loosed an arrow.

"No!" Max cried. The last thing he wanted to do was stick poor old Mr. Peterson—even in horrible monster form—with an arrow! But just before it struck, a beam of blue light knocked it from its trajectory, sending the arrow spinning over the edge of the cliff. Max turned to Megan, her staff pointed in front of her.

"He's still one of us," she said.

"That was awesome!" Dirk exclaimed. "Double zero roll for sure."

Melvin, however, looked flushed, and was reaching for another arrow. "You're wrong, Megan. It's *not* one of us! Not anymore!" But Sarah put her arm gently on Melvin's and stayed his hand. She leaned over to look Melvin in the eye.

"I refuse to believe that," she said.

Suddenly more cries broke forth as other howlers climbed over the cliff's edge. They had on the tattered remains of whatever clothing they had worn the day before. One howler, wearing a purple bathrobe and a head full of curlers, was waving a rolling pin in its hand.

"Mrs. Frankelburt?" Max asked. She was his elderly neighbor, who gave Max a handful of hard candy in exchange for mowing her lawn each week (which was something his mom made him do whether there was candy involved or not).

"You smell delicioussss," the monster version of Mrs. Frankelburt hissed, licking its lips with a forked tongue.

Wayne stepped forward. "We must press our attack while their backs are to the cliff. We can't let them get around us."

Max knew there wasn't much time. He pushed his mind into the *Codex* and found one of the Prime Spells: Liquidity. It would be impossible for him to describe how he knew which of the powerful forces was the right one, since the recognition came from the very blood that flowed through his veins. He felt himself shudder as he grabbed hold of the spell, ripping it from the *Codex*. Max could see the howlers rushing toward them. He also saw Wayne and Dwight out of the corner of his eye, leading their own charge. Max knew he only had one chance to get it right. He let it go, feeling the spell drop into the ground surrounding the ruined houses. There was a powerful thud, and a wave of energy pushed outward like a ripple in water. Then the earth beneath the houses bubbled and turned to mud. *Liquidity—to make flow.*

"Everyone, back!" Max managed to yell.

Wayne and Dwight scrambled backward as the row of houses were torn apart, caught in the massive current of the muddy earth. The howlers screamed in rage as they found themselves stuck, fighting desperately to get free. One managed to move within striking range of Wayne, but he brought his shield up in time to deflect the razor-sharp talons.

"Over here!" Sarah cried. She dropped her sword and ran to where Wayne and Dwight were starting also fighting with the mud. The two of them scrambled to pull themselves free as the howler pressed its attack, hammering blow after blow on Wayne's shield. Dwight yelled at the monster, getting its attention long enough for Wayne to bring his foot up and kick the beast square in the chest. The impact sent the howler flying backward and out of reach. Suddenly Dwight fell forward, the flowing mud catching hold and dragging him down. Wayne hurled himself forward with a grunt, grabbing the dwarf's foot and keeping Dwight from slipping farther toward the cliff.

Sarah rushed after them, just managing to grab Wayne, who was now stretched out on his stomach and holding fast to Dwight. Puff arrived next, biting down on Sarah's cloak and pulling backward. Melvin and Dirk ran through the mud after them, finally reaching

Sarah and seizing her cloak. They struggled to hold on to each other as crashes filled the air as the last of the houses disappeared over the collapsing cliff. The howlers screamed as they fought to free themselves, but they could do little as the ground melted under the power of the Prime Spell, turning into the world's largest mudslide. Max started to run toward his friends, plowing through the ankle-deep mud.

"Don't let go, boy!" Dwight shouted to Wayne. The big kid grimaced, beads of sweat breaking out on his ebony skin. He had to turn his head and fight for air as the mud flowed around him like a river.

Sarah groaned, pulling with all the strength she had. She knew they were in trouble. She thought back to the tugs-of-war her judo sensei would set up after class. In the end, it didn't always matter where the bigger and stronger kids ended up—what mattered was which team was pulling together. And that was exactly what they needed to do now! Sarah tightened her grip on Wayne's foot and yelled, "We have to work together! Everyone, pull with me!"

She then took a deep breath and began yelling "Pull!" in a steady rhythm. As the group started working together they managed to slow their slide toward the edge. It was a tiny victory, but it was enough to give them renewed strength. Sarah kept the cadence going, and they continued to work as one. They heaved and pulled against the terrible force of the liquid earth until they began inching in the opposite direction. Bit by bit, it was working!

Max finally reached the others, grabbing hold of Dirk and joining in. With his help they continued to back even farther away from the cliff's edge until Wayne heaved Dwight free and the rest went tumbling backward. Max landed on solid ground, and he felt an instant rush of relief. His body informed him it had just about had enough, however, so Max decided to stay on his back and catch his breath.

"Is everyone safe?" Max asked between gulps of air. He stared at the sky, seeing the tumbling clouds of the storm overhead. It was a reminder that the worst was still to come. A river of mud was nothing compared to the power of the Maelshadow.

"We're all here," Dwight answered.

"Yeah, that was epic!" Dirk exclaimed, jumping to his feet. Glenn had been slung over his shoulder and the magic lute spit out a mouthful of mud.

The rest were climbing back to their feet when Dirk suddenly yelled, "Over there!" He was pointing at Megan and Sydney, and the lone howler that had each of the sisters by the throat.

"I'm sorry," Megan said. "I didn't see it coming."

"No sudden moves," Sarah commanded. "And nobody raise a weapon."

The group watched as the howler glared back at them. It was wearing parts of a high school football uniform, including a helmet, shoulder pads, and padded pants.

"Just what we need," Dirk added, "a jock monster."

"Let me take the shot," Melvin said under his breath. He looked down at the bow lying at his feet. "I can make it."

"Nobody's doing anything," Max warned, standing with his hands in the air. "Did you hear that?" he called to the creature. "We're not going to do anything."

"Yousss going to die," the creature hissed back.

"Max?" Sydney cried out, looking frail against the taloned hand at her throat.

"Don't worry," Max replied, doing his best to keep his voice calm. "No one's going to die today."

"Foolsss!" the creature spat. "She'sss coming for you."

"She . . . ?" Melvin asked.

"No, *she'sss*," Dirk replied.

"Wait, are you talking about the Maelshadow?" Sarah asked, ignoring Dirk. "Is the Maelshadow a girl?"

"That would be kind of ironic, you know, because it's called the *male* shadow," Glenn added.

"I don't think knowing if the Maelshadow is a boy or a girl is important right now," Puff replied.

"It is if it wants to hold your hand," Dirk replied. "Just saying—it could happen."

"The Lord of Shadowssss does not want to hold your hand!" the howler screamed, losing patience. Then it suddenly lifted its nose and sniffed at the air. "Ssshe draws near! One for me and one for her! Better half than none at all!" The howler shoved Megan forward, causing her to stumble over her long white robe and fall to the ground. Then it whirled, throwing Sydney under its arm as it ran toward a small outcropping of rocks across the field. It used its free hand like a third leg as it flew toward its objective, and Max's heart sank—it was running far too fast for any of them to catch.

"Sydney!" Megan cried out. She turned to the others: "Help her!"

"Wait!" Wayne exclaimed. His voice thundered from his massive chest as he raised his hand and pointed at a black beast in the distance. It had crested a nearby hill and was looking down at them. Shaped like a horse, it was bigger and more terrifying than any horse imaginable. Flames rose from its hooves, the same crimson color as its eyes, and as it stepped forward they could make out a single, misshapen horn erupting from its head.

"Impossible," Dwight said as he stared at the beast.

"What is that?" Sarah asked. "Some kind of unicorn?"

"Princess . . . ?" Dirk began, holding his hand over his eyes. "Is that you, baby?" He had remained convinced that Princess was his girlfriend, even if she wouldn't admit it.

"If she was caught in the storm . . . ," Max began.

Wayne continued, his words measured. "That creature is a nightmare. It is born of the Shadrus and endowed with terrible power."

"It's more than that," Puff added. "It's also a unicorn. And that means it's much, much worse."

And then Dirk saw it: a single patch of pink within the layers of the coal-black mane. "It's her! It's Princess! What's happened?"

"She's changed, like everything else caught in the Cataclysm," Dwight said coolly.

"What about Sydney?" Melvin exclaimed, retrieving his bow. "We can't worry about some unicorn thing now; we have to go after her!"

Then the nightmare reared, fire dripping from its hooves and setting the surrounding grass aflame. "Time to keep an old promise," the creature bellowed. She sounded just like Princess as the wind rose and carried her voice across the open field. "Time to eat."

CHAPTER EIGHT

AN OLD FRIEND

THE BALL OF FIRE WAS PERFECTLY CAST.

It shot across the field and intersected with the running howler, hitting the creature square on its helmeted head and sending it toppling forward. Sydney flew from the creature's arm, managing to right herself in midair with a furious fluttering of wings. She quickly gained control and brought herself to a stop, hovering just above the ground.

The howler screamed in fury, picking itself up and charging the airborne pixie. But now that the thought of flight had occurred to her, Sydney beat her wings even harder, zipping higher into the air. The howler leapt for her, but she was too fast. She giggled, despite herself, watching from above as the frustrated monster jumped over and over again in an attempt to reach her. Then another perfectly aimed fireball struck the creature on the helmet again, sending the beast flying backward. It ripped the smoldering plastic from its head, looking for its unknown assailant. In the end, the howler decided the odds had shifted against it. It let out one last scream and ran for parts unknown, fighting strange memories that it used to do something similar while carrying a ball and in front of cheering crowds.

Max had watched as the events unfolded, confused at how fireballs had appeared without his doing. Then he saw a small orange-and-white kitten bound to the top of the rocks.

"Hi, Max!" Moki shouted at him. "Did you know there's a door over here?"

Max turned to the others. "Run!"

They took off in the direction of the fire kitten.

Princess, still in nightmare form, thundered down the hill after them.

"I can't believe we're running from a unicorn that wants to eat us again!" Sarah exclaimed. Max was too busy gasping for air to answer, but he worried that what she was really saying was *This is all your fault, Max Spencer. Just in case you've forgotten.*

Dirk was the fastest, and he pulled ahead of the group. Even then, he probably wasn't fast enough to outrun Nightmare-Princess. Max chanced a look over his shoulder and saw the black monster galloping toward them, a line of fire marking its path from the hill. He also saw Dwight falling behind. The dwarf could run fairly well, all things considered, but in his armor he just couldn't make the same strides as everyone else. Puff was galloping (Max hadn't realized that fluff dragons *could* gallop) alongside Dwight, but it was clear they weren't going to make the rocky outcropping in time. "Get everyone to the rocks!" Max called to Melvin. "Take cover!"

Melvin grunted, running with his bow in one hand and an arrow in the other. He'd tried to nock the arrow while he sprinted across the field, but he nearly tripped in the process. Max veered to the side, grabbing the *Codex* as he came to a stop. He began flipping through the pages—he needed to find a spell to buy the others time— he didn't have the strength to handle a Prime Spell again.

Nightmare-Princess lowered her head, aiming her horn at Max as she charged. The sound of thunder ripped through the air as the tainted magic made itself known.

"Max!" Sarah shouted behind him, but he couldn't

worry about her just then. He only hoped Melvin could keep the others running toward safety—or what he hoped was safety. He had no idea what Moki meant by a "door," but it was the best chance they had. The pages of the *Codex* flew through his fingers, suddenly stopping on a spell: *Magical Shaved Ice!* listed under Popular Spells at Parties. Max groaned, but there was no time left. He read the spell out loud, drawing it from the page and sending it at the charging, unholy unicorn. At the same time a lightning bolt ripped from Nightmare-Princess's horn and whizzed past him. The air exploded and Max was blinded by a field of dazzling lights. It nearly knocked him off his feet but he managed to stay upright, the *Codex* still clutched in his hands. Max did his best to clear his vision, anticipating the blow that was about to come. But when his vision cleared, he saw Nightmare-Princess on her side, screaming with rage. Then Max saw her hooves—instead of spitting fire they were covered in perfectly formed blocks of ice (just the right size, in fact, for shaving ice into snow cones). With each attempt to stand, Nightmare-Princess lost her footing and slammed back to the ground.

Max watched her for a moment, and supposed he had

the magic to defeat her right then and there. But Princess had become his friend, and it wasn't her fault she'd gotten caught up in the magical storm. In fact, it was squarely *his* fault. Max promised himself that none of his friends would pay the price for his mistake. He turned to find Sarah standing behind him, her sword in hand. *Of course she didn't keep running with the others,* Max said to himself. *She'll face the danger head-on.*

"Come on," Max said, grabbing Sarah by the hand and running toward the rocks. Max wasn't typically a hand grabber, especially when the other hand belonged to a girl.

Sydney fluttered down to her sister, and she and Megan gave each other a hug. When Max reached Moki, he let go of Sarah and grabbed the little fire kitten. "Moki!" he exclaimed, genuinely happy to see him.

"Wow, look at all your new friends," Moki announced.

"Wait a minute," Dwight said, pointing at the fire kitten. "How is it you survived the storm?"

Moki shrugged. "I was taking a nap."

"I don't think so," Dwight pressed. "The Cataclysm changes everything it touches. That monstrosity back there is Princess, and she's a freaking unicorn!"

Max looked Moki over and then noticed a change. "Look, the color of his eye is different." And in fact, one of Moki's eyes had gone from green to gray.

"I have a cat—but it doesn't talk and throw fireballs," Melvin added. "I was going to guess maybe that was it."

"No, Moki could always do that," Puff replied. "He's a fire kitten from the Magrus." Melvin nodded as if that was perfectly reasonable.

Dwight scratched at his beard. "So you're telling me that squirrels have suddenly militarized and turned into an army, people have become howler monsters, Princess is a nightmare, and all that happened to Moki was his eye changed color?"

"Fire kittens are a mysterious bunch," Puff added. "They pretty much keep to themselves."

The frustrated cries of Nightmare-Princess rang out behind them. "Moki, hurry and show us that door," Max commanded, feeling the urgency of the situation once again. Moki pointed to the outcropping, where a single smooth rock rose about five feet out of the ground. Behind it, the Malaspire with its twisting tornado was visible in the distance.

"Moki, that's just a rock," Sarah said.

But Puff moved over to the slab of stone and took a closer look. "Fire kittens have remarkably good eyesight," the fluff dragon said. "Maybe there's a hidden entrance or something?"

Max moved to join Puff and felt a warm vibration in the air. "There's some kind of magic going on," he announced.

"Yep. A door," Moki confirmed.

Wayne was keeping an eye on Nightmare-Princess. "Whatever you're going to do, you need to hurry."

"Moki, any idea how to get inside?" Max asked the fire kitten.

"Maybe we could scratch at it?" he suggested.

"Oh, move off," Dwight grunted, pushing past Max and looking the stone over. He felt around the smooth surface with his hands and stepped back, scratching at his beard. "Well, it's not mechanical."

"If it's magic, how do we get in?" Megan asked.

Dirk pointed to the door. "It's probably one of those riddle doors," And as soon as Dirk said the word "riddle," the rock began to twist and turn until a stone face stretched out and regarded them.

"A riddle then it is," the face said.

The group stared at the strange stone face for a moment—it was more or less shaped like a human, with large ears and a wide nose. Melvin cleared his throat and said, "You are obviously a great and powerful magical door—"

"Oh, please," the door answered, interrupting Melvin. "Flattery is not going to get you in." That seemed to throw Melvin off.

"I'm sorry," Sarah said, jumping into the conversation. "Are you saying there's a way you *will* let us past?"

"Let me guess, this is your first time at a magic door? Okay, everyone listen up so I don't have to repeat myself. I am a Select-O-Magic locking door and can be opened once every twenty-four hours. You may gain entry in one of the following ways: knocking three times, touching my surface with a magical item, or answering a riddle. You have selected the riddle."

"Oh no we didn't," Dwight said, motioning to Dirk. "This one doesn't speak for us, so it doesn't count."

"Well he did and it does," the door replied, sounding a little smug.

"You're telling me that if our lute-wielding Pirate here hadn't said anything, we could have just *knocked*?" Dwight asked, the irritation in his voice evident.

"Or touched you with something magical," Megan said, looking at her staff.

"Would have, could have, should have," the door replied. "Next time maybe you should think twice about letting pirates into your party."

"I'm not a pirate!" Dirk protested.

Melvin turned back to the group and warned, "Uh, guys, whatever spell Max cast is starting to wear off. That thing is about to get up."

"And be careful who you're calling a thing," Dirk said to Melvin. "That's my girlfriend—even if she does want to eat us at the moment."

"Can we just answer this stupid riddle!?" Sydney exclaimed, looking back and forth from Nightmare-Princess to the door.

"I like riddles," Moki added. "They're fun."

Dwight resisted the urge to pick the fire kitten up and punt him over the rocks. "Fine, then," he grunted. "Let's be quick about it."

The face cleared its throat and looked at Dirk. "Since

this one initiated the lock, he's the one who will give me the answer—and you only get *one chance*, so don't go asking me for more. Understood?"

"No problemo," Dirk answered, sounding way more confident then the others thought appropriate.

"Here it is, then," the face continued:

> Thirty-two white horses
> Upon a crimson hill:
> Each must rise and each must fall,
> A fate they'll all fulfill.
> What are they?

Dirk immediately started to reply, but Sarah managed to clasp her hand over his mouth before he could speak. "Let's talk this over before we give an answer, okay?"

Wayne, however, took several steps backward. "She's getting up," he said, his grip tightening around the axe in his hand. The others turned to see Nightmare-Princess slip the first hoof free from the ice.

Sarah turned to the face. "Are we allowed to talk things over?"

"It's allowed," the face replied.

Sarah carefully removed her hand from Dirk's mouth. "Dirk, tell *the group* what you think the answer is."

"Candy corn," he replied at once. Sarah blinked several times, trying to get her head around it. Dwight, on the other hand, took his finger and pointed it squarely at Dirk.

"What's wrong with you?" the dwarf asked. "That's the worst answer ever."

Dirk shrugged. "I don't know; I just went with my gut."

"We should at least consider the big five," Melvin suggested. "Mountain, wind, dark, fish, and time."

"I don't really think it's any of those," Megan added thoughtfully.

"Hurry it up . . . ," Wayne warned.

"'Horses' is probably a metaphor for something," Puff said. "I doubt it literally means horses."

"And I doubt any of you are going through that door anytime soon," Glenn piped in.

"What's a metaphor again?" Sydney asked.

Megan turned to her sister. "It's when you use one thing to describe another. Like 'laughter is the music of the soul.'"

Max ignored the others and focused on the riddle. He assumed the world could be easily divided between those who liked riddles and those who didn't. Max was decidedly in the camp that thought annoying riddles amounted to brain bullying. He also didn't care for corn mazes, puzzles, or math. But he did his best to try to visualize thirty-two horses on a red hill. His brain protested as a result, reminding him that he wasn't very good at this sort of thing.

"Thirty-two is a very specific number," Sarah said.

"I like the number thirty-two," Moki chimed in. "I like it one better than thirty-one."

"Blasted stupid door!" Dwight exclaimed as he kicked at the dirt. "I have no idea."

"Again, we need to hurry," Wayne said. Nightmare-Princess had risen on her front two hooves and was working to get the ice off her rear legs. The frozen blocks glowed orange and yellow as her magical flames fought to melt them.

"So looks like candy corn is the best option so far," Dirk suggested.

"Would you quit saying candy corn!" Melvin protested. "I can't stand them—they always get stuck in my teeth."

Sydney tilted her head. "Hey, I just remembered something."

"Time's up," Wayne said. In the distance, the creature had regained her footing and was staring across the field at them.

"It was always destined to be this way," Nightmare-Princess said. "You the prey and me the hunter." She began walking casually forward.

"Come on, guys, candy corn," Dirk insisted.

"Seriously stop saying that!" Sarah exclaimed. "I'm trying to figure this out."

Sydney rose up and down as her wings fluttered quickly. "I kind of remembered something," she said.

"Why do they all fall?" Puff said, thinking aloud. "There's got to be a simple explanation."

Max abandoned the door, hoping Sarah or someone else was smart enough to figure it out. Princess, in her horrible nightmare form, was steadily walking toward them. She was the same Princess who had hunted him in both the past and the future. And no matter how tired he was, he was the only one who stood a chance of defeating her.

Wayne matched Max's stride and stood next to him, shoulder to shoulder (or shoulder to top of head).

Wayne's muscles danced on his forearm as he squeezed his axe. Dwight joined them in his heavy plate armor, his battle-axe raised in the air. *It's the three of us, then,* Max said to himself. *It won't be enough.*

"Princess, this isn't who you are anymore," Max called out. "You and I are friends, remember? I saved you from the Mor Luin army. And you fought with me at the Wizard's Tower. We brought down Rezormoor Dreadbringer together."

"Then perhaps I am his revenge," Nightmare-Princess answered. "And yet he was nothing—simply a messenger of the true Lord of Shadows. I feel the presence of the Maelshadow even now . . . I feel his loathing of you. I feel his power as he destroys the old world and ushers in the new. You are part of that old world, Max. You will be consumed by the storm that rages around you. And as always, it was your blood that made it possible. From the might of the World Sunderer, who tried to rip magic from this realm, to the precious drops left at the fallen Tower. You have been there from the beginning. Now you will die at its end."

Max felt a hard lump in his throat and his hands went numb. He desperately reached into the *Codex*, but he was buffeted by the power of the Prime Spells. The fear that rose in his chest seemed as big and powerful as anything he'd ever known.

"Someone say something!" Puff shouted, running the riddle over and over in his head.

The others all looked at one another, unable to tease out the riddle's meaning. All except for Sydney, who had been desperately trying to say something. "Teeth!" she shouted as loud as she could. "That's what I remembered when Melvin said the candy corn got stuck in his teeth— we have thirty-two teeth in our mouths!"

"Of course, that's it!" Sarah exclaimed. "White horses are teeth . . . and the crimson hills are gums!"

Megan threw her arm around her sister. "And 'each must rise and each must fall' is about losing baby teeth!"

Sarah grabbed Dirk and turned him toward the door. "Hurry, give it the answer!"

"So we're not going with candy corn?" Dirk asked. Sarah's slug answered the question.

"The answer is teeth," Dirk announced as he rubbed his shoulder.

"That is correct," the face on the door acknowl-edged. Suddenly a white light began to run across the rock, tracing strange symbols that glowed with an other-worldly power. There was an audible click, and the door swung open.

"Hurry, Max, we're in!" Sarah shouted. She began ushering the group through the door one by one. Whatever lay beyond was sheathed in darkness, but it was less a risk than the dark nightmare walking toward them.

Max turned and saw his friends piling through the opening. Nightmare-Princess did as well, and her nostrils flared in anger. It was going to be a race, then, but if history was any guide, Max did not do well when it came to races. Of course, there was nothing like the fear of being chewed to death to get one moving. As Melvin, Megan, and Sydney scrambled through the small doorway, Max turned and started to sprint. He'd only moved a few yards away to confront Nightmare-Princess, but it seemed like forever as the thundering hooves came closer.

"Go on!" Wayne shouted, ushering Dwight and Max in front of him. Ahead, Moki had jumped on Puff's back as Sarah stood by the door and waved the fluff dragon through, followed by Dirk. Max ran with all the strength he could muster, but as he approached the door-way he could feel the ground shaking. Nightmare-Princess galloped after them, flames billowing from her nostrils and fluttering wildly from her hooves. Sarah's eyes went wide and she shoved Dwight inside. Time seemed to slow for Max, each stride mirrored by the pounding in his chest. His breath exploded from his lungs like the Old West trains billowing puffs of smoke. Sarah was there, just an arm's length ahead of him, reaching for him to pull him through the door. Wayne was somewhere behind him, most likely standing between him and the charging nightmare. Max desperately wanted to slow down, however—just enough to grab Sarah and send her through the doorway first. The sight of her in her black-and-gold armor, with her once-white cloak now soiled with mud around her shoulders, struck Max with feelings of both joy and sorrow. He had disrupted her well-planned life and had caused her to suffer much because of who and what he was.

Time continued to move in slow beats as Max came to the doorway. He could feel the hot breath of the monster behind him—the wicked flames reaching out and singeing the hair on the back of his neck. And then he locked eyes with Sarah. He could see the orange-and-yellow reflection of unearthly fire. Max began to veer away. It took only an instant for him to decide to lead Nightmare-Princess away and give Sarah and Wayne a chance to make it inside. It wasn't a particularly well-thought-out plan on his part, but it was the best he could do on short notice.

Then, without warning, Max felt a hard shove at his back. The force sent him flying forward, launching him through the small doorway. Time sped up again as he slammed against something hard.

"Max!" he heard Sarah cry. Then the door swung shut with a muffled thud as its massive weight settled into place. Darkness swallowed them, and Max spun around, dizzy from the impact and disoriented by the absence of light. He reached for where he thought the door was, stumbled forward, and fell to the ground.

And then he sank into a new kind of darkness, passing out on the cold, earthen floor.

CHAPTER NINE

BUFF SONGS

MAX OPENED HIS EYES. THE WORLD WAS A BLURRY MIX OF BLUE shadows, and he tasted mud and dried blood in his mouth. He blinked several times, and when he tried to move he felt a stabbing pain along his side.

"Hold still," he heard Megan say. His head was on something soft, and it took a moment for Max to realize he was resting on her lap. Then the world came into focus, and he looked up at her, seeing the long staff she held glowing blue and bathing the passageway in soft light.

"The door!" Max exclaimed, trying to sit up again. But he moaned as the sharp pain ripped through his side and he was forced back down.

The others had gathered around him. Moki pressed

close and Dirk leaned over him in his ridiculous purple-and-yellow tunic.

"It won't open," Dirk said, his voice heavy. "We tried, like a thousand times."

Melvin stood over Dirk, his ears and bow making him look very much an elf in the blue light. "The door won't open again for twenty-four hours," he said glumly. "I'm sorry."

Max didn't want to hear it. He refused to imagine Sarah and Wayne trapped on the other side with Nightmare-Princess.

"I know," Dwight said as if reading Max's thoughts. "We all feel it too. But there's nothing to be done."

"But," Max stammered. It was hard to even talk, and the pain in his side was intensifying with every passing second.

"First things first," Megan announced. "I've been thinking about this strange change in all of us, Max, and I believe I can help you. I think you should trust me and let me try."

"You should listen to her," Puff agreed. "You're no good to anyone right now."

Max wanted to protest—they had better things to do than worry about him. But he couldn't help Sarah like he was, and he'd do just about anything to fix that. "Okay," he agreed.

Megan nodded. Even though she and Max were the same age, Megan had one of those faces that made it easy to see her as a mom someday. It was a contrast to the youthfulness of her younger sister, but there was a strength and sensibility there that made Max feel instantly better. "I'm going to touch you with my staff," she announced.

That better feeling was suddenly gone.

There was no doubt that the glowing blue staff was magic—Max could feel the humming of it in the air. But just what *kind* of magic was the real question. The fact that it had appeared as part of the Cataclysm—even though Max's own spell had interfered with the process— made it dicey at best.

"I am a healer," Megan announced. "That's the character I always play, and that's who I am now. So I'm going to do what my character would do, and that is heal you with my magic."

"Yeah, you saw my awesomeness as a bard," Dirk said, his hand drifting to the strap that held Lute-Glenn over his shoulder. "I totally rocked my song, and I've never had lessons."

Melvin didn't look like he agreed entirely, but he added, "And I'm an elf and I know how to shoot a bow—even though I've never shot a real one before."

"And I have wings and can fly!" Sydney added.

"And I'm Moki!" Moki announced. He wasn't sure how this particular game worked, but he was enjoying it nonetheless.

Max looked around at the faces staring back at him and nodded.

Megan had her sister prepare a makeshift pillow before she carefully moved Max's head to rest on it. Then she stood, taking her staff in hand. Max noticed that it grew somewhat brighter, and he could see that they were in a long tunnel that sloped gently downward. The smooth rock door was close enough that Max could reach out and touch it, and he realized that he must have actually started to turn before he'd been shoved through the door. The weird angle must have sent him flying into the stone before blacking out.

"My character would usually pick which kind of healing spell to use at a time like this," Megan said. "I don't think it works like that here—I think the magic is in my staff and I just have to use it. If everything goes right, you'll be touched by a healing spell."

"Or a blue death ray," Glenn remarked. Max decided he preferred Glenn in motivational dagger form.

Megan lowered her staff, backing up several steps because of its length. As it grew closer, Max could feel more magic emanating from it. He immediately began to feel better, the strange power of the staff reminding him of being wrapped in a large blanket on a cold wintery night. He was instantly warm, and a feeling of peaceful tranquility settled over him. Then, when the staff actually touched him, that feeling exploded through his body. It wasn't uncomfortable at all, more like getting into a hot tub that was maybe a tad too hot. But tolerable. Max felt the pain in his side subside at once, and even the coppery taste of dried blood left his mouth. He saw the others staring at him, eyes wide in wonderment. He looked down to see small blue dots—like fireflies— drifting around his body. Each one touched his skin with a tingling sensation, flying around him—down his arms and legs and through his fingers. Then the small lights swarmed together and joined with the blue light of the staff, disappearing from sight.

"Whoa," Dirk said.

Max felt good. In fact, he felt better than good. He

quickly rose to his feet and began dusting himself off. "It worked," he said, smiling at Megan.

"I'm a healer," Megan said to herself. "I really am a healer."

"Very impressive," Puff agreed. "I've been around magic for most of my life, and healing magic is a lost art—it certainly wasn't taught at the Wizard's Tower."

Melvin offered Megan a formal bow. "You've always been our healer and you've never let us down," he said. She blushed a little. Max's attention returned to the door, however. He grabbed the *Codex* and felt the rush of power flow into him.

"There might be a door-opening spell of some kind here," he said. "But I don't want to waste time looking for it. I'll summon a Prime Spell and blow this thing off its hinges."

Suddenly the face in the door popped out and began protesting: "Now hold on just a minute," it said, looking perturbed. "There's no need for violence."

"Then you don't know us very well," Dwight replied flatly.

Dirk stepped forward. "Why don't you just open so Max doesn't have to turn you into rubble or something?"

The face regarded Max and then peered down at

the *Codex of Infinite Knowability* in his hand. "There's no doubt your magic is strong enough to destroy me," the door conceded. "But that won't do you any good."

"Of course it will," Max argued. "My *friends* are on the other side and they need my help—right now!"

"No they're not," the door replied.

"What do you mean?" Max asked, confused. "They were just there."

"Max," Puff said, moving toward him. "You were out for some time. A long time, in fact."

Max struggled with the thought—the mad flight through the door seemed like mere seconds ago. The feeling of dread began to creep over him as he found the courage to ask the question that terrified him most: "What happened to them?"

"The one in armor and the great beast led the female away," the door answered.

"Wait, what do you mean?" Max asked. "Led her away *where* . . . ?"

"To yonder tower, though I cannot see it myself. But I heard them say as much."

Dirk scratched his head. "You mean that Nightmare-

Princess led the *two* of them to the tower, right?"

The face shook its head. "No. The beast and the boy worked together."

Impossible, Max thought. Or was it? What did he truly know about Wayne? It was Wayne, after all, who had brought the portal. And Sarah had had her suspicions about him. If Wayne had used Max to open the portal on purpose, it was a betrayal beyond words. But he knew he couldn't get lost in such thoughts—what mattered was that Sarah was alive.

"It doesn't change anything," Max replied to the door. "We still need to get past you and go after my friends. I'm sorry."

The face seemed to brighten. "If it's the tower you seek, then look no further than this tunnel. It will lead you there through the secret route."

"And how do you know this, exactly?" Puff asked.

"Considering the sole purpose of my existence is to guard this hallway, it's not asking too much to know where it leads."

Max considered his alternatives: find a Prime Spell and remove the door or turn and follow the tunnel. He didn't really want to hurt the face, and the thought of running into more people turned into howlers wasn't exactly appealing. If the tunnel bypassed the obstacles on the surface, it just might be the fastest route to finding Sarah. "What do you guys think?" he asked. "The tunnel might be quicker, plus we'd avoid the howlers."

"Dude, this is like dungeon crawling," Dirk exclaimed. "If you find a tunnel behind a locked door, you *have* to follow it."

Melvin spoke next. "Our priorities have changed. We have to rescue the members of our party above all else." He turned to Max. "I vote we take the tunnel."

Max didn't really remember calling a vote, but as long as he and Melvin were like-minded, he figured he'd let it pass. He turned to the two sisters who said as one, "The tunnel."

"I agree," Puff added. Moki nodded, casting his vote as well. Then Max turned to Dwight, but he could see at once that something was wrong. The dwarf looked flushed, even in the blue light of Megan's staff. Drops of sweat broke out on his forehead, and he seemed to shrink under the weight of the surrounding walls.

"I can't do it," he blurted, the words forcing their way out. Melvin frowned, not understanding.

"What do you mean?" he asked, shifting his bow from one hand to the next. "It's just a tunnel."

"Look, you don't understand," Dirk answered. "Dwight has a problem with tight spaces."

"You mean he's claustrophobic?" Megan asked.

"I don't like talking about it," Dwight grunted. "It's a shameful thing to happen to a dwarf."

"But dude, you're totally like a hero now," Dirk shot back.

"Doesn't matter," Dwight said. "I can't go down no tunnel—hero, outcast, or something in between."

"Then we'll just go outside," Megan offered. But Dwight shook his head.

"No, too many dangers out there. You've got to follow the tunnel—it's your best chance to get to Sarah."

"What about you?" Max asked, not liking where the conversation was headed. They'd already lost two people, and going on without Dwight seemed like a bad idea.

"I'll just wait it out here. Don't need any light, either—it's better if I can't see the walls. And when the door's ready, I'll knock three times and be on my way."

"I guess we don't have any choice, then," Melvin said. "We can't expect a claustrophobic dwarf to walk down a narrow tunnel. Although I don't like what this does to our party—we've lost all our melee fighters, so now we're down to a wizard, a healer, a pixie, a ranged bowman, and two, uh . . . ," he started, looking over at Puff and Moki. "Pets."

"Watch who you're calling a pet!" Puff protested.

"And you forgot about me," Dirk said, looking annoyed.

"Oh yeah, a *bard*," Melvin continued, making the last word sound as appetizing as cod liver oil.

"Basically we're a party of magic users and others now," Melvin went on. "And that's not good."

"I'm not an 'other'," Dirk complained. But something Melvin had said was tickling at Max's brain.

"Actually, a bard is kind of a magic user when you think about it," Max began, working through his thoughts. "At least in the role-playing world, which is pretty much the characters we've become. And bards have a special kind of magic."

"Party buffs and stuff," Dirk answered. "It's like helper magic."

"Magic directed at us," Max continued. "Remember Sumyl and her carriage? That was magical too, and Dwight was able to go into the dwarf city as long as he stayed inside."

Dwight raised an eyebrow. "So . . . ?"

Dirk nodded, suddenly understanding. He grabbed Glenn and swung the lute off his shoulder.

"Are you sure this is a good idea?" Puff asked. But Moki was clapping his paws together excitedly:

"Songs are neat!" the fire kitten announced.

"We need Dwight with us," Max insisted.

"Well, I think it's a waste of time," Melvin added.

"As a warm-up," Dirk said, adjusting his shoulders and hips just like he'd seen an Elvis Presley impersonator do, "here's an old favorite called 'Melvin the Frail.'"

"Just get on with it!" Dwight shouted.

Dirk looked momentarily disappointed, but then grabbed Glenn's neck and fingered a new chord. He began singing, and his voice reverberated through the tunnel with a strange power.

Oh . . .
Let me tell you the story of a dwarf named Dwight,
Who when in tight spaces had such a fright!
He needed to go down a tunnel quite long

So the world's greatest bard sang him this song:
The rocks are not rocks waiting to crush!
They are giant stuffed pillows ever so plush!
You've nothing to fear, so please go ahead;
Now this song has been sung, so you'll do as I've said!

"That's the last time you will ever sing about—" Dwight started to say; then he stopped. The fear and anxiety that had played out on his face were suddenly gone. Instead, he looked around the tunnel with an odd expression. "I feel . . . better," he admitted.

Dirk twirled his lute around his shoulder and caught it in his hand, aiming it at Dwight like a rifle. "You've just been Dirked."

"Oh, I'm pretty sure we all have," Glenn added.

Moki began clapping his paws together. "Do it again!"

"We don't need any more of that," Dwight grunted, straightening his armor and slinging his axe off his back. There was a bounce to his step and an energy to his movements that Max hadn't seen before. "Now we have people to rescue and a tower to get to, so let's not be lollygagging. I'll go first, followed by Max. Moki, can you do that flame-on-your-tail trick of yours?"

Moki smiled and lifted his tail into the air. There was a muffled *whoosh*; then a bright orange flame erupted at the tip.

"Great," Dwight continued. "You ride on Puff by Max, lighting the way ahead. Megan, you light up the rear, and Sydney, you keep an eye out behind. Melvin and Dirk, you'll take the center."

Everyone got into place as Dwight had directed, and they began their march downward. The tunnel was just wide enough that two people could stand side by side, but the ceiling left little room over their heads. They traveled in silence for several minutes, listening to the sounds of their boots against the stone floor. After a time the tunnel leveled, and they pressed on. Dwight kept them moving at a brisk pace, and the flame from Moki's tail did a good job lighting the passage ahead.

"Dungeon crawling," Dirk said after a time. "Epic."

CHAPTER TEN

SHADRUS POCKETS

THEY HAD BEEN WALKING FOR A WHILE, WITH ONLY THE OCCASIONAL grumbling of Max's stomach to mark the passing of time. Max was slightly annoyed that in the middle of a cataclysmic storm and dark-lord invasion his stomach found it necessary to complain about the food situation. Stomachs seemed to have a mind of their own.

Ahead, the passageway opened into a large room. The group slowed, growing cautious as they approached. They paused for a moment at the entry, taking the place in. The room reminded Max of a restaurant after closing, filled with tables and upturned chairs. Shadows hung like heavy drapes as the fire kitten's tail did its best to push the darkness aside.

"This place kind of gives me the creeps," Sydney remarked.

"Yeah, like a Denny's," Dirk replied.

"And why is there a restaurant in the middle of a tunnel?" Megan asked, looking around. "Doesn't seem like you'd get much business."

"Let's have a look," Dwight said, "but stay close."

They entered the dining hall, the floorboards creaking with each step. As they pressed forward, Max caught sight of furniture that was both out of place and yet familiar— as if two different rooms had been mashed together.

"Look, there's a bed over there," Megan said, motioning to a great four-poster bed that was just visible in the blue light of her staff. "Do taverns usually have beds in the middle of them?"

Everyone looked at Dwight.

"Why are you looking at me?" he grumbled.

"We're just kids," Sydney said. "It's not like we've been in a tavern before."

"Although we did make one out of cardboard once for a LARP game," Megan added. "But then it rained so we changed it to a bog."

"Max and I were in a dwarf tavern once," Dirk said. "Just saying."

"No," Dwight said, growing impatient, "taverns don't have beds or dressers or any such things in them. Not that I can see worth a darn in this darkness."

"Oh, I can fix that!" Moki exclaimed. He jumped off Puff's back and darted into the middle of the room. Then he lifted his tail and the flame blossomed out like a gas-fed torch, chasing off the shadows and bathing the entire room in light.

"That's why fire kittens make the best traveling companions," Dirk said.

"Yes," Melvin said, thinking about how he might integrate that into his next LARPing adventure—likely a mix of house cats, tape, and flashlights. Max, however, was staring around the room.

"I've been here before," he said. And as he took the place in, he realized that the odd bits of furniture belonged to the regent's quarters—the very room where he'd stood before Rezormoor Dreadbringer as a captive. Max could see the large ornate chair where he'd nearly stumbled into the zombie duck during his hand-walking spell, and against the far wall stood Dreadbringer's stone fireplace. Only now the brick twisted and morphed into long wooden planks that eventually turned into a stage. But most striking was the black, obsidian stand where the *Codex of Infinite Knowability* had once rested as it waited to be rebooted and brought back to life. "This was the room that stood at the top of the Wizard's Tower," he continued. "At least, part of it is."

"You're right; I remember it too," Puff said, looking around. He'd been with Max during the pitched battle with Dreadbringer and his minions. "But why would it be *here*?"

"Who said that?" a gruff voice called out. Dwight stepped out in front of the group and motioned the others to get behind him, his axe at the ready. But Max recognized it. . . from somewhere.

"Do not trifle with me," the voice continued. "If you know who I am, you know what I do to thieves."

"The Wez . . . ?" Max said, remembering the goblin warlock who'd reached out to him when he was trapped in the future. There was a moment of silence before the voice answered.

"Even so. Now go while you have the power to do so."

Max motioned for the others to follow as he carefully walked toward the sound of the Wez's voice. Dwight kept close to Max as they moved past more tables and upturned chairs and then stepped behind the bar. On the other side they found a soft yellow light spilling out across the floor and leading to a back room. "We're not thieves," Max announced as they drew closer. "You invited me to find you."

"Not at this hour I didn't, so go away and *find me* when we're open."

Max continued to the back room and paused at the door. He couldn't be sure that the Wez remembered him—in fact, the warlock had warned him that he might not. The fact that the Wez had been able to reach through time to contact Max spoke to the goblin's power. Max took a breath and stepped into a small washroom with pipes of several different sizes running along the walls, including one that terminated at a lit gas lamp. At the far end the face of the Wez was reflected in a large mirror hanging over a basin. The goblin was running a straight razor over his green skin, and behind him the reflection of the same washroom was visible. He had long black hair, just as Max had remembered, with two clumps tied and braided so they ran down either side of his face. The Wez worked the razor around a tiny patch of black hair at his chin, his long ears wiggling with each stroke.

"Hey, that's one of those two-way parallel-world things, I bet," Dirk whispered, peering around the corner. "Sweet."

Max ignored his friend and approached the mirror, seeing the strange image of the Wez looking past him on the other side. "You said you might not remember me," Max continued. The Wez suddenly stopped shaving, and spun around to confront the unwanted intruder. But when he found himself still alone, he turned back to the mirror and leaned forward, squinting. Max wondered if he should say something or not, but then the Wez bent down to retrieve a feather-and-skull-covered staff. He shook it at the mirror twice, muttering something under his breath. Max felt a wave of magic wash over him as the Wez blinked, then locked eyes with him and frowned.

"Well, now, this doesn't bode well," the goblin warlock said.

"Then you remember me?" Max asked hopefully. The Wez had helped him once before, appearing prior to the great battle at Machine City and aiding him in wielding the Prime Spells. *You try and overthink magic that big and you'll never make it work. The key is flowing around in that red gook you call blood . . . just relax and listen for it.* Max had, and it had worked.

"I don't know you," the warlock continued. "And yet . . . ," he began, looking at Max. He studied him with a critical eye as the others made their way into the washroom behind him. "Such power. Old power . . . old blood. You are he, aren't you? You are the descendant of Maximilian Sporazo. You are the one who toppled the Wizard's Tower in Aardyre."

It wasn't really a question, but Max answered anyway. "I am. My name is Max Spencer."

"Interesting. I never expected you to be so old."

Max was confused for a moment and then remembered his hair. "Er, my hair isn't normally like this."

"What you need is a long wizardly beard and mustache," Dirk added, then he suddenly brightened. "Just think of your yearbook picture! That would be awesome!"

"And what is that book at your side?" the Wez continued, ignoring Dirk. "*The Book of Graves?* If so, it's a dangerous thing for a mortal to carry."

"No," Max said, looking down at the old magical tome. "It's the *Codex of Infinite Knowability*."

"Then the rumors are true. What have you done, Max Spencer?"

Max drew a breath, knowing what he had to say next was not easy. "I opened the Shadric Portal. I was only going to use it to go back to the Magrus, but something terrible happened."

"The Cataclysm."

"Aye," Dwight answered, stepping forward. "And now the Techrus is being transformed into a world of shadow. But how is it you are here, warlock, if you don't mind my asking?"

"I am here because you have done a very stupid thing," the Wez replied, looking at Max. "But as it stands, I know not who you serve nor what end you seek. You should know I am not in the habit of trusting wizards—especially ones with too little brains and too much power."

"You found me and helped me once," Max continued. "You warned me that you might not remember, so I should tell you something."

The Wez raised an eyebrow. "Is that so?"

"Yes," Max replied, searching his memories for the right words. "You said I should tell you to look in the mirror and count what you see."

The Wez stared at Max for several moments before replying. "I have such a mirror, wizard. And if you know about it then it is only because I have told you. It appears as if I am to trust you after all."

"So explain this place," Dwight pressed again. "How is it you are here?"

"It is a pocket," the warlock answered. "I have sprinkled many such across the umbraverse like seeds, hoping that they never take root and sprout. For if they do, it means that the barrier between the three realms has been broken. And *that* means the end of everything."

"Not everything," Dwight replied. "Behind it stands the Maelshadow."

"I see," the Wez answered, turning his back and pacing back and forth in the mirrored room. "Using the Shadric Portal to break the bonds of the umbraverse would allow black magic to taint it. Sporazo must have known this. It was said the artifact was locked away and guarded with powerful bindings." The Wez stopped pacing and turned to Max. "Blood bindings."

"Dwight told us only someone who was good could carry it," Megan added from the back of the room.

The Wez toweled the last of the shaving cream off his face. "A blood binding with an alignment lock— such magic would allow only one of Sporazo's blood to retrieve it from the Tower, and then only open it if they were good of heart. A prudent defense against the portal's misuse, I think. But obviously something went wrong."

"Max never took it," Dirk said. "This kid Wayne had it."

Max nodded in agreement. "He said the rulers of the Seven Kingdoms wanted me to come back, so they offered the use of the portal."

"This is not the doing of any king. You were obviously deceived by the one with the most to gain. Somehow the Lord of Shadows retrieved the Shadric Portal and employed this boy from the Magrus to bring it to you," the Wez continued.

"Excuse me, sir," Melvin said, offering a formal bow. "I am Melvin the elf. I have been listening to all of this, but it doesn't quite add up. How could our companion carry the portal for Max to use if he knew that it would destroy the world? That would make him decidedly evil, I think, and therefore unable to touch it."

"True," the Wez replied, looking Melvin over and raising an eyebrow—he'd seen many kinds of elves before, but this one looked odd. "Unless this Wayne was duped himself and had no idea of what was going to happen. Or he had some notion, but had lived such a life that the weight of his soul still remained good." Max wondered if Wayne had known what he was doing or not—a question he was going to ask the giant of a boy next time they met. That thought brought him back to what really mattered, however.

"My friend Sarah has been taken captive, and the people in our town have been turned into monsters," Max continued. "Please, is there anything you can do to help us?"

"I already have. You've found my secret place and it will lead you to the heart of the fracture. And as for the storm that has changed your citizens into monsters? You have one rotation of the sky—twenty-four hours. After that they can never go back to who they once were."

Max's mind desperately scrambled to calculate how much time had passed. Everything had started the day before, after school. Then they'd spent the night at the

Dragon's Den and set out the next morning. They'd done a lot of walking since, and he'd been knocked out for a while as well. Max felt a sinking sensation that time was running out.

"One more thing," the goblin continued through the mirror. "Alignment locks are double-sided. While you may have the power to activate the portal again, only someone *evil* can actually close it. It's an unsettling irony, I know, but I thought you should know."

It was too much for Max to think about just then. *One step at a time,* he told himself. *Rescue Sarah and then figure the rest of it out.*

"Thank you," Max said. "Again."

The Wez nodded, watching as the motley band turned to leave. Then he noticed something odd trailing behind them. It took a moment for the warlock to realize what it actually was. "And what in the world have you done to that fluff dragon?" he called out.

Puff paused and regarded the warlock. "If I told you, I doubt you'd believe it."

They made their way back through the strange room, seeing both elements of the Wez's Mesoshire nightclub and the regent's quarters. It occurred to Max that the "pocket" might draw on memories from both the Wez and those who traveled through it. That the top room in the Wizard's Tower had left its mark on the subconscious of those who'd been there wasn't surprising. Max reflected on this as Dwight led them to a doorway and the continuation of the tunnel. They assembled into their places and set out, walking two by two through the small passageway.

They had traveled for some time, noticing that the floor had begun to angle upward, when without warning they found themselves facing the tunnel's end. And as before, they were greeted by the strange swirling motion in the rock followed by a new face. It stretched out to meet them, only this time the face had feminine features. "Heard you coming for some time," it announced cheerily. "I suppose you'd like to get past."

"Yes," Dwight quickly answered. "And without any of that riddle nonsense either. I'll just knock three times and we'll call it good."

"Knock all you like if you wish," the face answered, "or trade riddles or touch me with magic. It won't make a difference because I'm not locked."

Dirk shrugged. "Well that was easy."

"Then let's get going—" Max began, but Melvin put a hand on his shoulder.

"I don't think it's a good idea to go blindly marching through a door when we don't know what's on the other side. I've played a lot of role-playing games and I've learned this lesson the hard way."

"Maybe the door can tell us?" Sydney offered.

All eyes turned to the face in the door. "Certainly," it replied, sounding thrilled to actually be talking with someone. "On the other side is a stone room with a gracon inside. And he doesn't look particularly happy."

"A what?" Megan asked, her staff still glowing blue in her hands.

"Oh no . . . ," Dwight sighed, shaking his head. "No, no, no."

"Dude, I think a gracon must be like a boss character or something," Dirk said to Max.

"I don't think you understand," Puff answered, his words measured and careful. Despite his recent condition he'd been a powerful dragon once, and as such he knew much about the darker things in the three realms.

"Take equal parts evil, power, death, and fury. Forge them together in the blackest depths of the Shadrus, and then add an ancient soul that yearns to destroy. Next give it liquid fire for blood and wrap it in flesh that rivals the strongest dwarven armor. And then, as if that weren't enough, place two horns on its head—each sharp enough to slice through stone and steel as if they were paper."

"Or butter," Dirk added, looking at Max.

"Imagine all *that*," Puff continued, ignoring Dirk, "and you'll barely understand what a gracon is."

They sat in silence as Puff's words hung over them.

"So tougher than a gnome," Dirk announced after thinking it over.

"And you're saying *that's* what's waiting for us on the other side of the door?" Megan asked.

"Yep," the door answered. "Exciting, isn't it?"

Max turned to Dwight. "So what do we do?"

"*We* can do very little. You're the only one with the power to face a gracon." The dwarf hesitated. "I think."

Max opened the *Codex of Infinite Knowability* and began flipping through the pages looking for a spell.

They simply had no alternative but to move forward—too much time had already passed.

"Everything has a weakness," Melvin offered, trying to help. "What would a gracon's be?"

"Not fire," Megan replied, "if it has lava for blood."

"Ice, then," Dirk suggested.

Max remembered a number of cold and frost spells in the *Codex*. He flipped ahead until he found one: "Okay, here's a first-level spell, Blunted Icicle Formation—"

"Dude, skip to the big ones," Dirk urged.

Max grabbed a handful of pages and flipped ahead. "Well, there's this one: Ice Age World Ender, level ninety."

"Too far."

Max nodded and started flipping back. "Okay, this one might work . . . Icening Bolt, level forty-four. Says it fires bolts of ice with the speed and power of lightning from the caster's fingers." Max looked down at his fingertips and tried to imagine bolts of ice-based lightning shooting from them.

"I take it you've never actually practiced this spell before?" Dwight asked.

"It's not like I can just go into my backyard and start throwing icening bolts around," Max protested.

Puff thought it over. "Maybe you should find a Prime Spell and cast that instead? We are talking about a gracon, after all."

"It's not like when I was in the Magrus," Max replied. "Casting a Prime Spell here . . . I can barely control it. And it takes everything I've got just to do that. So no matter how tough this gracon is, I've got to have enough left to deal with the Maelshadow."

Puff nodded. "I understand."

Max turned his attention to the spell. He read the words under his breath and felt the hairs on the back of his neck rise as he began to summon the magic. The Tower would train a wizard for years to be able to cast such a spell, and there was probably a certain way it was supposed to be done. But whatever Max lacked in knowledge he made up for with his connection to the *Codex*. Of course the ancient tome wasn't usually so helpful, which only made Max more nervous about how bad things had actually gotten. He cleared his head of such thoughts and focused on the spell, feeling it move from the pages of the book to his arms and hands. He had to hold it back with some effort—the power of it was like a huge dog pulling at a leash. Max stepped forward as the others prepared themselves. "Open," he commanded the door.

"This is going to be exciting," the face said as the slab of rock swung outward. With the spell bristling with energy, Max stepped through.

CHAPTER ELEVEN

THE MALASPIRE

THEY HAD ASCENDED INTO THE SKY ON THE BACK OF NIGHTMARE-PRINCESS, rising into the churning storm of the Cataclysm while lightning flashed and thunder exploded around them. Wayne had removed Sarah's sword and bound her wrists as the black beast lowered her twisted and malformed horn and warned: "Resist and I will burn you into memory." If all of Sarah's years of martial arts had taught her anything, it was that there was a time to stand firm and a time to yield—and now was the time to yield.

The winds that buffeted them were no match for the black, leathery wings that had unfolded from the monster's side. Sarah had glared at Wayne when he offered his hand to help her up. "Just do as they ask," he'd said as he hoisted her to the monster's back. She bit her lip and said nothing. The silence continued as she felt the powerful muscles driving the nightmare toward the Malaspire. An odd name, Sarah thought, but fitting. It had been formed from the bricks and stone that had once made up her school, but now they'd been torn apart and refashioned into a crooked tower that stretched much higher than any building in Madison ever had. On the roof the tornado continued its dance, and as they drew near, a pelting rain broke out around them. Sarah leaned forward on Nightmare-Princess's back, turning her head against the sudden fury of the storm.

They circled the top of the Malaspire, the lightning so close that static electricity filled the air. Sarah chanced a look at what was left of the town below. It was unrecognizable. Fires burned here and there, scattered between wooden huts with pitched roofs or crude stone fortifications. It was as if the world had suddenly lost five thousand years and reawakened in the Bronze Age.

Nightmare-Princess pitched forward, and Sarah had to squeeze her legs or risk slipping off the beast's wet back. She felt Wayne shift behind her, helping to prop her up. She didn't want his help. She didn't even want to be near him. They flew to a landing about midway up the tower, the otherworldly hooves of the nightmare shooting sparks from where they cut into the stone and slowed them to a stop. "Wait here," Nightmare-Princess said, ordering them off her back. Sarah hurried and slipped off before Wayne had a chance to help. She found herself in a small room filled with whitish candles in twisted metal sconces along the walls.

"Let the Maelshadow know we have her," Nightmare-Princess said to Wayne as she turned and made her way back out to the landing. "I return to the hunt." She leapt into the gray sky, more molten flame dripping from her hooves and smoke exploding from her nostrils. A flash of lightning caused Sarah and Wayne to turn their heads, and when they looked back the nightmare was gone. Sarah hurried over to the landing, confirming what she'd already suspected—it was too high to try to climb down.

"Don't do it," Wayne cautioned. "There's nowhere to go."

Sarah had had enough. "How *could* you?" she shouted. The sudden rebuke hit Wayne as hard as any blow, and he took a step backward. "He *trusted* you! You said you would protect him!"

"You wouldn't understand," he simply said, his eyes lowered. "I'm not one of you."

"What do you mean you're not one of us?"

"He means he's not human," a squeaky voice said, joining the conversation. Sarah turned to see a pink-faced macaque monkey staring back at her from the far corner. In addition to a coat of fine gray fur, it wore star- and moon-filled robes with a matching pointed hat. It was an outfit she had seen before.

"Magar . . . ?"

"Indeed. Only I seem to be a primate," the wizard sighed.

"A macaque, I think," Sarah said, remembering them from her textbooks. "If that helps, I mean."

"Not really."

Sarah turned her attention back to Wayne. "And what did you say about him not being human?"

"Exactly that. Your friend is clearly an ogre—although his transformation is quite good."

Wayne shrugged. "Like I said, I'm not one of you. Ogres and humans are enemies."

"Are we?" Sarah asked, stepping away from the landing and moving to where Magar sat. "Then let me ask you this: What has Max or any of us humans ever done to you?"

"It's . . . complicated."

"Is it? Because it must be pretty serious since you've decided to destroy our entire world."

Wayne slowly pulled the amulet of alignment from under his chain mail. The stone had turned black. "It's how someone like me becomes evil."

"Well, I guess congratulations are in order—you're certainly that."

"Ogre society is based on being evil," Magar added. "Every ogre youngling is given an exam upon graduating middle school."

"So let me guess," Sarah continued. "You were the star pupil—you were the valedictorian of evil school."

"The opposite," Wayne admitted. "I scored the very lowest. I was doomed to spend the rest of my life as an armor tester, except . . ." Wayne paused, remembering the strange events that took him from the career day festivities to the presence of the Maelshadow. The dark lord had found something important, but he couldn't touch it because it was protected. So that was where Wayne came in. He'd had such little evil in him that even the deception would keep him "mostly good"—and so long as he was mostly good, he could bring the artifact to Max. Of course Wayne had to take on the form of a human to pull it off. The magic that made the transformation had been old and powerful, and had left him with memories he'd just as soon forget.

"Except . . . ?" Sarah asked.

"Except I was recruited to work for the Maelshadow because I was good. They needed that."

"I see," Sarah continued. "So you were loyal to the one who used you, and then betrayed the one who accepted you. Sounds to me as if you got things backward."

"You still don't understand," Wayne protested. "It was the only way to become what everyone expected me to be!"

Sarah watched him for a moment, feeling sorry for him despite the anger that still burned inside. "Then perhaps you should be true to yourself, and stop worrying about what everybody else wants."

Wayne stared at her coldly, then turned and walked to a large door with a heavy lock. He knocked and called out, "Open it—I have business with the Maelshadow." Sarah heard the sounds of the door being unlocked before it was pulled open by unseen hands. Wayne paused in the doorway and spoke without looking back. "And my name is not Wayne. It's *Dwaine*!" And with that he walked out and slammed the heavy door behind him.

"So Wayne's true ogre name is Dwaine?" Sarah asked. "I guess I was expecting something a little more dramatic."

Magar shrugged. "Ogres aren't really known for their creativity. Here, give me your wrists."

Sarah took a seat on the floor and held her wrists out. Magar began working at the knots of cord, his small furry hands perfectly suited for the task. "I was quick enough to shield myself from much of the black mist," he continued, as if answering Sarah's unasked question. "Ultimately the storm changed me, but I kept my wits at least. Princess was not so lucky, as you've seen." The wizard managed to get the first knot free and pulled a length of cord through, working on the next. "Magic is not always about raw power, you know. Had Princess been schooled as I had, she might have been able to resist the change."

"Max protected us," she said. "Mostly."

Magar nodded. "That's good. Then he lives?"

"Yeah. And if I know him, he's headed this way."

Magar finished the last of the knots as Sarah freed herself and rubbed the bruised skin. He glanced out at the gray skies and rolling storm beyond. "There is not much time," he announced. "If Max can't close the portal soon, this world will be lost—and I'll be like this forever."

"I've seen Max do incredible things, but this is bigger than any of that." Sarah sighed and turned back to Magar. "Thanks for getting me untied. Anything I can do for you?

"Do you happen to have a banana?" Magar asked. "Seriously, I can't stop thinking about them."

Max stepped through the door and prepared to unleash his spell. He was in a circular room filled with heavy stones and red bricks that used to be part of Parkside Middle School. The gracon stood facing him, bound by a long branch that twisted around its entire body. The creature was tied to a black pillar was flecked with small white dots and vibrated with a deep and ancient magic. The gracon lifted its head, its small red eyes locking with Max's for the briefest of moments before it motioned to the far side of the room and groaned.

Max turned, the spell beginning to slip from his

grasp. He saw another gracon moving toward him, with the same hulking size and broad features, only this one was completely white. But not white, he realized—it was stone! Max turned his hands at the last moment and the spell leapt from him—dazzling blue streaks erupting from his fingertips, striking the stone gracon in the chest. The air snapped with the magical discharge as melon-sized chunks of rock exploded from the creature's torso, sending it stumbling backward. The bound gracon, however, was now motioning in the other direction. Max turned to see a second stone gracon charging like the first. Before he could react he heard the *thwunk* of a bowstring. An arrow suddenly appeared in the shoulder of the beast, quickly followed by two more. The impact twisted the monster and sent it careening into a pile of rubble.

Melvin jumped into the room, drawing more arrows from the quiver on his back. Dwight ran past, raising his axe and charging the second gracon. A fireball sizzled past Max's head and struck the first stone gracon as it struggled to rise.

"Moki, help the others!" Max called out. The fire kitten bounded through the doorway and began slinging fireball after fireball in the direction of the new target. Max turned to the *Codex* and began reading the Icening spell again, feeling the sensation of magic building in the air.

The second gracon tried to continue its charge, but it was driven back by a second volley of arrows and fire-balls. They found their mark in rapid succession, one after the other, until the stone monster had a half dozen burning arrows protruding from it. Dwight sprinted forward, diving as the gracon reached for him. He planted his axe in front of him and rolled over the weapon, bringing it up and across the leg of the monster in a single, fluid motion. The axe bit deeply into the stone with a spray of sparks that sent the beast spinning. Dwight skidded to a stop and swung his axe around, preparing for a second attack, when the sound of Dirk and his lute filled the room:

> *So we're battling some gracons;*
> *That seems pretty cool!*
> *Looks like Dwight just got one;*
> *Yeah, that dwarf's no fool.*
> *Oh, and there's another,*
> *And it's not looking very nice;*
> *Let's give old Max a boost now*
> *And power up his ice!*

Max had been faintly aware of his friend's singing when the spell suddenly leapt from the *Codex* and
exploded through him, exiting his hands with a force
that sent him backward. He felt the *Codex* roll from his
fingers as his other hand joined in on the icening storm.
Instead of single shafts of icening, the air erupted into
a series of connected bolts, splitting again and again,
until they enveloped the far side of the round room and
slammed into the stone monster. The gracon, swallowed by ice and lightning, stumbled backward and then
exploded. Max ducked as chunks of stone flew through
the room. He chanced a glance at Dirk, who was watching, wide-eyed—his hand in mid-strum and his mouth
hanging open.

"That . . . was . . . AWESOME!" his best friend
shouted.

There was a loud crack as the second stone gracon's
leg gave way where Dwight had hit it. The creature spun
around and dropped to its knees. The barrage of fireballs and arrows continued, finding their mark along the
monster's broad back until it looked like a giant flaming
pincushion.

Dwight rushed forward and made a quick end of the

creature, sending the great horned head rolling from its stone shoulders and landing on the ground with a heavy thud.

"That was no gracon!" Dwight exclaimed as he rejoined the others. Max retrieved the *Codex* and brushed himself off. They had done surprisingly well, all things considered. Megan insisted on looking everyone over, and once they'd passed her inspection, they turned their attention to the living gracon in the center of the room. The gracon let out a snort and watched Max with its small, crimson eyes. The creature was magnificent: at least four times the size of Max, with a spiderweb of molten lava crawling along its armored hide. It radiated with the kind of power that reminded Max of explorations within the *Codex*. But he could sense there was something wrong as well.

"Why is it bound like that?" Megan asked.

"Who cares?" Dwight said. "So long as it can't move, it can't get to us."

"It looks like it hurts," Sydney said. She watched as the branches woven around the gracon's body moved and constricted with a life of their own. At the sight of the bound creature Max felt a wave of pity. Nothing deserved to suffer like that, no matter what it had once been.

"What kind of magic could do something like this?" he asked.

"Shadrus magic," Puff answered. The fluff dragon strode up to the gracon and considered it. "The magic of the Maelshadow."

At the mention of the Maelshadow the gracon rolled its head, fighting against the branches that cinched tighter around its neck. It let out a woeful moan.

"That's it—we aren't going to leave it like this," Megan announced, stepping forward with her staff in her hand.

Dwight spun his axe off his shoulder and hefted it in his hand. "Put it out of its misery, then? I can live with that."

"What? No way!" Dirk protested. "We don't kill things that can't defend themselves."

"I have to agree," Melvin added, looking over at the burning remains of his arrows and sighing. "I was going to try and get those back, you know," he told the fire kitten.

Moki smiled. "Burning arrows are neat."

"You want to show pity to a gracon?" Dwight laughed.

"That just goes to show how much you don't know about the way things really work. That monster would tear you in half if you let it."

"I don't believe that," Megan argued.

Max agreed. "I think it tried to warn us."

Dwight laughed again. "Ha! And now you're a gracon whisperer, I suppose?"

"Don't listen to Dwight," Dirk said. "He doesn't like anything taller than he is. Which is why he hates everything."

"One more thought," Puff added. "I think we have to ask ourselves where the stone gracons came from."

Max motioned toward the black column. "There's some kind of magic coming off that."

"So you think there's a connection?" Melvin asked.

"I'd say if not then it's a pretty big coincidence," Puff continued. "A living gracon tied to a magical pillar, and suddenly there are animated stone gracons running around?"

"Oh yeah, total dark-lord move," Dirk agreed. "The Maelshadow is using the gracon to create magical versions of itself."

"But the gracon doesn't control the copies," Megan

offered. "If it did, it'd just use them to get free."

"So the real gracon doesn't control them, but it does make them come to life," Max said, thinking it over.

Puff frowned. "Shadric magic is known for using life energies. The gracon here is probably an unwilling captive that the Maelshadow uses to animate the stone guardians."

"So if we just leave it—" Melvin began.

Dwight finished his thought. "Then we'd likely be running into more of the stone horrors." Nobody relished the thought of having to fight more gracons—stone or otherwise.

"Well, we're not going to kill it," Megan insisted again. All eyes turned to Max as they waited for him to decide what to do. It was a horrible choice—the life of Sarah and everyone in the entire town depended on him getting to the portal and closing it in time. Having to battle stone gracons at every turn could slow them, if not stop them altogether. So was the life of one creature more important than the lives of his friends and family? Was it was necessary for him to do something that he normally wouldn't even consider doing? After he mulled the options over, he came to a decision.

"No, we're not going to kill it," Max announced. But saying that put a pit in the middle of his stomach—he hoped that he hadn't just doomed Sarah.

Dirk noticed the pained expression on Max's face and walked over to his friend and put his arm around his shoulder. "Dude, you made the right call. If you become the thing that you're fighting against, what's the point? Nobody said being the good guys was easy. It's part of being the good guys."

Max nodded, appreciating his friend's support. Dirk had always been there for him, and likely always would be. "One more thing," Max said, turning to Dwight. "Cut the gracon down."

Dwight was ready to protest, but something about the way Max said it made the dwarf stop. Sometimes when Dwight looked at Max he saw the slightly nerdy middle school kid looking for the next comic book. But other times he saw the boy whose blood flowed with that of the most powerful arch-sorcerer who had ever lived, who commanded the Fifteen Prime Spells through a sheer act of will, and who so frightened the most powerful across the three realms that they sought his destruction. *That* was the Max he was seeing now—and when *that* Max told you to do something, you did it.

Dwight silently took his axe and approached the gracon. "Ready yourselves," the dwarf called back as he took the weapon and began cutting at the barbed restraints. The living branch tightened in response, slithering like a giant constrictor and squeezing its prey. The gracon grunted as the branch tightened around its throat.

"It's killing him!" Max cried. Dwight tried to hurry, but the branch began wrapping itself even tighter around the gracon's neck. Max hurried and opened the *Codex*, looking for a spell that would free the creature. The names of the Prime Spells unconsciously rolled through his head: *Fixity—to hold fast and unchanging.* Maybe he could stop the branches with that?

Suddenly a blue light filled the room. Max looked up to see Megan, her long white robe flowing behind her, swinging her glowing staff at the living branch. There was a shriek that filled the air as it connected; then the whole of the branch twitched violently and began to shrivel. The gracon took a deep breath as the branch relaxed and fell loose, finally twisting upon itself and shrinking until it disappeared altogether. The gracon fell forward, dropping to its knees and falling on its two great fists.

The others jumped back and watched as the gracon, its back and chest heaving, remained still. Max let his mind drift into the *Codex*—if the gracon attacked, he needed to be ready. But instead of coming at them, the gracon carefully lowered itself into a sitting position. "I am free," it said, its voice gravelly and heavy.

"Mighty creature of the underworld, I am Melvin—" Melvin started, but Dwight elbowed him in the side.

"Oh, just give it up already," the dwarf grumbled.

"What are your intentions?" Puff demanded, doing his best to sound like he had when he was a fierce and magnificent dragon. He was fairly certain that being challenged by a giant mop in a spiked collar was some-what less intimidating. "And before you answer, know that the one who freed you carries the *Codex of Infinite Knowability* and is the very blood of the World Sunderer himself!"

The gracon slowly turned its great head, and Max couldn't help but notice just how sharp the large horns looked. The two of them locked eyes.

"I see," the beast rumbled.

"So I ask again, what are your intentions?" Puff pressed.

"Fear not, children of men. I have not the strength nor desire to see your end. I have long been embraced by the Tree of Abysmal Suffering, and my wounds run too deep."

Megan stepped forward, eager to help. "Allow me to heal you—"

The gracon raised its hand, stopping her. "Such magic and I are . . . incompatible." Megan nodded, stepping back.

Max broke his connection with the *Codex* and addressed the gracon. "Make your way back to the Shadrus, then. And do not harm any mortal on this world or else I will come and find you."

"And dude," Dirk said to the gracon, "when a white-haired wizard threatens you, you better know they mean business." Max frowned, not thinking the white-hair reference was necessary.

"Freedom for restraint—an acceptable bargain," the gracon announced. "Now leave me to my thoughts, for I have much to consider."

"Is there any more help you can offer us, friend gracon?" Melvin asked.

"Only this: I know naught of this spire's design, save

that we are at the bottom. If you seek to close the rift between the realms, you must journey to the top."

Sydney fluttered over to the gracon. "Thank you, uh—"

"Peaches."

"Peaches . . . ?" Dirk asked, suddenly confused. "We just had this totally awesome encounter with a Shadrus boss-type monster named *Peaches*?"

"It's a very impressive name in Gracon," the creature replied.

"I like peaches," Moki said, smiling to the group. "Both kinds."

CHAPTER TWELVE

SPIDERS AND MENTORS

MAY AND HIS FRIENDS LEFT THE GRACON AND MADE THEIR WAY FROM THE basement. They found a door at the far end of the room that opened onto a narrow staircase, and took the steps in single file. Candles burned everywhere, their dripping wax leaving long trails along the stone walls and making it unnecessary for Moki and Megan to light the way. They had only traveled a few feet when Puff asked, "Just how old was this school of yours?"

"Not old," Max answered. They spoke in hushed tones as they continued to climb. "Why?"

"The webs."

Max took a closer look along the winding staircase. There *were* a lot of spiderwebs along the walls. And with each step the webbing seemed to grow thicker. Max had a sudden flashback to the mechanical spiders that had chased him into the old cement factory when he'd first used the *Codex*. A shiver ran up his spine—spiders kind of freaked him out.

The staircase continued to turn until they found themselves face to face with a large door beneath a carving of a giant spider, its legs spanning the width of the hallway. The door itself was framed by the spider's two giant mandibles, each ending in a sharp claw.

"If you put a giant spider above your door, doesn't it basically mean go away?" Sydney asked. Max thought it was a reasonable observation.

"Stand back," Dwight said. He carefully poked at the stone spider with his axe. The density of spiderweb had markedly increased, hanging in thick sheets over the door and around the walls and ceiling.

"Seems to be stone," Megan said. "But that didn't stop the gracons."

Dirk poked at the spiderweb with Glenn. "Stone spiders don't make real webs."

"Could be a trap," Melvin suggested. "You know,

open the door and the spider comes to life—that sort of thing."

And then Megan began reciting a poem from memory:

"Will you walk into my parlour?" said the Spider
    to the Fly,
"'Tis the prettiest little parlour that ever you did spy;
The way into my parlour is up a winding stair,
And I've a many curious things to shew when you
    are there."
"Oh no, no," said the little Fly, "to ask me is in vain,
For who goes up your winding stair can ne'er come
    down again."

"*That* is super-creepy," Dirk said. "Thanks for sharing."

"I had to memorize it for a class," Megan replied. "It seemed . . . relevant."

"It's not like we have much choice in the matter," Puff said.

Suddenly a mass of swirling lights formed in front of Max and Dwight. They retreated several steps and Max opened the *Codex*, readying himself for an attack. But the lights took on a form he recognized, and he let out a sigh of relief.

"Bellstro!" Dirk exclaimed.

The old wizard hovered slightly above the stone steps, glowing with an otherworldly light. "It is I!" he announced.

"You know this spirit?" Melvin asked.

"He's like our mentor," Dirk offered, as if it was the most reasonable thing in the world to say.

"I have come to give you wisdom and counsel from beyond the grave," Bellstro continued. "Soon you will face a gracon! But not all is as it seems—"

"We know," Max said. "We've already been through that part." He was hesitant to interrupt the old wizard, but time was of the essence.

"You have? Oh, well . . . good. I mean, you survived that without my advice? Weird."

"I'm sure it would have been easier with your help," Puff suggested, addressing his old friend.

"Haven't I warned you about rushing headlong into things without the proper mentoring to guide you along? We all have jobs to do, you know. The mentor's job is just as important as the hero's."

"You have," Max replied. "And I know. Sorry about that. We're just in a hurry."

The glowing wizard frowned. "I wonder if I should tell you about the floating islands of ice?" Bellstro stroked his long white beard as he thought it over.

"I don't like ice," Moki added. "Especially ice puppies."

"We don't have time for your babbling, wizard," Dwight grumbled, dropping his axe to his side.

Melvin said, "If you have any boons to share concerning spiders, O great spirit, we who walk the mortal realm would be glad to hear it."

Dirk rolled his eyes. "Elves don't talk like that, you know. I've met *real* elves."

Bellstro nodded, ignoring Dirk. He liked the way the funny-looking elf addressed him. "Spiders, eh? Yes, I remember reading something about them in my mentoring packet. Now let me think—"

"You get a mentoring packet?" Megan asked, slightly confused.

"Just because I'm dead doesn't mean I know everything about everything, young lady."

"You were saying something about spiders?" Max urged, trying to get his spectral mentor back on track.

"Ah yes," Bellstro exclaimed, suddenly remembering. "The Giant Tarantula of Transmogrification! A nasty creature that one." The wizard noticed the giant stone spider perched over the doorway. "Looks just like that, in fact. Now that's an interesting coincidence."

"Just what do these tarantulas do?" Megan asked.

"Well, obviously they bite, don't they, dear?" Bellstro said, pointing to one of the stone spider's claws to drive the point home.

"And there's one of *those* inside?" Sydney asked, not liking the thought of that very much.

"The important thing is *not* the spider," Bellstro said, looking at Max. "It's the spider's *web*. They're not all the same, you know. I mean, they are, more or less, but they aren't. You get my point."

Max didn't.

"Okay, fine," Dwight grumbled. "There's a giant spider with its more-or-less web behind the door. Max, you prepare some fireballs and we'll roast that thing and be done with it." The dwarf looked down at Moki. "You can join in if you want."

Moki nodded. "Spiders are gross."

Bellstro frowned at Dwight. "You have ears but you

don't hear. Stubborn, thick-headed dwarfs, the whole lot of you!" The wizard began to fade, waving his hands in the air. More lights, like tiny fireflies, swarmed around him, before he and the lights disappeared.

"We should totally get experience points for that," Dirk announced.

Melvin scratched his ear. "You have a very odd mentor."

"He was a great and powerful wizard once," Max said. "I think he's kind of new at the whole mentoring thing."

Dirk motioned to the spider door. "So let's hurry and take this thing out!"

"You seem awfully enthusiastic," Puff said to Dirk.

"All epic stories have giant spiders in them. It's like a rule or something."

Megan thought it over. "I think he might be right."

Max flipped through the *Codex* looking for a fireball spell. He'd had some luck with level three Spontaneous Combustion, but he wasn't sure that was big enough for a giant tarantula. He flipped a few more pages and stopped. "Here's a level twenty-nine spell of Creature Conflagration. Says it's the first component in weaving together the mighty inferno chain."

"Fine, but let's avoid doing anything with the word *inferno* in it," Dwight cautioned. He'd been on the hunting grounds when Max had turned the entire sky into a firestorm, and besides nearly being engulfed in drops of liquid fire, he'd had his beard singed in three places.

Max nodded and began reading the spell, feeling the magic build around him. He looked at Moki, who smiled and produced a flame on the end of his tail. "Moki and I will go in first," Max announced. "Hopefully we'll catch it by surprise."

"And if there's a beautiful elf princess caught in a web or something, try not to burn her," Melvin suggested.

Dwight put his hand on the door. "Why in the world would there be an elf princess in there?"

Melvin shrugged. "A guy can hope, can't he?"

"Just for the record," Dirk said, "*my* girlfriend is an actual princess."

Max ignored his friend and concentrated on the spell. He looked up and nodded. "I'm ready."

Wayne was escorted through the Malaspire by one of the hooded servants. Their faces were lost in the shadows of their black cowls, with only the occasional strands of long, ghostly white hair any evidence of something within. It was strange to think that he served the same master as they. As he continued to climb it occurred to him that he was still thinking of himself in terms of his human name, despite what he had said to Sarah.

They stopped at the doorway that led to what had once been the school gymnasium. The creature that stood before the door had been a human once—the school's janitor, in fact. But now it was something else. The former custodian opened the door and ushered Wayne and the servants of the Lord of Shadows through. Wayne noticed that the thing carried a mop over its shoulder, but the thick strands of coarse cloth seemed to move of their own accord.

"You like 'em, eh?" the unholy and largely toothless janitor hissed to Wayne.

"Sorry, are you talking to me?" Wayne asked.

"Saw you looking at my pretty. Thought you'd like to know her name."

"Oh. Sure. Very nice mop."

"Not nice—and not no mop, neither."

"Great," Wayne said, wanting to get through the door.

The creature raised a bucket he was holding in his other hand. "And this here is my secret weapon."

Wayne looked over the bucket's edge. "Looks like the Maelshadow spared no expense getting you set up."

"Ha!" the creature spat. "Made these myself, I did."

"Well, good luck with all of that," Wayne said, slipping through the door and shutting it behind him. He hurried and caught up with the cowled servants as they stood before the tear between the realms. Outside, Wayne could hear the rain pelting the roof, interrupted by the blasts of rolling thunder. The two servants lifted their hands—each a pallid form of tautly stretched skin over skeletal bones—and pointed at the vortex in the air. Wayne looked up at the twisting hole and swallowed, knowing what was being asked of him. To stand before the Maelshadow required that he cross into the umbraverse.

He wasn't sure how much time had passed, only that the harrowing journey to the Maelshadow's throne was not something he wanted to repeat. The throne itself was twisted and chaotic, forged from some unknown metal that seemed to have exploded from the ground and then frozen into place. Suddenly there was a sense of something moving, and Wayne realized that the Maelshadow had been within the folds of shadows that fell about the throne's jagged features. "The good ogre," the Maelshadow intoned. Wayne felt the voice reverberate around the stone columns of the temple as he dropped to his knee.

"That name does not fit you anymore. Rise."

Wayne stood but kept his eyes lowered. He supposed his parents would be proud if they could see him like this, standing before the Lord of Shadows and doing his bidding. But the thought felt empty as he considered the long journey that had taken him from his home, through the lives of Max and his human friends, to where he now stood.

"Your amulet glows black," the Maelshadow continued. Wayne looked down at the Amulet of Alignment hanging around his neck. "It is as I promised it would be, is it not?"

To be evil was the goal of every ogre. It meant everything. So why did Wayne have to be born so different? *Why do I feel like an impostor?* He gathered his wits and addressed the ruler of the Shadrus: "It is as you've promised."

"But not completely black, I see. Curious. Such an act of betrayal, and yet . . ."

There was an awkward pause before Wayne spoke up again. "I had a long way to go."

"Indeed," the Maelshadow said after a time. "And you played an important role. You have not failed me as so many others have."

"That's good," Wayne answered, and then thought better of it. "I mean, not good, but evil. The good kind of evil."

The shadows shifted on the throne. "Tell me of Max Spencer."

"He and his friends survived the Cataclysm. He carries a powerful book that protects him."

"*The Codex of Infinite Knowability*," the Maelshadow said. "Rezormoor Dreadbringer was foolish enough to try and use the boy to command the Prime Spells within. "Hubris is the rot from which the powerful are made weak. I will not make the same mistake—I will not be tempted to use the boy to gain access to the book. Instead, I shall end the bloodline of Sporazo and be done with it."

Wayne had always known that the Maelshadow had a great interest in Max Spencer and his book, but this was the first time he'd heard the Lord of Shadows pronounce what amounted to a death sentence on the boy. And truly, Max was just a boy, close to Wayne's own age. Max had done nothing to provoke such an enemy, except to be born with the wrong blood coursing through his veins.

"Does this not sit well with you?" the Maelshadow asked, catching something in Wayne's expression.

"I was just wondering," Wayne replied, mustering enough courage to ask what he was thinking. "What will you do *after*? You destroy Max Spencer and remove his book as a threat, and you drive the umbraverse into the three realms until they've all become like the Shadrus. So when you're in charge of everything and you don't have any enemies left, what then?"

"No one has ever asked me that. But I will give you your answer, ogre. You see, the heart of evil yearns for power. The heart of good yearns for meaning. I am evil and thus I yearn for power."

"And when you have it? When the entire universe is yours?"

"Ah, yes. Well, then it's about getting into shape."

Wayne blinked several times at the shadowy throne.

"The acquisition of power leaves little time for working out. I plan to hit the weights, tone up, maybe even run a marathon." Wayne blinked several times before continuing.

"What about the girl?" he asked, ready to change the subject. "You commanded me to bring her to the Malaspire if the opportunity presented itself. It did."

"Go and bring her to me then, and she will draw Spencer here."

"Like a moth to a flame!" a bald priest in the corner added, obviously enthused about the whole conversation.

The Maelshadow whirled. "I told you no idioms!" The Maelshadow clenched his fist and the priest suddenly vanished into a puff of black ash. Wayne realized two important things about the Maelshadow: First, he had a fitness plan for after he conquered the universe; second, he had very strong feelings about certain types of grammar.

"Will Sarah be . . . harmed?" Wayne managed to say.

"That's entirely up to her," the Maelshadow continued.

"If she bows to me, I am not without my mercies." From what Wayne knew of Sarah, he didn't think bowing was very likely.

"And if she doesn't—" Wayne started.

"Then she and Max Spencer will enjoy the same fate."

CHAPTER THIRTEEN

WEBS

MAX HEARD THE SOUND OF THE OCEAN.

He blinked several times, his eyes protesting against bright shafts of light. A curtain was moving, catching the warm breeze that pushed past an open window and filled the room with the smell of salt. Bells sounded in the distance—the kind Max had heard when he'd visited a harbor once with his mom. He rolled from his bed and walked toward the opening. He was fairly high up, maybe six stories or so, and below him ocean waves crashed into rocks formed from the seaside cliff. In the distance, square-sailed ships moved across the blue horizon.

He turned back and regarded the room. Near the window was a desk, and rounded shelves full of books ran along the walls. A rapping at the door was followed by the creak of it opening. Max turned and was relieved to find the face of Dirk poking through.

"Dude, today's the day! Get out of your pajama robes and into your wizard robes."

Max frowned and looked down at what he was wearing. He was dressed in light blue robes adorned with wands and stars. "How do I know which are which?"

Dirk smiled, stepping inside and closing the door behind him. "Because they're not black. The regent of the Tower wears black robes. What's wrong with you?"

"I, uh, don't know."

Dirk grabbed Max by the shoulders and gently led him to a closet, where eight or nine versions of the same black robe were hanging.

"So hurry up already." Dirk turned and made his way to the window and stared out. "Too bad you don't have a view of the port from here."

"Oh yeah?" Max asked as he changed.

"Yeah. There's an Aaredt warship out of Thannis that arrived last night. Plus that Schil warship from Caprigo is pretty cool."

"You don't say."

"There are even rumors that there's a dwarven

submarine around. Of course, you know the dwarfs—
they won't say anything about it and nobody's actually
seen one before."

Having changed clothes, Max walked over to a full-
length mirror and regarded himself. The black robes
seemed to shimmer, and he could make out intricate pat-
terns in the fabric that looked like dragons in flight. Dirk
joined him in the mirror, wearing comfortable-looking
leather with a thin elven sword at his side. "Yeah, we
rock," Dirk announced. "And just think, Sarah almost
talked you out of coming."

"She did?" Max asked. He couldn't escape the feeling
that there was something important he was supposed to be
doing—something that involved Sarah. "Where is she?"

"Madison," Dirk said. He walked over and plopped
on the edge of Max's bed. "This place was never really for
her, anyway. I mean, we all know Sarah's like the coolest
non-unicorn chick around, but she was never like us. She
wasn't a gamer and she never read comic books or got
into any of the same things we did."

"But she's our friend."

"Hey, you gave her the choice to come. She didn't
want to and we have to respect that."

Max walked to a large stuffed chair and sank down in it. "I'm having problems remembering things."

"Oh. Well, that explains why you're acting so weird."

"But shouldn't I be able to remember stuff? You know, like how I got here?"

"Wait, you don't remember coming here?" Dirk asked as one of his eyebrows lifted for dramatic effect.

Max shook his head.

"Dude, you opened the Shadric Portal. The wizards said there'd be some temporary memory loss and stuff."

"They did?"

"And bad dreams, possibly."

Max sighed. "I do feel like something bad is happening."

"I don't know what to tell you. You opened the portal and we walked through. Sarah was a little upset, of course. But you said you'd come back and visit her."

Max did his best to remember, but he was drawing a blank. "And then what?"

"We were taken to the castle and met the barbarian king. He totally hated Rezormoor Dreadbringer and loved the fact you whaled on him, so he made you regent of the Tower, said you work for him now, and sent us here."

"Here?"

"To the new Tower in Dorse. King Kronac left the old Tower a pile of rubble as a reminder to those who want to challenge his authority. It's like a messed-up monument or something."

"Where is Dorse exactly?"

"It's down the coast a ways from Aardyre—that's the capital. Do you remember Aardyre?"

"Yeah, I remember," Max admitted. It hadn't been that long ago that he and his friends had snuck into the city on their way to the Tower.

"So basically everyone is coming here to celebrate your arrival," Dirk continued.

"I'm really the regent of the Wizard's Tower?"

"Yep. Seriously, who's going to challenge the kid who can read from the *Codex of Infinite Knowability*?"

At the mention of the book Max felt a sudden energy coming from the bookshelf. "Where is it?" he asked, somehow knowing the answer already.

Dirk motioned to the bookshelf. "I think you put it in there someplace."

Max felt a strong pull to go over and retrieve it.

"But dude, you don't want to take the *Codex* with

you," Dirk said, following Max's eyes to the bookshelf. "Don't you remember? It kind of freaks people out."

"I don't remember."

Dirk shook his head. "When you get your memories back this is all going to be a lot easier. But hey, we need to go or you're going to miss your party. Although I guess you can do what you want, since like I said, everyone is pretty much afraid of you."

"I don't want people to be afraid of me."

"Then don't go dragging the *Codex* around with you, and don't be late to your own party."

Max stood. "We really did just walk through the portal?"

"Yeah, dude. You know you can trust me." Max nodded, and the two of them made their way from the room and out of the Tower. Max couldn't shake the feeling that things were wrong, however, and that they were getting worse with each step. But as he felt the warm sun on his face and greeted the various townspeople who clapped and wanted to shake his hand, the feeling of dread began to diminish.

That was until he walked past the bookstore.

Dorse turned out to be a picturesque seaside city. A

good deal smaller than the capital, it nevertheless had a number of streets and open marketplaces where goods from around the Seven Kingdoms were sold. It was a common stop for the traders heading north along the Crystal Sea or west from Mor Luin, and Max found the people warm and friendly. The fact that they knew the black-robed wizard could blast them into oblivion might have also helped them appear cheerful—nobody was interested in offending the regent of the Wizard's Tower.

The bookstore was on a narrow, shop-filled street. As he approached, Max felt a pull from within, similar to what he'd felt in the Tower. He decided to investigate further (whether the owner, a small piggish-looking man, was happy or not about it, he couldn't tell). Dirk followed him inside.

"The Great Sorcerer, Regent of the Wizard's Tower, Reader of the *Codex of Infinite Knowability*, Tearer-Down of Towers, Time Traveler, and Friend to the Dragon King has entered your store!" Dirk proclaimed. "He shall be given all courtesies, full browsing privileges, and the frequent-buyer discount."

The little pig-faced shopkeeper nodded. "I'll tell all my customers that the great Max Spencer shopped here!"

"Well, we haven't bought anything yet," Dirk countered.

Max had been drawn to a large bookcase where a number of very old books were stored. The shopkeeper hurried after him. "I see you've found our special collection. A great eye for books you have, sir. A great eye!" Max nodded, feeling the familiar pull that led him past various large volumes until he came to the book he recognized. It was a ruddy color that looked a bit like blood, and along the spine was a pattern of symbols made up of tiny, interlocking dragons. He reached for the tome, and the moment he touched it, a kind of electric power ran through his body. On the cover was the gold, eight-pointed star that separated colorfully dressed humans on one side from a mix of strange, otherworldly creatures on the other. He heard the shopkeeper gasp.

"That's the, the—" the man began.

"*Codex of Infinite Knowability*," Max finished.

"How did it get here?" Dirk asked, eyeing the small man suspiciously.

The shopkeeper raised his hands and took several steps backward. "Please, I have no idea!"

Max ran his hand along the familiar magical tome. "It has a mind of its own," he said, doing his best to ease the shopkeeper's fears. "It must have followed me here."

"Followed . . . ?" the pig-faced man said, his eyes darting back and forth between Max and Dirk. "Please, just take it out. I don't want it influencing any of my other books to do . . . things."

"Does the Tower have some kind of treasury?" Max asked Dirk.

"Totally." Dirk produced a small coin purse.

"Pay the man for the inconvenience," Max said, walking over to a small table and sitting down. He wasn't ready to leave just yet. And while Dirk dropped coins into the shopkeeper's hand, Max opened the *Codex*.

The page showed a tall, misshapen tower with a tornado rising from its roof and connecting with a great boiling storm overhead. Beneath the picture the caption read: *When the Shadric Portal was opened, the Maelshadow seized the breach and allowed the umbraverse to flow into the world, causing the Cataclysm.* Max turned the page and found another illustration. It showed a band of eight adventurers running along a narrow tunnel. There was a dwarf in armor, followed by some kind of dog with a flaming cat on its back, then a wizard, an elf, a bard, a pixie, and a priestess. The caption read: *The band of nine had been betrayed. Two were lost and one was found. Together they flew through the secret places to find the breach and save the world.* On the opposite page was an illustration of a giant spider, wrapping the bodies of the eight adventurers in a silken web. *But deadly fangs found open flesh, and the adventurers succumbed to the poison in their minds.*

"What's going on?" Dirk asked, pulling up a chair next to Max. "Why is the *Codex* following you around?"

Max turned the book so Dirk could see the illustrations. "What do you see?"

"Weird," Dirk answered after a moment. "That bard fella kind of looks like me."

"More than kind of. I think that cat is Moki. And the dwarf there is Dwight."

"So you're like the old wizard dude?"

Max frowned. "I think so." He took the book back and showed Dirk the previous page. Then flipped forward, but following the spider illustration the rest of the *Codex* was blank. "I think it's trying to tell us something."

"Like what?"

"Like things aren't right. Doesn't this all feel off to you? Like we're not supposed to be here?"

Dirk thought about it for a moment. "I have been

feeling kind of anxious, like when I drink too many caffeinated sodas."

"Yeah, me too," Max agreed. He thumped his finger on the book. "I think all of this really happened. I think we opened the portal but we didn't just walk through. I think we created this." He turned to the page showing the tower and the storm. Suddenly the world around them shook. But it wasn't like an earthquake, and stranger still, it didn't affect Dirk or Max. It was as if they were watching something on TV.

"Whoa," Dirk said, looking around after everything had returned to its proper place.

Max flipped the page. "I'm sure this is us, trying to get to the portal and shut it. But something happened. Something bad."

Dirk stared at the picture of the spider. "What if that's what's happening right now? What if we're all lying on the floor someplace, trapped by that spider thing?"

The world suddenly vibrated again, blurring and shaking like all of reality had been hooked up to a paint mixer. It lasted for several seconds.

"The caption said a mind poison!" Max exclaimed, letting go of the table he had instinctively grabbed onto.

"That's it! Somehow we've been trapped, like in a dream or something—"

Without warning the world blew apart. They were lost, tumbling through a black void. Max felt the *Codex* slip through his fingers.

When reality slammed back together, Max was sitting in a saddle, reins in one hand and a mallet in the other. The air rushed past him as he suddenly dropped, spinning toward a well-manicured lawn below. Large tentacles flapped in the air around him, and he realized they belonged to the creature he was strapped to. Not knowing what else to do, Max yanked on the reins. He felt the muscles of the creature tighten beneath him and then his insides seemed to drop to his feet as he pulled out of the fall and soared into the air. He heard an explosion of applause as he passed a giant banner: 111TH ANNUAL SQUIDDITCH CHAMPIONSHIPS!

Squidditch? Max asked himself as he turned his attention back to the beast he was riding. And now that he got a closer look, he knew exactly what it was—a squid! His saddle was mounted just behind the creature's collar on the posterior surface. *Wait, why do I know that?* Suddenly

Max had a memory of his old biology textbook—he'd learned about squids in school. He didn't recall that they could fly, however.

Max looked over his shoulder and saw that he was in a giant stadium where other Squidditch players were darting about. They all seemed to be chasing something, riding the beasts and swatting at opposing players with their mount's tentacles.

"Hey, Max!" a voice called out.

Max turned to see the girl from the *Codex*. *Megan— her name is Megan.*

Max swung his squid around and flew toward her, nearly colliding with an opposing player in the process. He looked down and realized both he and Megan were wearing the same uniform, and she was positioned in front of a floating hoop. *She must be the goalie.*

"Isn't this great!" she exclaimed.

"Megan, what's the last thing you remember—before this?"

She frowned for a moment. "I was talking to you in the Dragon's Den."

"How did we get here?"

A roar exploded from the crowd as Max turned in

9781442450196220 Platte F. Clark

time to see a very small book with wings go flying past. An opposing player was chasing after it, guiding her mount to try and close on the zigzagging object. Max knew at once that it was a pocket-sized version of the *Codex of Infinite Knowability*. How or why it was showing up like this was another question.

"Don't let her get it!" Megan exclaimed, pointing at the miniaturized *Codex*.

"I need to talk to you—" Max started to protest.

"Go get the book or we'll lose!" Megan shouted. She gave Max's squid a swat with her mallet and the beast took off, surprising Max and nearly sending him toppling out of his saddle. He managed to get control of the creature and pulled the reins hard, sending the airborne squid down and toward the *Codex*. He flew past the stands and managed to catch sight of a small, blond cheerleader.

"Go, Max! Go!" she shouted. Max did a double take as he flew past. *Sydney,* he remembered. *I know her.*

Max leaned forward in the saddle and spurred the squid on. The flapping tentacles suddenly pitched forward, forming together into an aerodynamic point. He shot forward, the stands blurring next to him, and focused on the weaving book. He managed to get along-side the opposing player—she was cute, Max thought. The player turned and smiled at him, and Max smiled back. Then she tapped the side of her squid with her mallet and it launched a long, wet tentacle across Max's face. The sound reminded him of the time he'd belly flopped in the swimming pool, and it hurt just as bad. the blow sent Max flying backward and out of his saddle. He barely managed to grab hold of his squid's back as the girl turned and flashed him a wicked smile before pressing her own squid forward.

Max saw the flying winged *Codex* suddenly stop and double back. The girl reached out to grab it, but she wasn't quick enough. The *Codex* flew by as Max struggled to reach out and catch it. But he wasn't in his saddle and the squid was more slimy than what would have been useful. He lost his grip and flew through the air, hitting the grass with a thud and toppling head over heels before coming to a stop on his back. He lay there for several moments, watching the points of light that circled his vision. Then a loud whistle pierced the air.

"Time!" someone shouted.

Max blinked, staring up at the blue sky and watching as

the two teams separated to their respective ends of the field. His squid landed next to him, its large eyes staring down and watching him with a blank expression. Max sighed, climbing to his feet and then back onto the saddle. The squid took off, flying over to where his team was gathered.

"Max, you have to try and stay on your squid," Megan chastised him. It appeared she was the team captain as well. Max looked at the rest of the team, recognizing several kids from school.

"Megan, there's something important we need to be doing," Max said.

"Yeah, we need to be out there *scoring*."

Max looked around, wondering what had happened to Dirk. Then he spotted him, hanging from a tall flagpole. Dirk waved back and shouted, "I'm okay!" It looked as if several crews were hoisting ladders to get to him. Max turned his attention back to Megan.

"Megan, look, you need to listen to me. None of this is real."

She laughed, but it wasn't rude or condescending. "Good one, Max."

"It's not a joke. We were doing something together— something important. I'm starting to remember bits and pieces of it, but only because the *Codex* showed me."

Megan smiled, but her eyes betrayed a suspicion that all was not right in the world.

"I mean, just look around," Max continued, motioning to the stands and playing field. "Isn't this all a bit familiar?"

"Maybe," Megan admitted.

"Familiar on one level, but kind of messed up on another. Like these squids—isn't there seem something wrong with flying squids?"

"I remember studying them in biology," Megan said after a moment of reflection. Suddenly the world shifted and blurred, just like it had before.

"See?" Max continued. "When we remember stuff everything starts to change."

"Like a dream," Megan continued. The world suddenly spun and threatened to break apart, but in the end it came back together. Max looked around as a whistle blew.

"Time!" a referee called out.

"I think I need to show you," he said, turning back to Megan. "I think you have to see the pages in the *Codex* to break free from whatever this is."

"Then it looks like we need to win," Megan said, a

smile returning to her face. But winning a game was the last thing on his mind. He thought back to the image of their bodies being cocooned in webbing. Prepared, no doubt, to be eaten by the spider. And he thought about Sarah, knowing that her life was in danger. And if that wasn't enough, he remembered that time was running out for everyone else as well.

CHAPTER FOURTEEN

SQUIDS AND BEARS

MAX SPURRED THE SQUID INTO THE AIR AND TOOK HIS PLACE OPPOSITE the girl who had tentacle-slapped him earlier. Between them, the *Codex* hovered in the air, its small wings looking very much like a hummingbird in flight.

"You're not very good at sports, are you?" the girl taunted. She was right, of course, but Max wasn't about to let her know it.

"I didn't have the hang of it back then," Max replied, referring to his less than graceful crash. "But I do now."

"You mean 'then' as in three minutes ago?"

Max frowned.

The whistle blew and the field erupted into frantic movement. The crowed roared again, either from their places in the stands or from the tall towers that framed the rectangular field. Most of the squidditch players were chasing a ball around and trying to drive it toward the hoops on either end. But Max wasn't worried about them—he needed to catch the *Codex* and show it to Megan. He spurred his squid on and the tentacles wrapped forward again, sending him and his ride diving toward the ground. Max pulled the reins as he swooped past the grass, using the speed to come up and around the edges of the field as he looked back and forth for the flying book. It took him a moment before he found it, and he spurred the creature forward, weaving in and out of a pair of opposing players as he took chase.

The girl following the *Codex* was just ahead of him, doing her best to match the erratic movements of the magical book. Max stayed with her, following as she pitched up and down, left and right, and then broke across the field just inches above the grass. She managed to get within ten yards or so of the *Codex*, but never closer. The whole thing reminded Max of the World War II dogfighting game that he liked to play online. At the beginning of the campaign the Japanese Zeros were faster and more maneuverable than the US fighters. If you tried to chase after them, they would outrun and outclimb you, eventually getting behind and shooting you down. The only way to beat them was to come at them fast and from their blind spot, and the only way to do *that* was to climb until you were much higher than they were.

Max spurred his squid and pulled on the reins. He had no idea of the mechanics at work that could actually make a squid fly, but he didn't think it really mattered. As he gained altitude, he thought about waking up in the Tower earlier. Coming to the Magrus as heroes was something Dirk had always dreamed about. And Megan had called their present situation just that—a dream. Max recalled the caption under the illustration of the spider: *But deadly fangs found open flesh, and the adventurers succumbed to the poison in their minds.* Max had vague memories of standing before a door and preparing to fight a giant monster on the other side. They must have done that, only it didn't go as planned. They must have lost. Then the words of Bellstro pushed their way through his murky memory: *The important thing is not the spider. It's the spider's web.* The old wizard must have been trying to warn them that the spider had its own kind of web—one that trapped the mind, not just the body. Its poison had not only caused them to dream, but to forget. The only thread that bound them all together was the *Codex*—and the one person bound to the *Codex* was Max. It must have taken him inside the dreams of the others. And although he'd forgotten what had happened, the *Codex* hadn't.

Max took a deep breath, looking down at the pea-sized players as they moved across the field. He would have to try to catch sight of the *Codex* as he dove—then pull up with enough speed to overtake it. He kicked the squid and pointed it down. The drop was gradual at first but quickly gained momentum. Max tried to think back to the flying skills he'd developed playing dogfighting games. He didn't have to contend with actual wind and g-forces online, but the game physics were probably the same. He needed to have enough room to pull up and avoid crashing into the ground. He also needed to give himself enough space to turn, because when you were traveling fast everything required more room.

Max leaned forward and gripped the saddle tighter with his legs as he fought to keep his eyes open against the blast of wind from his fall. The world was coming up to meet him at an alarming rate as he continued to scan the other players—he needed to find the single rider who wasn't with the others. And then he had her, near the far edge of the playing field and circling just above the stands. Max kicked the squid to come about, heading for the opposite end. He twisted his head to take a final look as the girl continued her route around the field. Max then pulled the reins hard, and the force hit him in the pit of his stomach. He lost his breath and his vision blurred as it felt like every organ in his body suddenly dropped a foot or two. *I know how to do this,* Max told himself as he brought the flying squid around and banked against the far side of the field. *I've done this a million times.*

Max whipped around the far edge of the field as he continued to pull the reins and force the squid to turn. He flew past several players as he shot across the entire length of the grass and approached the other side. Max could just make out the girl ahead of him as he calculated the angle necessary to come up from behind and intercept the flying book. It wasn't something Max had learned to do in geometry (although he wondered if he'd paid better attention if it might have helped), but rather an instinct honed after years of gaming. His mind quickly worked out his speed, his angle of attack, and where the target was likely to be. There would be no room for error, and he'd only get one chance. Max swallowed and readied himself.

He closed on the rider as if she were standing still, coming up just beneath her. The suddenness of his arrival surprised the girl, and she yanked on the reins to avoid a collision. Max saw her disappear out of the corner of his eye, but he remained focused on the flying book as it dipped and weaved. Max had never been particularly good at catching things. He had a baseball mitt that wasn't broken in (mostly because it had never been used), and all his Frisbees were on the roof of his house. Max knew himself well enough to know that the odds of him just reaching out and snatching the winged *Codex* were not good. So he aimed directly at it, and the book flew into his chest with a stinging THUMP! Max let go of the reins and encircled his arms around it.

The squid, as if on instinct, began to slow. Max heard a great horn bellow, followed by an explosion of cheers from around the stadium. It took another full circle around the field for him to slow enough to land, and on the ground he was joined by the excited members of his team. They patted him on the back and whooped and hollered.

"You did it! We won!" Megan shouted. The crowd exploded again, and if Max hadn't had both hands wrapped tightly around the *Codex*, he would have waved. It was a strange feeling—Max had never won any kind of sport before, and certainly not something that had actual fans. Dirk came running across the field (apparently his rescue had been a success), grinning from ear to ear.

"Dude, that was epic!" he exclaimed.

Max wanted to savor the moment, but he knew he couldn't. He looked down at the *Codex* and watched as the wings fell away and the book grew to its normal size. He ran over to Megan and opened it.

"Look here," he said, pointing to the first illustration. "This is what happened back in Madison. This is what is happening now."

The world shook and vibrated as it had before. Max continued flipping pages, and Megan looked on in horror when she saw the image of the giant spider attending to their web-wrapped bodies. "Oh my gosh," she said, a tremble in her voice. "I remember—"

The world came apart again, and the three of them tumbled through the darkness. For a brief moment Max caught a glimpse of the real world, feeling his real eyelids, heavy with sleep, prying themselves apart. There was a stinging sensation near his shoulder blades, and his head ached. He was hanging upside down, bound from head to foot, and the others were hanging next to him, cocooned in webs that ran from their necks to their feet. The spider—a monstrosity the size of a small moving van— was attaching the last of them to the web that ran along the ceiling. It was Melvin. But Max's eyes grew heavy and the world pinched shut. Then just as quickly, he was falling in the nothingness between reality and dreams.

They were standing in the great throne room. On either side of them large banners hung between white and gold columns, each portraying a smiling bear with a large emblem on its snow-white belly. At the bottom were various names: Sir Friendly Bear, Sir Sunshine Bear, Sir Luck Bear, Sir Peaceful Bear, and so on.

Max turned to Dirk and Megan. "Where the heck are we?"

"I think I might have an idea," Megan answered. But suddenly a trumpet sounded and a purple bear came bounding toward them. It looked more like a stuffed animal come to life than an actual bear, and it had a small rainbow on its chest connecting a diamond and a heart.

"Hello! Hello!" the bear shouted as it approached. "Are you here to see the queen?"

"Now don't be rude!" came another voice from behind the throne. This time a small panda ran around the other side and joined the others. "We haven't even introduced ourselves."

"Quite right!" the purple bear agreed. "My name is Friendly Bear."

"And I'm Considerate Panda," the black-and-white panda offered.

And then they said in unison, "We're flair bears!"

"Flair bears?" Max repeated.

"Will you be my friend?" Friendly Bear asked.

"Can I pick you up and hug you if I say yes?" Dirk asked.

The purple bear giggled. "Of course!"

"Deal!" Dirk announced, picking up the bear and giving it a squeeze. The flair bear giggled again, only louder. "Yep, just like the one I had as a kid," Dirk said as he put it back down.

Max turned to his friend. "Is this *your* dream, then?"

"I'm pretty sure I don't dream about flair bears," Dirk replied. "At least I hope not."

"No, but my sister probably does," Megan said as she motioned to the throne. The others looked to see Sydney, dressed in a pink dress and sparkling tiara, sitting and watching them.

"Welcome to Flair Bear Kingdom," she said, flashing Max a smile. "As queen I am ever so busy and don't have much time for company, but it's nice having friends to visit with."

"I love friends!" Friendly Bear announced.

"Especially when they're polite and mind their manners," Considerate Panda chimed in.

"Polite friends are the best kind," Sydney agreed.

"What's the last thing you remember, Syd?" Megan asked her sister. "Before coming here, I mean?"

"You must always address the queen as *Her Royal Highness*," Considerate Panda said, casting Megan a distressed look.

"Okay, it was kind of cool at first, but I'm pretty much over them now," Dirk announced.

Sydney cocked her head as she considered her sister's question. "I don't like to remember the places before Flair Bear Kingdom. In fact, I write them in my journal so I don't have to remember them at all."

Something about the word "journal" caught Max's attention. "Sydney, what does your journal look like? Is it red with a golden star on the front?"

Sydney smiled. "It is! How did you know that!"

Max guessed the *Codex* had taken the form of Sydney's journal. "Do you think you could show it to us?"

Considerate Panda frowned. "It's definitely not polite to read someone's journal," it said, waving a finger at Max. Max had a sudden urge to kick Considerate Panda through the window.

"Well . . . ," Sydney said, thinking it over. "I suppose it would be okay since you're really good friends. You are a really good friend, aren't you, Max?"

"Oh, uh, sure."

Sydney smiled again. "Then I would be happy to show you."

"Do we really have time to read journals?" Dirk asked Max.

"It's the *Codex*," Megan answered.

"Oh."

"Only there's a teensy-weensy little problem," Sydney continued. "My journal was stolen and taken to Scare Bear Island!"

236 Platte F. Clark

"We don't care for scare bears very much," Friendly Bear said.

"But I know!" Sydney suddenly exclaimed. "You could go and get it for me! I'm sure the three of you are brave enough to go to Scare Bear Island!"

"Yeah, I'd hope so," Dirk said. "They're probably like soft and furry and stuff."

"True," Sydney admitted, "except for their claws and teeth."

Friendly Bear frowned. "It's not very nice to file your teeth down to sharp points." Max didn't like the sound of that.

"You'll have to get past the four guardians," Sydney told them. "Do Your Worst Bear, Share Your Secret Bear, Bad Pun Bear, and worst of all, Surprise You're Dead Bear."

Max knew they had very little choice in the matter. Even though the *Codex* managed to interject itself into the minds of his dreaming friends, it seemed to be bound by whatever logic was controlling the dream. In this case, a sleeping Sydney who apparently had a thing for flair bears. "Okay then, show us the way to Scare Bear Island."

The boat was shaped like an upside-down rainbow. It's Your Birthday Bear was steering the vessel across a shimmering body of blue water, while Champion Bear stood watch on the boat's bow, a shiny gold trophy in its hand.

"I thought you were a 'champion' as in you were a knight or something," Dirk said as they crossed the lake. The two of them had struck up a conversation shortly after leaving.

"But I am a champion," the blue-and-white bear announced proudly. "I even have a trophy." Dirk moved over to take a closer look.

"It says 'Everyone Gets a Trophy Day.'"

"Yep!" the bear exclaimed, holding it up. "A champion."

As the small boat moved across the water, the blue sky became overcast. By the time they reached Scare Bear Island the world had turned gray and the air had chilled.

"My birthday wish is to never have to come here again," It's Your Birthday Bear announced as the boat pulled up to a decrepit dock. Along the beach a number of pikes had been driven into the sand, adorned with the heads of various stuffed animals.

"I don't think they have trophies here," Champion Bear said, unnecessarily.

Dirk jumped off the boat and tied the rope to the dock (the rope had a certain red-licorice vibe to it). "Don't leave without us," he commanded the two flair bears. They nodded, not looking especially thrilled at the idea.

"We'll wait," It's Your Birthday Bear replied. "But are you *sure* it's not your birthday today? I always keep a slice of cake in my pouch, just in case."

"Ew," Megan replied.

Max, Dirk, and Megan climbed off the boat and made their way to the beach. They walked past the row of pikes and found a small trail that led into a dense jungle beyond, marked by a wooden sign painted with a skull and crossbones.

"I'd say it's probably this way," Dirk said, motioning to the sign.

"We need to be careful," Megan cautioned. "As sweet and innocent as those flair bears are, I think the scare bears might be the opposite."

They hurried, driven by thoughts of their unconscious

bodies as ready-made snacks back in the real world. The jungle eventually gave way to a small clearing, where two torches burned by the mouth of a cave. The cave itself was set into the stone face of a rocky hillside.

"I think we go inside—" Dirk started to say, when a blur of movement exploded from the opening and hit Dirk square in the chest. He was driven backward and fell to the ground, his hands wrapped tightly around the neck of a snarling scare bear. It looked like a flair bear—if a flair bear had been dropped in a damp hole for a decade and gnawed on by rats. Add to that a set of sharp claws and gnashing, pointed teeth.

"Get it off me!" Dirk screamed as he struggled with the snarling scare bear.

Reaching for the *Codex* was instinctual. Max drew out the level two Spontaneous Combustion Spell and flung it at the berserking scare bear. The creature burst into flames, and Dirk managed to toss it toward the jungle and roll away. The small, flaming bear landed in a section of thick foliage as Dirk scrambled to his feet and drew the elven sword from his belt. "That thing is super creepy," he announced.

Suddenly the scare bear jumped from the jungle,

completely engulfed in flames. It took a step forward, calling out in a harsh voice: "Is that the best you got, or the *worst*?"

"Looks like we found Do Your Worst Bear," Dirk said, raising his sword.

The flaming bear took another step forward and then fell to the ground, bursting into a final orange fireball. Dirk walked over to it and poked it with the edge of his blade. "I think that's that. Also, I'm totally going to get rid of my stuffed animals when I get home."

Megan reached down and found a heavy branch. "We'd better be ready for more of those things," she said. "It moved awfully fast."

"Nice job with the spell," Dirk said to Max. "Just be careful where you're aiming that thing, you know, because you've had problems in the past."

"A long time ago," Max replied. "But I've got a handle on it now. But more importantly, the *Codex* is close. I can feel it."

Dirk nodded. "Cool. You must have leveled up or something. I bet you're level ten. Good things usually happen at level ten, because you're now a double digit."

Max shrugged. "Let's just keep moving." He grabbed one of the torches as he led the others into the cave. The opening stretched out to a passage large enough for them to walk down. They followed the path, feeling the dampness and cold wrap around them with each step. Along the walls they could make out drawings of small bears with thick claws and long teeth in battles with various creatures. *What is it with Sydney and scare bears?* he wondered. Then he felt the presence of the *Codex* grow stronger—they were heading in the right direction.

The passage opened into a larger, well-lit chamber. The place stretched up a hundred or more feet to a huge glass dome, and in the center was a rock pillar encased in a cage that looked as if it had been carved from a single, giant diamond. Inside, the *Codex of Infinite Knowability* rested on a pedestal of rocks. But there were also three more of the scare bears there. They had the same old-and-worn look as the first, but each with its own unique design: Share Your Secret Bear was blood red and had the faded image of an open lock on its stained, off-white belly; Bad Pun Bear had baby blue fur with a frowny face on its front; Surprise You're Dead Bear was midnight black, with a gray tombstone on the patch of dirty white fur. It was Share Your Secret Bear that spoke first.

"How did you get past Do Your Worst bear?"

"Oh, him?" Dirk replied. "You might want to change his name to *Impaired* Bear."

"I'm not sure we need to be antagonizing them," Megan cautioned.

"I know we don't *need* to . . ."

"Tell me why you're here," the scare bear continued. "I can keep a secret—I promise."

"I don't think we should trust a guy named Share Your Secret Bear," Dirk replied. "Just saying."

"Don't feed us your lies," Bad Pun Bear injected, "because we're already *stuffed*. Get it? Stuffed? Because we're all full of stuffing on the inside."

Max rolled his eyes. "Look, we don't want any trouble. Just give us the *Codex*—uh, journal—and we'll be on our way."

The three scare bears began to laugh, but it wasn't the kind of adorable cartoon bear laugh you'd see on television. It was a creepy, crackling laugh that suggested they might want to pay a visit to Family Physician Bear fairly soon.

"You are all going to die here," Bad Pun Bear continued. "*Fur* sure."

"You there," Max said, pointing to Surprise You're
Dead Bear. "Are you in charge?"

Surprise You're Dead Bear smiled, its yellow, sharpened teeth contrasting with its black fur. "You could say
that."

"Then you should know that I don't want to hurt
you, but I have to get that book back. The lives of my
friends depend on it, and I'm not going to let anything
happen to them."

Bad Pun Bear groaned. "Can we just kill them
already? All this talking is un–*bear*-able."

Max took a step forward. "My name is Max Spencer.
I am the last living descendant of the World Sunderer,
Maximilian Sporazo. I am the keeper of the *Codex of
Infinite Knowability* and wielder of the Prime Spells. Do
not test me."

"Kill them!" Surprise You're Dead Bear rasped before
arching its head back and howling. And then the stuffed
scare bear began to grow—its body expanding until it
stood twice Max's height. Its chest had thickened, its
limbs had lengthened, and as it turned to glare down at

them, it had a wolfish aspect to it. "Surprise," it growled.

"Werebear!" Dirk shouted. Max had no idea how Dirk had come to that conclusion, but it seemed reasonable.

The two scare bears rushed them, one coming at Dirk and the other at Megan. They would have to fend for themselves, Max knew—he was going to have his hands full with the werebear. He caught a glimpse of Megan swinging her branch while Dirk began circling with his sword raised. Dirk had had some training at the hands of Prince Conall back in the Magrus, and at the very least he knew how to defend himself. Megan, however, was a different story. He wasn't sure if LARPing translated into actual combat skills or not.

Suddenly the werebear attacked. It covered the distance between itself and Max in the blink of an eye, and Max swung the torch in response. The werebear knocked it out of his hand with a head-sized paw, then swung the other. The impact hit Max on the shoulder, and his arm went numb as he flew through the air and landed on the stone floor. He barely managed to turn as the werebear ran toward him, driving both clawed fists into the ground. Unbelievably, the hard stone floor exploded, and bits of rock and debris flew into the air. Whatever the werebear was, not only was it fast, but it was strong. *Too strong.*

Max rolled again, just avoiding the next blow. He reached out to the *Codex*, but the snarling monster grabbed hold of him. The beast lifted Max over its head, and his connection with the *Codex* faltered. Max panicked, helpless, his limbs flailing. He could see Megan, her branch now glowing a bright blue, driving Share Your Secret Bear back. Then the world blurred as he was launched into the air. Max slammed into the side of the cave wall with a thud that sent electric shocks through his body.

He didn't remember hitting the ground, but he could feel the cold stone under his cheek as spots of light danced around his eyes. Claws encircled him again, and Max was hoisted back into the air. His vision had all but narrowed into a tiny tunnel of light, and the sounds of combat echoed strangely as if far away and through a tin can. He could feel himself losing consciousness, and with it came a profound and deep sorrow. His failure meant not only the end of his friends, but the end of the world. It was too much to face. Max reached for the *Codex* again, but the magical book felt far away. He could barely sense it when the rush of wind and the sensation of falling returned. And then another explosion of pain, and his world turned white, for just a moment, before being swallowed by the numbing blackness.

CHAPTER FIFTEEN

ROCKY AND COMPANY

"MAX!"

Max opened his eyes to see Megan leaning over him. She had the glowing blue branch in her hands and she touched him with it. Suddenly the pain and weakness fell away. He drew in a deep breath, and with it came a renewed strength and clarity. The change must have been obvious because Megan said, "Now go destroy that thing so we can get out of here."

Max climbed to his feet and saw Dirk dancing around the werebear with his sword. The monster was fast, but so was Dirk as he used the sword to parry the creature's attacks. He and Megan had been able to take care of the other scare bears before coming to his rescue—but the werebear wasn't going to go down so easy. Max reached out to the *Codex* and dove into the part of the book where the Prime Spells were hidden.

"Tutelary!" Max shouted, his voice shaking the cavern and causing the werebear to stumble. The creature whirled, snarling, but it seemed insignificant compared to the power of the Prime Spell. Max drove the magic into the rock itself. He watched as the stones shifted and came together, taking shape. What rose from the cavern floor was larger than the werebear by half. It had four arms and two legs, formed by great masses of rock and bound together by glowing magma. Steam rose off its body as it stepped between the werebear and Dirk, its fingers clenching and unclenching with the sound of grinding stone. Its two eyes were fiery pools of light, and a red glow emanated from its mouth. The werebear charged its new opponent, dragging its long claws against the heaving, steaming chest of the rock now come to life. The rock creature was unfazed, however, and responded by driving its two fists into the werebear, sending it flying.

Dirk hurried and scrambled away from the fighting, circling over to where Max and Megan were standing. Max watched as the werebear decided it had had enough, and ducked into a passageway and retreated.

"Whoa!" Dirk exclaimed. "You made a rock golem. How come you never did *that* before?"

Max shrugged. "It's not like I've been trained or anything—I kind of make it up as I go." He turned and put his hand on Megan's shoulder. "You saved me—again."

Megan smiled. "It's what a healer does."

"Yeah, every party needs a quality healer," Dirk added.

Max turned his attention to the rock golem and called out, "Hey, uh . . ."

"Rocky," Dirk suggested.

Max frowned. "You there," he continued, trying to sound polite. "Would you mind breaking this cage open for us?" He pointed to the diamondlike bars that surrounded the *Codex*. The rock golem moved to the center of the chamber, each step sending vibrations through the floor. It raised its giant fists and struck the cage with a mighty blow, shattering it into a thousand shimmering pieces.

Max ran up to the stand where the *Codex* lay. He grabbed it, feeling the magic tingle in his hand.

"Back to the queen?" Dirk asked.

"Yeah." Max turned to the golem. "Thanks for your

help." The rock creature regarded him for a moment, but did not speak. Instead, Max heard a voice in his head:

The one who seeks your end cowers in its den. I will stay here and ensure it does not harm you. Then I will return to whence I came.

Max nodded and then led the others from the cavern and out of the cave. They followed the trail through the jungle, leaving Max a moment to reflect on what had happened. He had summoned a Prime Spell, but it hadn't exhausted him. Whether it was a part of whatever rules governed the dream or something else, he wasn't sure. But he took it as a good sign—he'd need all the strength he could muster to face and defeat the Maelshadow. He'd also need to be more careful. If not for Megan and Dirk the werebear would have beaten him. He was fairly certain that no matter how dangerous the werebear was, it was nothing compared to the Lord of Shadows. He needed to remember that lesson—he would need to use every advantage he could find.

"Rocky was awesome," Dirk said to Max as they stepped out of the jungle and back to the beach. To their shared relief, the rainbow boat was still tied to the dock and waiting for them.

"I'm pretty sure that's not his name."

"Well, that's what I'm calling him in the song I'm writing. Need something that rhymes with Rocky . . ."

They returned to the dock and made their way to the boat, Max pausing to help Megan aboard.

"You found the queen's journal," Champion Bear announced. "I've won!"

Max rolled his eyes as they boarded the boat and made for Flair Bear Kingdom. He wasn't sure of the mechanisms involved that actually made the vessel move, but when you were in a dream, he supposed, details like that didn't matter. But the whole scenario was becoming problematic—Max didn't want to jump from dream to dream in order to pull everyone back to reality. If things continued like they had, he'd have to move through Dwight's and Melvin's minds next. Not to mention Fluff's and Moki's—and Max was pretty sure he didn't want to know what fire kittens dreamed about. More frightening, however, was the thought that if sweet little Sydney could conjure something as horrible as scare bears what would be waiting for him in Dwight's or Melvin's head? *No—there's got to be a way to pull all of us back at once.*

By the time they returned to the docks at the foot of

the flair bear castle, Max had come up with a plan. They disembarked from the rainbow boat and he moved to a secluded spot just outside the castle wall.

"I'm going to see if I can short-circuit all this dream stuff," he announced. Max tightened his grip on the *Codex* and made the connection with the Prime Spells. He knew them all, having spent long days memorizing the list on their travels in the Magrus: Captivity, to imprison or enslave; Density, to compact or make heavy; Elemenity, to affect through fire, earth, water, or air; Fixity, to hold fast and unchanging; Futurity, to move forward in time; Gallimaufry, to create a mixture of diverse things; Gravity, to attract; Irony, to disrupt the expected and the realized; Liquidity, to make flow; Nimiety, to copy and make excess; Panoply, to cover and protect; Parity, to balance and make equivalent; Tutelary, to summon protection; Unity, to unite into one; Vacuity, to empty.

Max found what he was looking for. Taking hold of a Prime Spell was always strange, and he felt a part of the universe shift as the power and enormity of it rose around him. He focused on the others: Fluff, Moki, Dwight, and Melvin. He then imagined them united with him in

Sydney's dream. "Unity," he said under his breath. The whole of the world seemed to fold in on itself, and for a brief moment Max thought he was going to be dragged into some nether region and lost forever. He continued to focus on his companions, imagining them one after the other, each standing at his side.

When the world righted itself, Max took a breath and opened his eyes. To his delight, his friends were all there! Dwight was sitting on some kind of royal dais, his mouth open as a female dwarf fed him from a silver tray, while Melvin was putting the finishing touches on a long bow he'd been carving. Moki was there too, chasing a ball of yarn around a giant catnip plant. Then the screaming started, and terrified flair bears began running for cover and pointing frantically down the beach.

Max turned to find a giant dragon perched on the sand. He watched as it opened its wings, casting a shadow over the whole of the dock. But there was something strangely familiar about it.

"Puff . . . ?" he began.

"Oh, wow, a real live dragon!" Sydney exclaimed as she ran toward them. A group of terrified flair bears followed her, all eyes locked on the ancient monster. When

Sydney noticed the *Codex* in Max's hand, however, she began clapping. "And you found my journal! This is like the best day ever!"

"I had the strangest dream," the dragon said. "I had been transformed into a fluff dragon."

"Puff, that is you . . . right?" Dwight called out. The presence of a dragon had made him forget all about grapes.

"It is I," the ancient voice rumbled.

"Okay, dude," Dirk added, "I just want to say you might not like what you're about to hear, so don't go breathing fire or anything."

"What's going on?" Melvin asked.

"I can explain," Max said, waving the others over to join him as he walked to Puff. "We all forgot something important, but the *Codex* didn't." They gathered around and watched as Max flipped through the pages, explaining what had happened. None of them liked the idea that they were all held captive in a dream while their bodies were defenseless. Puff took it especially hard, having to face the truth that he was actually a fluff dragon dreaming he was his old self. But as they stared at the final image, the fog that had obscured their memories lifted. The world jumped and blurred as it had before, and together they fell through the poison of their dreams.

The Giant Tarantula of Transmogrification was about the size of a fifteen-passenger van, and even upside down it looked threatening. Not that the spider was upside down—Max and his friends were hanging from webbing on the room's ceiling, wrapped tightly in cocoons that made them look like giant dangling Q-tips. Except for their heads, which were left untouched—presumably so they could breathe.

"You wake now," a small voice whispered. Max managed to look over his shoulder and see a small kobold hanging next to him. Or at least it looked like the kobolds from his fantasy games: short, grayish creatures with elongated noses and long, pointed ears. This one also had an explosion of red hair.

"Who are you?" Max asked, wondering if he was back to reality or not. He squinted against the pounding in his head.

"Name Broduken. Or you can call me spider dinner."

Max frowned, casting another look at the spider.

"Kobold humor," Broduken continued. "Not well appreciated. So how come you wake?"

"It's a long story."

"Kobolds don't dream. Wish me could. Me rather be sleeping when spider comes."

The room where Max and the others were hanging was long and narrow, and contained a series of columns that ran along each side. There was a door at the far end, opposite the one they had entered through. Max could only remember bits and pieces of what had happened, but it seemed to add up to an ambush.

"I need to get down," Max said as he started to push against the web.

"No!" Broduken whispered as loud as he dared. "Don't twitch. Spider feels."

Max froze as the spider turned. It was multicolored, with brown and black legs, and a black and white body. Max couldn't see the eyes under the fine hair, but he sensed it was staring at him. He held as still as he could, until the creature turned back around.

"Max?" he heard Puff whisper.

"Yeah. Is everyone here? Is everyone okay?"

Max couldn't see the others from where he was

hanging—only the little kobold. There was a pause before Dwight whispered back: "We're all here and awake. Everyone's okay."

"Spiders are gross," Moki added from somewhere in the back.

"Everyone stay still and be as quiet as possible," Max warned them.

"We heard you whispering before," Melvin added. "We sort of figured that much out."

"Max, we need to do something fairly quickly," Puff said. "That spider is not going to wait very long before it eats one of us."

"More humans awake?" Broduken asked. Apparently he couldn't see the others either. "You must be buffet."

"We're not all humans," Puff whispered back. "Just for the record."

"Hey, that spider might want an appetizer before dinner," Dirk announced. "We have to save Dwight."

"Who you calling an appetizer?" Dwight whispered, a little too loudly for Max's liking.

"We don't have time for this," Megan warned. "Max, do you have a plan?"

Max didn't have a plan, but he could see the *Codex*

lying on the floor below him. He knew he could draw upon the Prime Spells, but he summoned one, there'd be consequences.

"I think I have to use a Prime Spell," Max announced to the group. "I don't think the fire one I have memorized is strong enough."

"Web burn good," the kobold added. "So does everything in it."

"I can cast Captivity to enslave the spider," Max suggested after a moment. "Then Elemenity to carefully burn through the webs."

"You're going to use one of the most powerful spells in the universe to burn through web?" Puff asked, sounding shocked.

"Yeah, dude," Dirk added. "That's like using a nuclear bomb to cook a hot dog."

At the sound of "hot dog" Max's stomach rumbled loudly. Unfortunately, Max's stomach was loud enough that the spider spun back around to face them. It studied the group a moment before starting toward them.

"Just do it!" Dwight shouted. "We're out of time!"

At the sound of Dwight's voice the spider sprang into action, suddenly moving much faster than it had any right to. Max narrowed his focus on the *Codex*, trying not to think about the monster bearing down on him. He found the familiar magic of the book waiting for him, and pressed deeper to where the Prime Spells were hidden. But as before, it felt as if the spells pushed back, refusing to be summoned. He chanced a look at the rushing spider and realized he wasn't going to make it.

"Why did you have to say 'hot dog'!" Sydney exclaimed. "You've doomed us all!"

Max made a clumsy grab for one of the Prime Spells. He no longer cared which one—any one of them would have to do.

"Hope we die quick," the kobold said.

Suddenly there was a sizzling sound and the smell of something burning. Max lost hold of the *Codex* and tried desperately to twist so he could see what was happening. Then he caught sight of an orange-and-white blur on the ground. It was Moki. The little fire kitten snarled, arching his back as a bright blue flame came to life on the end of his tail.

"Nasty spider!" Moki called out. Then he began flinging crackling blue balls of fire at the tarantula. They were so hot that Max could feel them on his skin even as they traveled across the room. The tarantula didn't stand a chance: It ignited with a horrible screeching sound, falling from the web as it landed and continued to burn, finally shriveling into black ash.

"Moki!" Max exclaimed.

"And you didn't hit the web!" Melvin shouted. "That's some sharpshooting there!"

Moki frowned, the flame on his tail going out with a puff of white smoke. He hadn't thought about the web at all. "It's not nice to eat people," he finally announced. Moki backed up and made a run at Max, leaping into the air and grabbing hold of the webbing with his claws. He used them to cut through the silken layers. Max fell to the floor, landing less than gracefully but without injury. He watched as the fire kitten bounded from person to person, freeing each of them in turn.

"I'm officially declaring fire kittens the ultimate bane of spiders," Dirk announced.

Broduken approached Max, bowing slightly. "Broduken will live now. Thank you."

"How did you come to be trapped here, woodland creature?" Melvin asked.

The kobold shrugged. "Broduken work at Malaspire."

Dwight hesitated pulling the last of the spider web from his beard. "Wait, you mean this evil, Shadrus-inspired tower has a *staff*?"

Broduken nodded. "Of course. Who do you think does all the work?"

Megan kneeled down before the kobold. "Were you forced to serve here? Are you a slave?"

"Yes," Broduken announced. "Me work for temp agency."

"Can you help us, Broduken?" Max asked. "I'm looking for my friend. A girl with auburn hair, wearing a white cloak."

"I can help," the kobold said. "The master take her to temple."

Max shared a look with the others—at least Sarah was still alive. "I have to get to her," he continued. "Do you know the way?"

Broduken nodded again. "Sure. We on level one. Door to temple on level twenty-seven."

"So *twenty-six* more to go?" Dwight asked, not liking the sound of it.

"Yes. Level one is spider level."

Melvin frowned. "What's on level two?"

"Level two Ice Yeti of Boombasa. Very bad. No good level two."

"I don't think I like this spire thing very much," Sydney said.

"Just what else do we have to look forward to?" Puff asked. "How many traps and monsters are there?"

Broduken stroked his chin before answering: "Level three swarming vorpal hornets; level four mechanical spinning wheel of death; level five lava snake pit; level six Theater of Unfathomable Horror—"

"Unfathomable horror . . . ?" Megan asked.

The kobold shuddered. "Yes—only plays Jaden Smith movies. No one makes it past level six."

"*Every* level has something horrible in it?" Melvin asked.

"Monsters and traps till level twelve. That fitness room."

"Looks like that's as far as Max gets," Glenn chimed in.

"Me work kitchen. Level sixteen."

"Then how'd you get down here?" Dwight asked, sounding suspicious.

"Dumbwaiter take Broduken to wrong floor," the kobold replied, motioning to a far wall. "I show you."

They followed the little kobold to the far corner where he pointed to the stove. It appeared just like a normal wall, but when Broduken gently knocked a small door swung open, revealing a narrow elevator shaft.

"Oh, I get it," Melvin said. "Not a *dumb* waiter, but an actual dumbwaiter."

"A dumb what?" Sydney asked, looking confused.

"It's what they used to call these small elevators a long time ago," Dirk answered. "People used them to carry food and stuff up and down to different floors."

"I don't think that's a very nice name," Sydney added.

"I ride dumbwaiter," Broduken continued. "Take to wrong floor. Spider waiting. Big mistake."

Max scratched his head. "So you're saying this elevator goes all the way to the top?"

"Ah, smart human. Now know spire secret."

Max turned to the others. "Are you guys thinking what I am?"

"That there's still no way you're getting past the workout room?" Dirk replied.

"No," Dwight said, swatting Dirk on the back of the head. "We ride the dumbwaiter all the way to the top."

"I like going up," Moki added.

"Me show you how to work it," Broduken continued. "Even now for saving Broduken's life."

Max agreed, happy to accept a bit of good luck for a change. He just hoped it would last.

CHAPTER SIXTEEN

BATHROOM BUDDIES

THEY HAD TO RIDE THE DUMBWAITER ONE AT A TIME. THERE WAS A MOMENT when they weren't sure Max was going to fit, but he sucked his breath in and squeezed. Max wasn't exactly fond of tight spaces: Once when his Boy Scout troop decided to go hiking, he'd been forced to crawl through a drainage pipe. Three hours, seven firemen, and one industrial winch later, they managed to pull him free. Max tried not to think about *that* while the elevator made its slow crawl upward.

They were ultimately deposited in a small alcove on the twenty-seventh floor. They said their farewells to Broduken and moved into a large hallway. The floors and ceilings had lost the random scattering of red brick and gray stone. Instead, the hallway was lined with what looked like black marble. On closer inspection, however, the veins in the stone actually pulsed. It was also free of dust and debris—so much so that the hallway practically glittered under the light of the torches that lined the wall.

"Looks clean," Dirk said. "A little *too* clean."

"What's that supposed to mean?" Melvin asked.

"Can't trust anything so spotless," Dirk continued.

"What in the world are you talking about?" Megan asked.

Dirk sighed. "Think about it. . . . Carnivals, zoos, arcades, movie theaters—all basically dirty yet awesome. Hospitals, schools, clothing stores—very clean and to be avoided at all costs."

"I like shopping for clothes," Sydney protested. But Max had long since learned that you shouldn't always dismiss one of Dirk's crazy thoughts. There *was* something suspicious about a place that was too clean.

Suddenly a figure stepped out ahead of them. "Urinal cakes aren't really cakes, you know," the man said. Max recognized the voice—or at least a version of the voice, which had once belonged to the school custodian,

Mr. Lizar. There wasn't a kid in the entire middle school who wasn't already afraid of Mr. Lizar, even before the umbraverse messed everything up. He had wild, thick hair that rose straight up on his head and small lips that stretched across a mouth crammed full of yellow, uneven teeth. He was tall and thin, and wore a threadbare scarf and gray tweed jacket that was decorated with several old army medals. His eyes seemed a little too close and a little too big, and each was topped with a thick brown eyebrow that clung to his forehead like a fuzzy caterpillar. The person standing before them now was essentially the same, with a mop slung over his shoulder and a bucket in his hand—only now he wore an eye patch.

"Hey, that's Mr. Lizar," Melvin noted.

"Except something happened to his eye," Megan added.

"Eye patch—the sure sign of evil," Dirk announced.

Max scanned the place for exits: Behind Mr. Lizar was a large door, but just ahead there were two other doors, one pink and one blue, on opposite sides of the hallway. The bright colors seemed especially out of place given the pulsing black marble.

"Like the patch, do ya?" the former Mr. Lizar called out to them. "See, I'm the Jan Man now. And the Jan Man has the power to wield the one and only mop-dusa!" The Jan Man gave the mop on his shoulder a twirl and Max noticed something very strange about the way the mop seemed to keep moving—like it was alive.

"What's more," the Jan Man continued, "I don't scrub and clean for ungrateful kids. Not no more."

"I'm not ungrateful," Sydney added. "I appreciate all you do to keep our school clean."

"Me too," Megan pointed out. "I thought you did a great job."

The Jan Man lowered his bucket to the floor. "You did?"

"And that time someone wrote about me on the wall, it was gone by the next day," Melvin said.

Dirk smiled. "Oh yeah, I remember that one: 'Melvin is a dork' written in big letters by the shop-class door. Classic."

"If you think we didn't appreciate you, well, that's just not true," Max insisted, building on what the others had said. They seemed to be onto something—maybe they could reach Mr. Lizar with a little kindness? Maybe all he needed was to know that he mattered, and it would break whatever spell he was under?

"I never knew. Excuse me for just a moment," the Jan Man said, fighting back a sniffle. He pulled what looked like a long handkerchief from his pocket and then lowered it into the bucket.

"I think he's crying," Sydney said. "I think we touched his heart with our kindness."

"He just needed to know we cared," Melvin noted. "Not all monsters on the outside are monsters on the inside."

Max was about to move toward the Jan Man when he heard the sound of muffled laughter. The Jan Man straightened, something about the size of a hockey puck hanging from his handkerchief. The laughter continued to build, filling the hallway until the former Mr. Lizar was practically howling.

"Oh, how sweet!" the Jan Man mocked. "You actually thought that would work, didn't you? That your kind words would turn me from my evil ways?"

"Maybe a little," Max admitted.

"The poor misunderstood monster," the Jan Man continued. "Just needed a friend to tell me how wonderful I am and everything's all better. What'd you do, read that in a comic book or something?"

Dirk bristled at the remark. "Don't go mocking comic books."

The Jan Man raised the handkerchief over his head and began swinging it like a sling. "Poor little children. I think you just need some friends to play with. I make friends, you know . . . just like I make the urinal cakes. Kind of ironic, since *urine* a lot of trouble."

"That's like the worst pun ever," Melvin remarked.

The Jan Man frowned and continued swinging the urinal cake over his head, taking aim at the group.

"What the heck's a urinal cake anyway?" Sydney asked.

"It's that stupid thing in the bottom of boys' toilets. Like a deodorizer or something," Dirk answered.

Sydney frowned, looking even more confused. "Why would anybody name that *cake*?"

"No idea, but maybe not the most important thing at the moment," Max called back. "I think we better take cover!" He pointed to the blue door. "In there!"

Nobody argued. Max ran to the blue door just as the

Jan Man launched the urinal cake. It careened toward them, then dipped and smashed on the floor.

"Incoming!" Dirk shouted.

Max pulled the door open and held it as the others scrambled in. The Jan Man had loaded a new urinal cake in his makeshift sling and was preparing another attack. "Hurry up!" he shouted, not liking the idea of being exposed while some kind of urinal cake projectile was being flung at him. The others ran past; only Sydney stopped in the doorway, her eyes wide.

"I can't go in THERE!" she protested.

There was a whizzing sound as another urinal cake flew down the hall. This one also seemed to veer off course and slam to the floor. Max was about to think the Jan Man was a pretty horrible shot when he noticed something was growing out of the black, pulsing marble— something very much the consistency of a blue urinal cake, only with a head, torso, and arms. To his disbelief, the urinal cakes were turning into urinal . . . men? That seemed like the absolute worst name for a monster *ever.*

"Sydney, get in there!" Megan shouted behind her pixie sister.

"I can't! It's the *boys'* bathroom!"

Max watched as the urinal man moved forward, stepping out of the strange marble stone like it was climbing out of a swimming pool.

"We don't have time to argue about this!" Megan shouted, giving her sister a shove through the doorway.

"Eww!" Max heard her scream as she flew inside.

The urinal man started toward them as another began to grow from the projectile remains. The Jan Man whooped and sent a third projectile flying in their direction. The urinal cake smashed into the ground and exploded just as the others had.

Max followed Megan into the boys' bathroom. He slammed the door and called the others over. "Hold this while I try and lock it!"

The others ran to the door and pressed their weight against it.

BOOM!

The door opened a few inches as the urinal man crashed into it, but the group managed to push it closed again. Max opened the *Codex* and began looking for a locking spell.

BOOM! This time the door opened further before

they were able to shut it. "That felt like more than one!" Dwight grunted through clenched teeth. "Hurry it up, Max!"

Max moved through the old spell book as quickly as he could: level four spell of Grass Leveling; level twelve spell of Insect Speak; level twenty spell of Pantaloon Protection.

BOOM! The door flew halfway open.

"Dude!" Dirk yelled as he and the others tried to force the door closed. Blue hands wrapped around the door as the magical creatures fought to force their way in.

Max flipped the page and found what he was looking for: level twenty-two Dead Bolt of Extreme Awesomeness. "I think I've got something—just get the door shut!"

"Oh, sure, good idea," Dwight exclaimed. "Why didn't I think of that?" The dwarf groaned as he and the others pushed against the bathroom door.

"They're too strong!" Megan called out.

Puff had backed into the door and was pushing with all he had. He looked down at Moki, who was standing upright with two paws on the blue surface. It was more cute than actually effective. Then Puff had an idea. "Moki, why don't you try flinging a few fireballs at them?" The fire kitten nodded, liking any idea that involved making fireballs, and left his spot to circle toward the opening. He produced a small orange flame and closed his eye, taking aim.

Max began uttering the spell under his breath.

BOOM! This time the door flew open and the group fell backward. But Moki was ready, and began flinging softball-sized fireballs through the opening. The volley went on several moments before the urinal men slipped back, their blue skin melting from the heat. Dwight sprang to his feet and shoved the door closed.

Max followed with the spell. Suddenly a giant dead bolt, made from heavy iron and a complex series of gears, materialized in the door. The gears spun, and a heavy bar slammed into place, locking the door with an impressive *clank.*

There was a collective sigh of relief as the others stooped to catch their breaths. The pounding on the door resumed, but the lock held fast. The door, however, was another matter. Eventually the urinal men would break through.

Max turned to take a better look at the bathroom. It was definitely a boys' bathroom, with a long row of urinals along the wall and bathroom stalls that stretched from the ceiling to the floor, but each had a heavy key lock attached to the front. Sydney noticed the locks as well. "Wait a second, boys get locking stalls? No fair!"

"I wish," Dirk said, climbing back to his feet with the others. Max approached the first stall. "Weird . . . these are much bigger than I remember."

Meanwhile Sydney had inched toward the closest urinal and peeked in. "Oh, so that's a urinal cake. Boys are gross."

Melvin frowned. "Maybe we should, you know, use the facilities as long as we're here? There seem to be plenty of private stalls."

"True," Dirk said, walking toward one of them. "No one can be truly heroic with a full bladder." He turned and pulled on the handle, but it refused to open. Shrugging, he moved to the next, but with the same result. There were at least twenty stalls stretched out along the blue tiled bathroom, and not one of them appeared to be open. "Now I get it!" Dirk exclaimed. "All these toilets and they're locked? The Maelshadow is a true monster!"

In response to Dirk's cry, a voice came from one of the closed stalls. "Hey, who's out there?"

Max and the others shared a look, then cautiously moved to the door. In the background, the pounding of the urinal men against the door continued.

"Who are you?" Max asked.

"Max? Max Spencer?"

"Nice try," Dirk said. "Max is out here."

"No duh," the voice continued. "And you're Dirk, aren't you? Figures."

Suddenly Max knew exactly who it was. "Ricky? Ricky Reynolds?"

"Yep."

Melvin frowned.

"Ricky 'the Kraken' Reynolds?" Megan asked. "That's who's in there?" Max nodded. Of course Megan, Sydney, and Melvin had no idea of his history with Ricky, but that didn't matter. Ricky's reputation around the school with kids like them was bad enough.

"Well, that's easy," Dirk said. "As long as he's locked in there he's not a problem." But something didn't seem right to Max. Why was Ricky locked inside a bathroom stall that was more like a prison cell?

"What happened?" Max asked through the door.

"You tell me. We were just in the bathroom after practice and everything went crazy. We got sucked into these stalls. I'm going nuts in here—you gotta get me out, Spencer."

"What else changed?" Dirk called out. "Are you like some horrible creature with tentacles now?"

"What? What are talking about?"

"Is your skin more scale-based than usual," Dirk continued, "or do you now have more talons than you used to?"

"Max," Ricky cried out, "I don't know what Dirk's talking about. Get me out of here . . . *please.*" Max had never known Ricky to use the *P* word before. Things must have been really desperate in there.

"So you're still . . . you?" Max asked. He really didn't know how else to put it.

"Of course—what are you talking about? What's going on out there? This has something to do with you, doesn't it?"

"Why would he say that?" Melvin asked.

"Dude, it's a long story," Dirk answered. "But Ricky knows that Max is a wizard."

Megan frowned. "Who else knows? Is this like some secret the whole school knows except for us?"

"Nobody else," Ricky answered through the door. "At least I never said anything. Why would I? Who'd believe me?"

Max considered his options. The bane of his existence, his archenemy, the kid who terrorized him and everyone like him, was locked safely away on the other side of the door. And he *claimed* to be his old normal human self—a very muscular, athletic, and proficient-at-delivering-pain self. But if he had been turned into some kind of horrible monster like most of the town, why would he be locked in a bathroom? Maybe a freak accident . . . maybe not.

"Hey Max," Ricky continued, "I know I'm kind of a jerk, okay? I don't know why I do what I do."

"It's not a big mystery," Melvin said, leaning toward the stall door. "I mean, if you really want answers, you pick on people like us because you have no self-esteem. Being the best athlete and winning all those trophies doesn't cut it for you. You don't like yourself—for whatever reason—so you hurt the people who can't fight back. You're a bully—but it has nothing to do with us. We're fine. Your problem is with you."

There was a moment of silence as Melvin's words sunk in.

"So you going to let me out or what?" Ricky continued, but his voice had softened. "Look, I get it—if I were you I totally wouldn't let me out either. You have no reason to trust me. But I have no interest in hurting you. That's the truth."

Max turned to the others and considered them for a moment. Here they were, the nerds and geeks—the kids on the lowest rung of the social ladder—and they were doing their best to save the world. He thought back to what Dirk had said when they found the gracon helpless in the basement. *If you become the thing that you're fighting against, what's the point? Nobody said being the good guys was easy.* He put his hand on his friend's shoulder:

"Dirk, you're like one of the wisest people I know."

Dirk nodded as if Max's compliment was the most appropriate thing he could have said at that moment. "As a bard, I probably have like a sixteen or seventeen wisdom. So yeah, you're probably right."

"What would you do with old Ricky here?" Max asked.

"We let him out. And if he's lying to us, that's not

very smart. He's seen what you do, Max, when you're all wizardly and stuff."

Max nodded and turned to the others. "I agree."

"Are you sure?" Dwight asked. "This is the same guy who took you to the Tower as a prisoner. The same guy who fought alongside Rezormoor Dreadbringer and tried to destroy you."

"Maybe," Max answered. "Or maybe not." He turned to Moki. "Moki, can I ask you and your tail to do us another favor?"

Moki beamed at the thought of being helpful. "Do I get to burn something?"

"Absolutely. Would you mind melting through this lock? You know, like you did at the Tower?"

Dirk lifted the small fire kitten to the stall door. Moki produced the bright blue flame on his tail and inserted it into the mechanism.

"You're letting me out?" Ricky asked.

"We're letting you out," Max confirmed.

Moki turned the metal lock bright red and then withdrew his tail. "It's all gooey now."

Max looked at Dwight and the dwarf understood.

"I'll draw my axe and stand here, just in case." The others moved back as Dwight took his place. Max moved back as well, recalling the combustion spell he'd memorized long ago.

"Okay, open it," Max said.

There was no resistance from the lock as the door swung open. Max had been prepared for all kinds of monstrous things to come spilling out, but instead Ricky just stood there, dressed in his wrestling singlet, with dark rings beneath his eyes. Not everyone was built to pull off wearing the skin-tight wrestling singlet, but somehow Ricky did. He didn't have the huge, hulking muscles that Wayne had, but he had the thick neck, broad chest, and powerful arms of a kid with the right genetics and a life-time spent in the wrestling room.

"Can I come out?" Ricky asked.

Max nodded and Ricky walked out of the stall. He paused at the sight of Dwight holding his axe at the ready. The dwarf shrugged. "Hey there."

"Uh, hey." Ricky went to the sink and turned the water on, cupping his hand beneath the faucet and drinking for at least a minute. When he finished, he turned the faucet off and wiped his mouth dry.

"I guess you were thirsty," Melvin said.

Dirk nodded knowingly. "Toilets . . . lots of water— but probably not worth drinking."

"Yeah, pretty much," Ricky admitted. He then looked the group over. "So I guess you guys hit a costume store on the way here? I sort of get what you were going for, except for Grandpa." Ricky smiled at Max. There was a heartbeat or two of silence; then everyone looked at Max and began to laugh.

CHAPTER SEVENTEEN

PENUMBRA

AS IT TURNED OUT, RICKY WASN'T THE ONLY WRESTLER LOCKED IN THE bathroom. Five more of his pals (other kids in the school might have used the word "gang") were also trapped. They had had a similar change of heart when it came to how they viewed their rescuers—even if those rescuers were dressed like they'd walked off the set of a fantasy movie. Apparently spending the night in a toilet stall presented a lot of time for soul-searching.

Dirk took on the job of getting the wrestlers up to speed. "I am a bard, after all," he announced. "Storytelling is what I do."

Meanwhile the pounding on the door continued. Max had grown quiet, sitting near a shiny silver garbage

can and flipping through the pages of the *Codex*. He paused
when he saw the next heading, then carefully read on:

ON THE MAELSHADOW

⋕

EVERY CENTURY OR SO A HERO, WIZARD,
or other champion decides it is their destiny to
challenge the Maelshadow and defeat the Lord of
Shadows for the good of the three realms. Such indi-
viduals have probably been spending too much time
pondering their greatness while neglecting their studies. As a result, their quests have ended badly. The
Maelshadow, you see, is wholly unnatural (much like
the McNugget). And therein lies the problem: You
can't simply poke a noncorporeal creature with a
sword. Shadow cannot be harmed.

There is a legend, however, as old as language
itself. It whispers not of a chosen boy, descended from
the bloodline of an arch-sorcerer, who finds the courage to defeat the Maelshadow with a ragtag group of
friends and a magical book (sorry to get your hopes
up), but rather that a creature born of the Shadrus
might ultimately defeat the Ruler of the Shadrus:

"For only shadow may drive shadow to light." Either that or the legend is actually a marketing slogan for sunscreen.

So whether going into battle against an intangible malicious entity who commands great reserves of dark magic, or avoiding red, painful skin due to spending too much time outdoors, try to get a little shadow working on your side. Because without it, you don't stand a chance.

Max sighed and closed the book. He'd been struggling to figure out a way to defeat the Maelshadow, and the truth was, he really didn't know much about him. He remembered Rezormoor Dreadbringer's words when the sorcerer threatened to turn him over to the Lord of Shadows: *There's something about your blood, and I believe the Lord of Shadows would like to make a withdrawal.* What was it about his blood that was so important? Max had thought everything was connected to the *Codex of Infinite Knowability*, but now he wasn't so sure. Dreadbringer was the one who wanted the magical book, and the one who had been secretly working against the Maelshadow. That thought suddenly gave Max an idea.

"I have a plan," he announced to the group. Puff blinked at him several times.

"You mean you didn't have one before?"

"Er, not so much."

"There's always the headlong-rush-into-battle-and-just-hope-it-works-out strategy," Dirk said.

"And does it?" Megan asked. "Work out, I mean?"

"Not without a lot of respawning," Dirk admitted.

Max put his hands up to stop the discussion. "It doesn't matter, because now I have a plan."

"So you think you know how to defeat the Maelshadow, then?" Dwight asked. "I saw you reading from the *Codex*. You figured it out?"

"No, not really," Max replied. "You see, the only thing I know about the Maelshadow is that it doesn't seem interested in the *Codex* like everyone else that's been chasing me. The Maelshadow is after my blood."

"Gross," Sydney added.

"You think the Maelshadow is a vampire?" Dirk asked. "Because that would be—"

"No it wouldn't," Megan interrupted, knowing exactly what Dirk was going to say.

"Maybe a little," Dirk said, sulking.

"But that's not the point," Max continued, getting the conversation back on track. "I may not know much about the Maelshadow, but I know a lot about the person who tried to destroy him."

"Rezormoor Dreadbringer," Puff said.

"Exactly. So I don't have to come up with some kind of ingenious way to beat him—I just need to pick up where Rezormoor left off."

"Because what he needed was you and your book," Dwight said, catching on. "Which you already have."

"Yeah, but he also needed that special scale thingy," Dirk added.

"The serpent's escutcheon," Puff replied. "But we don't have any of that."

"Don't we?" Max said, looking at Puff.

Moki looked back and forth between Max and Puff. "I have no idea what's going on, but it's very exciting."

"Well, technically . . . ," Puff began, looking down at his chest.

"Oh, dude, I get it!" Dirk exclaimed. "Puff still has all his armor on—it's just inside out. That's how a regular dragon gets turned into a fluff dragon—they put their scales on backward."

"And then the serpent's escutcheon turns against us," Puff continued. "It changes us."

Dirk turned to the others and explained. "The serpent's escutcheon is like a special scale over a dragon's heart, and it's awesome. It can't be pierced by a normal weapon, and it reflects magic away. Rezormoor Breadbringer—"

"Dreadbringer," Dwight corrected.

"Yeah, that guy—he had this whole plan to capture Max and use him. Because the only magic powerful enough to shape those scales into armor is the Prime Spells, and the only place you can find the Prime Spells is in the *Codex of Infinite Knowability*."

"Which only Max can read," Sydney said.

Megan shifted her staff, pulling it close. "So this Rezormoor guy is the one who sent the unicorn after you."

"Exactly," Max agreed. "And he threatened to kill my friends if I didn't do what he said. I mean, you can't just hand the most powerful spell book in the universe over to someone without some leverage."

"Only Max tricked him," Puff continued. "Made him think the *Codex* wasn't working. And we used that time to escape, get the book back, and take Rezormoor and his minions out." They all looked at Ricky, who shrugged.

"What can I say. I picked the wrong team," he said. The other wrestlers looked at their captain strangely. "I'll tell you guys about it later. Or maybe I won't—I'll have to think about it."

"But all of this is to say that Rezormoor Dreadbringer had a plan to defeat the Maelshadow," Max said. "I know what that plan was, and I have the ability to finish it."

"What are you getting at exactly?" Melvin asked. "You're going to make that suit of armor?"

"I am," Max announced.

"And that's what the *Codex* said to do?" Megan asked him.

Max frowned. "Not exactly. But all I can hope is that Rezormoor knew something that I didn't, and that once I'm in the armor, I'll figure it out."

"Besides," Dirk added, "you have the *Codex* and all its spells."

Max nodded. "Okay then, I was able to do this in the Magrus once before. But it's the magical realm, and I had the *Codex* at its birthplace. It's not going to be that easy here. In fact, it may take everything I've got. I guess I'm just saying that this is going to have to work,

290 Platte F. Clark

because I won't have the strength to do anything else if it doesn't."

"No problemo," Dirk said. "Like you said—you've done it once; you can do it again."

It turned out to be much harder than Max ever imagined.

He had the *Codex* in both hands and pressed his will into it. Where the sensation in the Magrus had been like two magnets coming together, doing it in the strange Malaspire, which bridged the realms of the Shadrus, the Techrus, and the umbraverse, was like walking headlong into a hurricane. When he came upon the Prime Spells, his mind called out: *Parity!* Sweat broke out on his forehead as he focused the power of the spell.

"Point at it," he said to Puff. The fluff dragon nodded and drew his paw to his chest.

Max let the Prime Spell Go. *Parity—to balance or make equivalent.* A second version of the magical scale appeared before Puff as a tremor rumbled through the room. The rhythmic banging at the door paused.

"Max magic," Dirk explained. "Big stuff."

Max kept hold of the spell as it threatened to return to the *Codex*. He clenched his jaw and forced it to fold over itself, redirecting its surge back to where he wanted. He directed the spell to touch both the scale on the floor and Puff's. *Parity,* he thought again. The vibration moved through the room, knocking one of the glass mirrors sideways. But there were three scales on the floor now.

"Max, something strange is going on—" Puff started to say, but Max interrupted his friend, talking through clenched teeth:

"Hold on—just don't move!" Max had to perform the same folding and grouping procedure twice more, until there were fifteen of the most precious dragon scales on earth spread across the blue tiles of the bathroom. Sweat dripped from him now and he felt his body shaking. But Max wasn't done yet.

He let go of the spell and felt it retreat into the magical book, his mind chasing after it, like a race car drafting behind the leader. He'd never done that before, but then again, he'd never had to. *Unity,* he called out, and he felt the spell move toward him. "Stand back," he managed to say, the words barely escaping his labored breathing. Puff nodded and stepped back, but he kept looking at his chest with a strange expression.

"Max, are you okay?" Megan asked. "Can I help you?"

"Please, just stay back," he answered. He didn't want Megan close as he tried to focus on what he was doing. He probably sounded angry, but it wasn't his intention. It was all he could do to keep the spell under control. He brought it over the armor and spoke the word: "Unity."

The room shook more violently now. His friends had to grab hold of whatever was near them in order to keep from stumbling.

"Max is doing all this?" Ricky asked, wide-eyed.

"Max is the most powerful wizard in the three realms," Dwight answered.

The Prime Spell did as it was directed, suddenly merging the small pieces of scale into one large piece.

"Wow," Melvin said, his jaw hanging open. "I mean, wow . . ."

Max released the spell, and he felt muscle spasms shoot up and down his back. He blinked, trying to clear his eyes. He took a deep breath, but it must have sounded like a gasp.

"Max, stop," Megan insisted. "It's too much."

Max shook his head, unable to waste the energy needed to speak. He followed the spell back into the

Codex, resting for just a moment as its powerful gravity pulled him along with it. He found the next spell at once, and pulled it from the *Codex*. His vision narrowed and he felt the world spin—he nearly blacked out. But he grabbed hold of the wall and commanded the spell: "Panoply!" He pictured the unique set of armor in his mind, as if he had been the very smith who had fashioned it in the first place. Such knowledge had come to him once before at the top of the Wizard's Tower, and as before he was unsure of its source. But for now it was simply enough that he could bend the scale with the Prime Spell and force it into an intricate, nearly impossible design.

A wave of power crashed through the room, breaking every mirror and cracking the sinks. Bits of blue tile shattered as a large crack formed in the wall. Then there was a loud groan that emanated from the Malaspire itself, and they felt the whole structure shift.

"Whoa!" Ricky exclaimed. He stared through the dust and debris at a black, shimmering suit of armor. The back of it was rippling and moving like liquid. They all watched as Max stepped forward, but he suddenly collapsed on his hands and knees.

Dirk was the first to his side, followed by Ricky.

They helped Max up, and he managed to steady himself. He took another step toward the armor, and then with a final movement he stepped *into* it. The liquidity vanished and the armor formed into a solid piece. Max stood there, looking like a medieval knight in shimmering black plate mail. And because it had been designed by Rezormoor Dreadbringer, who'd thought in terms of speed and maneuverability, it was perfectly balanced. The sleek armor covered Max from head to toe, and as the others stared at him, they noted a faint black mist that drifted off it, carried by unseen magical currents. Max radiated power—so much so that even Puff could feel it through his inside-out scale. *That* hadn't happened in a long time.

Max dropped to one knee, but he refused to surrender to the exhaustion that was beckoning to swallow him. There was too much to do, and too little time. And he had one more Prime Spell to cast.

Megan rushed over. "Let me heal you," she said, lowering her staff. But when it touched the armor it shot backward, flying through the air. The staff careened toward one of the wrestlers, who managed to dive out of the way at the last second.

"Magic can't reach him now," Puff said, stepping forward. "He's enshrined in the most powerful armor ever conceived. Powerful enough for the wearer to take over the entire world, if that's what they desire."

"It's . . . it's . . . ," Melvin tried to say, struggling to get the words out. "It's magnificent."

"No one person should ever have that much power," Dwight grumbled, and then spat dust from his mouth.

"Yeah, but that's Max in there," Dirk said. "He's not like that."

"You mean the same kid who opened the portal and started all of this?" Dwight shot back. "Yeah, I know who it is. I'm not worried about his intentions—frankly, they don't matter. There are consequences for that much power, and it's always people like you and me who end up paying the price."

Max regained his feet, but there was no heavy thud from the sabaton that covered his foot. And the way that Max moved, it wasn't like he was struggling under the armor's weight at all. In fact, he moved as if the armor weighed practically nothing.

"Dreadbringer must have spent years designing this,"

Max said as he caught his breath. He could feel his strength returning to him—perhaps aided by the suit itself? Who knew what secrets Rezormoor Dreadbringer had woven into his life's work?

"How did you learn how to do that?" Megan asked, still a little shaken from it all. One of the wrestlers had retrieved her staff and brought it back to her.

"In the Tower. Dreadbringer's thoughts blended with the *Codex* when I first made the attempt. But there's more to it than even I imagined."

"Like what?" Melvin asked.

Max lifted his gauntleted left arm and a symbol began to glow on his wrist. It was a blue circle with eight arrows pointing inward. He touched it with his other hand and suddenly the whole suit began to collapse in on itself. Pieces slid beneath others, the helmet rolled back from around Max's head, and plates moved away, compacted, and folded until the entire set of armor had retreated into a single band around his wrist.

"DUDE!" Dirk exclaimed.

Max smiled. "And that's how Rezormoor Dread-bringer decided to take his armor on and off. Of course the wristband is kind of permanent, I think."

"Who cares," Dirk continued, his excitement showing on his face. "That is the most epic suit of armor, ever!"

Max nodded, turning to Puff. "Thanks for letting me do that. I couldn't have done it without the serpent's escutcheon."

"I'm glad I could help," the fluff dragon answered. He still felt strange after being touched by the prime spell, however, but Max had enough things to worry about.

"So I have one more spell to cast," Max announced, turning to Ricky. "That is, if you guys are willing to help us."

Ricky swallowed. "Look, Max, I've been wanting to say something, so I guess now is as good a time as any. I'm sorry for everything I've done to you, at school and in the messed-up places you go." He turned to Max's friends. "And that goes for the rest of you. I'm just going to be honest here: I kind of envy you guys. You dress up and do all this crazy stuff, but you know who you are. And you seem happy—until I come along and mess it up. But it's not up to me or anybody else to tell you its wrong, or dorky, or whatever. So I'm sorry—and I guess that's pretty much it."

"That took a lot of guts," Megan said, after a moment

of silence. "I'll tell you something I heard once: When you destroy it makes you sad. When you create it makes you happy. That's all we do: create worlds and characters, and even armor and costumes. If you want to be happy, Ricky, just find something you want to create and go do it. Destroying others, their work, even your own self, will only leave you empty."

Ricky nodded, turning to his former gang of troublemakers. "Just so you guys know, I like ballroom dancing. If you have a problem with that, tough."

A skinny wrestler stepped forward. "I wanted to play the flute but I was afraid of what people would think."

"Yeah," a short and thick wrestler agreed. "I always dreamed of acting on the stage. And not just because sometimes you get to kiss girls."

George Lobowski, football star and heavyweight wrestler, stepped forward. "And I love to bake!" he blurted out. "I love to bake cupcakes and frost them and make them pretty and delicious and I don't care who knows it!"

"I like cupcakes," Moki agreed. He thought the idea of baking cupcakes was an especially good one.

"But I need you all to do something first," Max

continued. "I need you to help me fight our way to the Maelshadow and save Sarah, Madison, and pretty much the rest of the world."

The wrestlers nodded as they grew serious. "You picked the right bunch of guys for that," Ricky announced.

"Okay, then," Max continued. "Step back." He pressed his mind into the *Codex* and found the limitless space within, summoning the next spell: *Gallimaufry—to create a mixture of diverse things.*

Max had never been properly instructed on how to be a wizard. But he was learning, and he was beginning to understand that he could shape things as he bought the *Codex*'s magic into effect. This time he imagined the kind of supply shop he used to go to online as he played his games. He concentrated specifically on racks of armor and weapons, pushing that images into the spell and feeling them take hold. Then he concentrated on something else—a memory that was not his. It was, he knew, his father's, and it had been captured within the *Codex* long ago. It was of a world of shadows and gray skies, where a large volcano spewed and coughed rivers of hot lava across an ebony landscape. A forge sat at the foot of the volcano, where a solitary figure hammered on an anvil. *Dagda the blacksmith—smithing her steel over the everlasting flame.* The knowledge came with the ancient memory of the place. Then Max found what he was looking for—a solid black sword hanging near the master blacksmith. The blade was like obsidian, and translucent enough to show a volcanic fire bubbling and trapped within. The hilt was shaped into a dragon—the guard formed by two outstretched wings and the grip by the tail. Max focused on the mythical blade and brought it to the Prime Spell. The room shook violently and the spire itself seemed to shift in protest.

Dust floated through the blue bathroom, and several tiles fell from the ceiling. But all around bits and pieces of armor and weapons were scattered on the floor. And at the center was *Penumbra*, the Shadrus weapon now given form.

Max stepped forward, wiping the sweat from his eyes. His gray hair was matted against his head and his body shook from the exertion of the last few minutes. He walked to Penumbra and picked it up. Unlike his armor, the sword was heavy. "The *Codex* said only shadow can destroy the Maelshadow. This sword was forged in the Shadrus, and I intend to use it to drive the Lord of Shadows away." But that wasn't exactly true—the *Codex* had said that a *creature* of shadow would have to sacrifice itself. He hoped wielding Penumbra was close enough. As far as the sacrifice part, he was ready to do it. But he couldn't tell the others . . . they wouldn't understand.

CHAPTER EIGHTEEN

MAX, THE BLUE MEN, AND GRAVITY

THEY UNLOCKED THE BATHROOM DOOR AND STREAMED INTO THE hallway, yelling at the top of their lungs. Ricky was the first through, followed by Dwight and the rest of the wrestlers. They were wearing armor now, and had found weapons that suited them. Max was next, followed by Melvin, Dirk (who had Glenn across his back and a thin sword in hand), Moki, and Puff, with Megan and Sydney bringing up the rear. Max was back in his armor, feeling more tired than he could ever remember. They pressed forward into the hallway filled with at least fifty urinal men—blue, featureless, and looking like the clothes mannequins at the mall.

The wrestlers slammed into the blue creatures like a

wave crashing on the beach. They were strong, athletic, and still upset at the whole toilet-stall thing. They cut, shoved, bludgeoned, and stabbed their way forward. A strong minty smell began to fill the air.

Melvin was busy firing arrows into the ranks of the enemy, while Moki lobbed the occasional fireball. Max moved in the near-weightless armor as he fought to control the Shadric sword. Penumbra was heavy, and he felt unbalanced as used it. He could hear the voice of the Jan Man calling out from the back: "Attack! Attack! Get them, my pretties!" Max figured anyone who called living urinal cakes "pretty" probably lived alone and ate a lot of microwaved dinners. Then Max remembered the strange mop carried by the Jan Man.

"Clear me a path to the janitor," Max called out. "But stay away from his mop."

Ricky grunted an affirmative and Max watched as urinal man after urinal man fell beneath the fury of the wrestlers. It wasn't long before an opening presented itself, and Max rushed toward the Jan Man. He brushed past the remaining blue monsters as the former janitor swung his mop-dusa to meet him. Max saw the twisting, slithering snakes, their small tongues darting in and out as their slitted eyes met his. The Jan Man paused, his eyes wide with expectation. Then he frowned.

"You didn't change! You're supposed to change!" The Jan Man stamped his foot in protest. Max knew no amount of mop-based magic was going to penetrate his armor, however. He brought his sword around and sliced through the handle of the mop. The chaotic bundle of snakes turned into thick coils of cloth as it fell to the floor.

"No!" the Jan Man cried.

The others dispatched the last of the urinal men and rejoined Max. The Jan Man backed up a foot or two toward the large door behind him. "I'm not supposed to let anyone past," he protested.

"We're going through," Max said, trying to be sympathetic to Mr. Lizar's plight.

"The hard way or the easy way," Dirk chimed in. "That's what you say at a time like this."

The Jan Man looked at the remains of his mop on the floor. "So my mop-dusa was just a mop?" he asked.

"Yeah," Melvin answered. "And this building used to be our school." The Jan Man tilted his head in thought.

"Park—something or other," he said.

"Parkside," Max answered.

"Go, Eagles!" Sydney added, then suddenly looked embarrassed.

"None of this is right, is it?" the former Mr. Lizar asked. He looked at Max. "You gonna put it right?"

"Yes."

The Jan Man nodded and moved to the side, motioning toward the door. "Then you should go and do that. I suppose I'll just wait here and see how it all turns out."

"Or . . . ," Dirk said, getting an idea. "You could clean up this big mess." The hallway was filled with bits and pieces of urinal cakes.

"Bathroom could use some attention too," Dwight added.

The Jan Man scratched his chin as he thought it over. I *could* clean up this mess, *or* I could go find a quiet place and take a nap." He turned to Max. "No offense here, but if you guys lose, better to look like I put up a fight." And with that the Jan Man headed off.

"Well, at least we didn't have to hurt him," Megan said after he left.

Max sheathed his sword. "It's not his fault—it's mine."

"So now what?" Ricky asked.

"Duh," Dirk answered. "We go through the door."

On the other side of the door was the old gym where everything had started. There was no sign of the bleachers where Max had sat with Wayne, or the basketball hoops, the scoreboard, or the banner on the wall that had read PUMMEL THE PANTHERS! Instead, they found themselves at the highest point in the Malaspire. The room had started off more or less a square, but as it rose a good twenty feet or so, it twisted and bent, as if it couldn't support its own weight. In the center a single rope fell from the ceiling to the floor, swaying slightly as the wind howled outside and the rain pounded the roof. But it wasn't just any rope—it was *the* rope. Max's nemesis—the ever-present reminder of his failures and the object of shame and humiliation that had embarrassed him in front of half the school. And above it, pulsing with reddish light, lay the opening through the Shadric Portal.

"No way," Dirk said, pointing to the rope. "You have to climb the rope to enter the portal? You only climbed like six inches last time."

Max's heart sank. Dirk was right, of course. He had

no chance whatsoever of doing it. Did he risk casting a Prime Spell again? He'd done it before, by accident, at the great hunting grounds when he'd lifted Sarah, Dirk, and himself to the top of a ziggurat pyramid. He'd been frustrated and emotional, but it had been the thought of Sarah that had given him the strength to summon the spell. He'd also set a frobbit adrift for several days, but he couldn't really be blamed for that.

"So where to next?" Ricky asked, looking more enthused about things than Max thought appropriate. "Up the rope, I guess?"

Max commanded the armor to retract into the single wrist piece, and he slumped to the floor. Megan walked up and shared a concerned look with the others. "What's wrong?"

"Max can't climb ropes," Dirk answered.

"Yeah, I saw his epic fail the other day," Melvin added.

Dwight looked up at the twenty-foot climb. "Just use some of your magic again. No problem."

"Maybe," Max sighed. "But I'm running out of gas. Am I so pathetic I have to use *magic* to climb a stupid rope? I need the magic I have for the Maelshadow."

"Can't Megan just heal you again?" Sydney asked.

Puff shook his head. "Maybe, but there are limits. More than once can be dangerous."

"But I've healed him twice already," Megan replied. "Remember?"

"Three times in one day is too much," Puff answered.

"But we can't just stop here," Dirk protested. "We fought howlers, answered the door riddle, evaded Princess, defeated gracon statues, wailed on a giant were-bear and his scare bear pals, beat the spider, and *then* battled a whole bunch of urinal men—all to be stopped by a stupid rope?"

"You forgot singing our way past the army of squirrels," Sydney offered, trying to be helpful.

"Look, we're talking about the fate of the world here," Dwight reminded them. "If another healing spell can work, we need to just try it, even if it's risky."

Max looked up. "I'm willing to do it."

Puff shook his head. "You don't understand—we're talking life and death here. It could kill him."

Max shrugged. "I don't have a choice."

"And if you're dead, then what? Are we supposed to just pick up and go on without you?" Puff snapped angrily. "What's going to happen to Sarah then? What's going to happen to the entire Techrus? It's not just about *you*."

"You know what your problem is?" Ricky said. "You're so used to all this magic stuff that you think it's the answer to everything."

"So what are you suggesting?" Dwight asked. "You think you're strong enough to carry Max all the way to the top?"

"No," Ricky answered after a moment. "The only person who's going to get Max up that rope is Max."

Melvin threw his hands in the air. "Then we're back to where we started."

"I happen to know for a fact that Max can climb it," Ricky said. "Without magic, without being carried—all on his own."

"Oh, I get it," Dirk said. "We're going to yell at him until he makes it, right? My dad was in the army and he said that's how you motivate people."

Ricky approached the rope. "You know, for a bunch of brainiacs you guys still don't get it. Yelling isn't going to do any good either—I'm going to *teach* Max how to climb."

"What do you mean?" Max asked as he stared at the thick rope. "Don't you just grab hold and pull?"

"Maybe if you're built like me," Ricky said matter-of-factly. "But there's a better way." He turned to Megan and Sydney. "I can teach all of you how to do it."

"It's worth a shot," Melvin said. "Max . . . ?"

"What have I got to lose?" Max replied. "But if it doesn't work, then I'm using magic and Megan's going to heal me—that's the deal."

"It's going to work—trust me," Ricky said. But trusting Ricky "the Kraken" Reynolds wasn't something that came easy. Max realized that despite the apology and battle in the hallway, he still was unsure about the one-time bully. If he was going to make this work, Max knew he'd have to let go of all that.

"Okay, Ricky," Max said as he climbed to his feet. "I'll trust you." And he realized that he really did.

"Cool. So here's what we're going to do—it's called the break-and-squat technique."

"Sounds like the time I ate a taco out of the garbage," Dirk added. Ricky ignored him and kept going, grabbing the rope with two hands.

"Rope climbing is all about what you do with your feet. Most people don't know that because they see some-one just pull themselves up with their arms. But if you get your feet right you don't have to have a strong upper body. The trick is to just let the rope slide along your right hip as you grab hold, then use your feet to make a kind of rung, like on a ladder. Here, let me show you."

Ricky jumped and grabbed hold of the rope. Then he raised his right leg high enough that his left foot was able to get under it and lift it about a half foot so the rope looked like an *S* turned on its side. He dropped his other leg into the "rung" and as he lowered his weight, it drew taut. Ricky let go of the rope with one hand and sat there looking perfectly relaxed.

"I'm not using my arms at all," Ricky announced. "I can sit here and rest as long as I want, then just do the same thing over and over until I'm at the top."

Max had never seen anyone climb a rope like that before. He hadn't known it was even *possible* to climb a rope like that. Ricky let go and dropped to the floor. "See?" he said. "No magic, just one person willing to teach another."

"You might want to teach the rope not to break, too," Glenn piped in.

Max slipped the *Codex* into the leather satchel and then handed Penumbra to Ricky. "Probably should still try and be as light as possible," he said. Max jumped on the rope and began working his feet the way he'd seen Ricky do it. It wasn't graceful at first, but with a little help Max got the hang of it. And amazingly, Ricky had been right. Max could stand on the rope and rest as long as it took to reach up and inch his way a little higher. By the time he reached the top, his arms were burning and he was out of breath. He didn't rest as long as he should have as the thought of time running out pushed him forward. He neared the entrance to the Shadric Portal and saw a mass of swirling red smoke. The rope ran up and into it, and there was nothing to do but follow. He took a final breath and pushed himself higher—into the swirling mist of the umbraverse.

CHAPTER NINETEEN

THE UMBRAVERSE

THE PLACE REMINDED MAX OF THE TUBE HE USED TO RUN THROUGH AT THE carnival fun house—a spinning tunnel that turned on its axis as giggling kids tried to keep from losing their balance, the barbershop pole–like stripes making it appear as if the walkway was spinning and not the tube. Max had that same disoriented feeling as he watched the spinning layer of clouds churn around him. A part of him knew that he'd climbed *inside* the tornado that fed the storm around the town. It was an unsettling thought.

He made it through the spinning vortex and found himself in a strange place. A black castle rose in the distance, floating on a great island of ice. It glowed with strange blue and green lights that seemed to be reflected in the boiling clouds overhead. Max was good at sensing magic by now, and the waves of power that rolled from the castle made him feel sick.He had found the Maelshadow.

One by one the others crawled through the portal and joined him. Moki rode on one of the wrestlers' shoulders, while Ricky held Puff in his legs and pulled the pair of them up using only his arms. The others used the technique Ricky had shared and were able to climb to the top as well. Dwight struggled a bit in his armor, but he refused to take it off and eventually climbed through.

"This place is crazy," Dirk said, looking around. They were all gathered on one of the frozen islands. Around them, mounds of icicles rose like frozen jellyfish. And at the top, shafts of ice rose into the air like a wall of sharpened stakes. There were other ice islands adrift in the air, defying gravity as they floated within the eye of the storm. They made a path of sorts from the Shadric Portal to the castle, but it would take an Olympic-caliber jump to get from one to the next. Too far for Max and his friends to make it. Too far even for Ricky and his band of wrestlers.

Suddenly a great horn blared, and two huge doors at the front of the ebony castle opened. Then came the sound of marching as a tremendous column of creatures funneled from the castle and made their way down a wide ice path.

"That's an invasion," Melvin said solemnly.

"The Maelshadow's army," Dwight added, watching as the column, some six men wide (if they could be called men), continue to advance. "This is the future if we fail."

Without thinking Max spun around and grabbed hold of the Shadric Portal. It had grown since he'd first opened it. He pushed with all he had, but it would not close. In fact, he felt it grow wider beneath his fingers.

"Remember, only somebody who's evil can close it," Dirk said. "Because only someone good could open it." Max let go of the portal with a groan.

"I had to try something," he said.

"Our path to closing the portal leads through the Maelshadow," Dwight answered, his voice heavy.

"And now his army too," Melvin added.

Max turned to look at the black ribbon of soldiers moving away from the castle. Eventually they'd have to cross the gaps between the floating islands. But armies were good at that sort of thing—bridging rivers was a common enough problem.

"I might be able to make the jump," Ricky offered.

"Maybe we should try and build a human chain or something," one of the wrestlers suggested.

Max considered it, but it felt too risky.

"You could always toss the dwarf," Glenn suggested.

Everyone turned to Dwight, expecting an angry rebuttal. Instead Dwight shrugged. "Might work."

Dirk shook his head. "No, you're supposed to say 'nobody tosses a dwarf!'"

Dwight lowered his axe. "Says who?"

"Says everybody. It's like against your code."

Dwight harrumphed. "My cousin Brohimir Stone-garden was tossed over the wall at the battle of Elyshiem. Did a full somersault in the air, just for dramatic effect, then broke past the elf lines and opened the gate."

Dirk frowned, not liking the idea of dwarfs being tossed around in strategic ways.

"Any other ideas?" Max asked, getting back to the problem at hand.

"We could build a snowman," Moki suggested, eagerly.

"Any *good* ideas?" Glenn asked.

"I might have one," Puff said stepping forward. He

turned to Max. "Ever since you cast the Prime Spell on me, I haven't felt right."

Megan stepped forward. "What's wrong?"

"Not 'wrong' so much as . . ."

Dwight approached the fluff dragon—they had become friends despite their rocky start in the Magrus (and a long-standing mistrust between dragons and dwarfs). "What do you mean by that?"

"I think Max's spell broke through my scales. I've been feeling things I've haven't felt in years—magic, for instance."

"Wait, what are you saying?" Max asked.

"Perhaps you should give me some room," Puff said. Max and the others took several steps backward. "Farther," Puff coaxed until they had moved a good distance away.

"What exactly is going on here?" Melvin asked.

"Hopefully it's snowman related," Moki offered.

Puff took a deep breath and closed his eyes. Suddenly a blue light formed on his chest. Then it grew, tracing a line along the edge of the serpent's escutcheon. The light hesitated for a moment, then split, racing around the fluff dragon and forming into the image of a great serpent. *No, not a serpent,* Max realized. *A dragon.*

The blue light turned red as a thunderclap rang out overhead. The red light became so bright that Max and the others were forced to turn their heads. They heard what sounded like old leather unfolding, and then a wave of magic rushed over them, causing Max's entire body to tingle. When they were able to look back, they saw a full-sized dragon stretching his wings and raising his head. The beast gave out a tremendous roar, full of raw and ancient power. Max recognized the dragon as the one in the dream world—the dragon that Puff truly was!

"I am myself again!" Puff exclaimed, his voice deep and cavernous. He lowered his great head and regarded Max. "Do you recognize me?"

The dragon looked nothing like a fluff dragon, but there was something in his eyes that reminded him of his friend. "I think I'll always recognize you," Max said.

"That pleases me, but we have no time to tarry. Now, I can carry three of you on my back, so come and we will go and meet this army. I am eager to show you what a dragon can do."

Max activated his armor so that it flowed back around him. He took his sword from Ricky and addressed the others. "Dwight, I need you to stay here to organize a defensive line. Dirk and Melvin, you two come with me." Puff lowered his wing and allowed the three adventurers—the wizard, the elf, and the bard—to climb on his back.

"Go and save the world again, kid," Dwight called out to Max.

Max nodded as Puff leapt into the air, a powerful stroke of his wings propelling them skyward. The tendrils of black mist from Max's armor spun in the swirling currents before dissipating across the ice.

"I guess it's up to them now," Rick siad.

They watched as the dragon flew toward the castle.

"Yeah," Dwight replied after a moment. It was all he could think of to say.

Max decided that riding a dragon was pretty cool. They passed over several floating islands as they made their way toward the castle, and Max began to make out familiar forms within the ranks of the Maelshadow's army.

"Shadrus necromancers," he announced to the others.

They watched as the necromancers gathered at the edge of the ice to perform some kind of an incantation. As they wove their spell together, Max could feel the sickly sensation that accompanied Shadric magic. Suddenly new ice formed, muddy and grayish in color. It flowed outward until it spanned the gap to the next island, hardening into a bridge. The necromancers fell in line with the others as the army moved to march across it.

"What are they?" Melvin asked, pointing his bow at the long ribbon of soldiers still marching from the great castle gate. "They don't look human."

"The necromancers are their spell casters, but their soldiers are called Shadekin," Puff answered. "Undead."

"No way, *zombies*?" Dirk asked excitedly.

Max studied the orderly march of the heavily armored troops. "I don't think so," he replied. "Not enough lurching."

A blast of flame suddenly ripped toward them. Puff reacted at once, turning in to the blast and managing to shield the others. Nightmare-Princess raced by, her wings beating as she circled around.

"So you brought a dragon for me to play with," she called out. "How thoughtful."

"You'll have to do better than that, *horse*!" Puff roared back.

Max prepared himself for another attack (the one thing you didn't call a unicorn was a *horse*), but instead she turned and flew toward something large and monstrous rising above the castle. A wave of sickly tainted magic crashed over Max, and he felt Puff shudder beneath him.

"Witness the coming of my master," Nightmare Princess called to them.

"The Maelshadow!" Puff exclaimed, seeing the monstrosity.

Max saw it too as it rose into the sky. It appeared as if it were a colossal collection of sharpened antlers, woven together and erupting from a foul black cloud. The Maelshadow's head was a series of outstretched spikes, like long taloned fingers and almost indistinguishable from two similarly shaped claws, attached to limbs long enough to engulf the entire island. The thing before them was unlike anything Max had ever seen.

It took Melvin's voice to bring Max out of his stupor. "Hey, that's Sarah!"

Max blinked and focused his attention where Melvin was pointing. Near the top of the castle was a single spire, and Sarah was there, chained to a post. Max had flashbacks to the cruel games where she'd been similarly bound before the Machine City. Standing over her was Wayne, and at the sight of him Max felt a cold rage begin to build. The supposed protector was now her guard.

"Your time is nearly over, Max Spencer," the Maelshadow said. There was no mouth as such, only the sound of the words and an unwholesome presence that filled the air. Puff drew back and hovered, keeping his distance from the horror in front of them. "Am I what you thought I would be?"

"You mean a giant twig?" Dirk called back. Max shushed him—there was no sense getting a destroyer of worlds more irritated than necessary.

"You have surprised me," the Maelshadow continued. "And that does not happen often, mortal. You are adorned in the armor of Rezormoor Dreadbringer— fitting that his destroyer wears such as a trophy. You were more powerful and clever than he anticipated. Or perhaps he did not sense the strength of Sporazo's blood in you—too strong to be centuries removed. What are you to him?"

"His son," Max called out, seeing no reason to hide the fact now.

"Yes . . . it explains how you command the *Codex* so easily. Blood is the key to everything, isn't it? Blood is why I ordered Dreadbringer and the unicorn to hunt you."

"Just so you could retrieve the Shadric Portal?" Max shouted at the entity in front of him. "All the things we've gone through, everything . . . just for this?"

"Why else? You were the key that opened the lock. And now that you've done so, the key must be destroyed."

"Not if I destroy you first!" Max shouted back.

"I am honored by the attempt," the Maelshadow replied. "I will await you in my temple. We shall fight eye to eye, as it were, as was done in ancient times. That is, if you survive long enough to get there."

The Maelshadow began to descend, his body of thorns retreating into the mass of smoke and shadow.

"He thinks highly of you to challenge you so," Puff said.

"Funny way of showing it," Melvin said.

"Max," Puff called back to him. "Do you know where the Prime Spells came from?" Max remembered reading about that in the *Codex*: *The origins of the Fifteen Prime Spells are unknown, having not so much been created as found.*

"My father found them somewhere," he replied.

"The legends of my kin say that the World Sunderer found them here, in the umbraverse."

"What does that mean?"

"It means that the spells may be even more difficult to control—or less. Or that they will not work as you think. The Prime Spells have always been affected by the realm you were in, and this realm is like no other."

"So Max may not have his magic," Melvin said.

"It's possible."

"Then we'll have to figure it out as we go," Max said. Suddenly the sky around them exploded in shafts of green light. Below, dozens of the Shadrus necromancers had taken aim and were attacking.

"Doom's breath!" Puff shouted. "Poisoned magic!" The dragon dove, giving Max and the others barely a chance to hold on. "Careful! A single touch will destroy you!" Puff roared.

Somehow, Melvin managed to nock an arrow and let

it fly. It raced to one of the necromancers and struck it in the chest, sending it tumbling off the edge of the ice.

"Dude!" Dirk exclaimed. "Nice shot!"

Melvin nodded and nocked another arrow. "I am an elven archer, and I will not miss my foes this day."

Puff continued to dive as more of the twisting shafts of light erupted around them. Suddenly one connected with Max, striking him on the shoulder. He closed his eyes on reflex and tightened his grip on the dragon's neck, hoping the armor was as good against poison as it was magic. The answer, left from the impression of Dreadbringer's mind, seemed to say that it was.

Puff swooped down, opening his mouth and feeling flame building in the back of his throat. It erupted into a billowing, orange fireball that cut a long swath across the necromancers and Shadekin. The undead instinctively dove from the mythical flame, but many were engulfed and burned. Puff banked hard, gliding across the ice and past the castle. Arrows began to fall around them, but Puff was moving too fast to be an easy target.

"You okay?" Puff asked, craning his head back. "I thought the spell struck you."

"It did," Max replied.

There was a momentary pause. "Your armor appears to be all that you had thought."

They continued to bank as Melvin let arrow after arrow fly, but given the size of the enemy force, it made little difference. The Maelshadow's army continued its advance, bridging the next divide between the floating islands of ice. Several squads of archers and pike men broke off from the main body, the archers taking aim and firing at the dragon and his passengers.

Puff began climbing, zigzagging to avoid the arrows flying in their direction. Max regarded the army beneath him—he had to stop them from reaching the portal, or his friends wouldn't stand a chance. Having a dragon on his side was a tremendous advantage, but no dragon could defeat an entire army. Max needed to do something himself.

"Dude, just think of it like a game," Dirk yelled above the pounding thrusts of Puff's wings, and as if reading Max's thoughts. "You've done this online like a million times. You know what to do."

You respawn when you die online, Max answered silently. Then he turned his attention to the magical bridges—those were the weak points. He placed his gauntleted hand against the *Codex* and entered it with his mind. The *Codex* seemed barren—stripped of everything except for the space where the Prime Spells dwelled. But more importantly, the Prime Spells seemed to be slipping *past* the boundary Maximilian Sporazo had put into place!

Only the blood of a Sporazo will bind them here, the familiar voice came to him, just as it had on that first trip back through time. *They will obey you, son, if you choose to make it so.*

Max focused on the crumbling barrier, rebuilding it with a force of will he summoned from deep within. There was a push as if the spells were testing him, and then they gathered at the edge of the magical barricade as if eager to be released. "Puff, take me to that bridge!" Max shouted, his voice a little shaky after the effort to bind the spells.

The dragon veered, flying through a new flurry of arrows until they closed on the bridge.

"Liquidity!" Max shouted. The spell flew forward, slamming into the gray ice and turning it into water. Hundreds of soldiers who'd been crossing dropped at once, falling through the floating landscape and into the churning storm below.

"Nice!" Dirk exclaimed.

Max pointed to the next bridge. "Take me there!"

Puff banked hard, skimming across the ice as he prepared to gain altitude. Suddenly a form flashed ahead of them, and Nightmare-Princess struck Max with her hooves, sending him flying off the dragon. He tumbled several times before slamming into the ice. Stars exploded across his eyes and he fought to clear his head. He managed to climb to his feet just in time to see Nightmare-Princess descend on him, her flaming, goo-dripping hoofs driving into his chest and sending him flying. He rolled on the ground and slid against an icy overhang.

The nightmare-unicorn came around and landed just ahead of him, lowering her misshapen horn and pointing it in his direction. "Time to finish what we started," she said, her crimson eyes blazing. "I doubt your new armor can deflect what my horn has become. And even so, I will simply thrust it through your visor and suck you out like a clam from a shell."

Max rose to his feat, his legs unsteady. He scanned the horizon for Puff but there was no sign of the dragon.

"So now you will die, as it was meant to be from

the very beginning," the creature that was once Princess continued.

"Elemenity!" Max shouted. He formed a great river of wind and threw it like an uppercut at Nightmare-Princess. The gale-force stream of air hit her with unimaginable power, and her wings became unwilling accomplices as she was blasted into the sky. Then Max caught sight of a half dozen Shadekin scrambling toward him on the ice. They were roughly man-sized and covered in mismatched bits of armor, save for silver spiked plates that covered the skeletal heads beneath. They carried jagged swords, morning stars, and other weapons of war, and their eyes burned with an otherworldly fury as they descended on him.

As the first prepared to leap down and crush Max with a large war hammer, an arrow flew by and caught it in the shoulder, sending the Shadekin spinning backward. Max drew Penumbra and met the next attacker with an awkward thrust. The Shadric sword shattered the Shadekin's blade, continuing until it struck the creature through the chest. Max heard the snap of an arrow fly past as another Shadekin was struck; then, before he could pull his sword free, a ringing sound exploded in his left ear. The unseen blow sent him stumbling, and it was all he could do to keep hold of his blade. Above him the Shadekin advanced, swinging a spiked morning star. Max's armor was unscathed, but the kinetic energy had hit him like a punch to the side of the head. He prepared to raise his sword and fend off the next attack, when a stream of liquid fire cut across the Shadekin, igniting the undead creature like a tinderbox. Puff dropped with his talons extended, grabbing hold of the last of the undead soldiers and flinging them off the island.

"It's about time," Max said as he climbed to his feet.

"Dude, you got company," Dirk yelled from Puff's back. "Lots of company."

Max turned to see the entire force of Shadekin breaking from their march and charging toward him. He thrust his sword in its sheath—he was never going to be a melee fighter. Instead he reached into the *Codex* and found the spell he was looking for: "Tutelary!"

The wave of power created by the spell crashed into the charging Shadekin, knocking the entire line backward. A single spectral knight stood before Max, glimmering in white armor. It turned to face the horde of Shadekin, who were quickly reforming their charge.

"I need more of you," Max said to the knight. Then he drew the next spell and shouted, "Nimiety!" *Nimiety—to copy and make excess.* The Prime Spell roared into existence, filling the air with ice and frost. When the icy haze cleared, the single knight had been joined by tens of thousands more. The Shadekin, to their credit, did not falter in their attack. The misshapen and skeletal force crashed into the line of knights, and the battle commenced, army against army.

"Over here!" Dirk cried. Puff had landed on a small outcropping and Max hurried over. Melvin rose with his elven longbow and fired a volley of arrows into the Shadekin troops.

"Where's Princess?" Max asked as he climbed on the back of the dragon.

"Dude, careful with my girlfriend—she's still a good person under all that evil and junk."

"I lost sight of her," Puff admitted.

Melvin sat back down as Puff took to the air. The three of them could clearly see the battle below. The Shadekin outnumbered the knights, but Max's spectral army held their ranks, moving with a determined order and unshakable discipline. The forces of the Shadekin rushed headlong in a series of frenzied charges, like wave after wave crashing against the shore. It was a costly strategy, but eventually the endless ocean of Shadekin would have its way.

Max turned his attention to the bridge. "They're getting reinforcements—we need to take the bridge out."

Puff flew toward the ice structure, diving through a sudden downpour of arrows. Dirk and Melvin leaned in, using Max's armor to shield themselves as best they could. It only took a few seconds to clear the barrage and close on the ranks of undead streaming over the bridge.

"Liquidity!" Max shouted as they flew past.

Nothing happened.

"Max . . . ?" Puff called back to him. The dragon veered, preparing to take another run at the bridge as more arrows chased them. Max reached into the *Codex*, confused. He found the place where the Prime Spells dwelled, but something was different—the Liquidity spell was gone! Max panicked, wondering if he was losing his connection with the book. Then he realized it wasn't just the Liquidity spell that had gone missing—several of the other Prime Spells were gone too! Panic swelled in Max's chest; then he heard the voice address him again:

There is a price to be paid here. Eventually everything returns home.

Max realized what was happening—once a Prime Spell was cast in the umbraverse it left the *Codex* for good. Suddenly the Fifteen Prime Spells had become Eleven. The sobering truth was that while Max had the power to cast the ancient spells in the umbraverse, he was not his father—he had no idea how to command them to return to the *Codex* when they were done. That meant he'd have to be very careful—each Prime Spell was like a single bullet that could only be fired once.

"Puff, can you melt the bridge with fire?" Max asked, desperately trying to find a solution to the stream of reinforcements flowing into the battleground.

The dragon veered and dove for the bridge. The crossing undead scattered as he unleashed more of his dragon fire, but the magical ice held. "It's too laced with dark magic!" Puff shouted back as he climbed. All around them the storm continued to churn, a mirror of the chaos that Max felt in his heart—he was running out of options.

He turned his attention back to the Shadekin soldiers

crossing the bridge. He couldn't summon any more of the spectral knights, nor could he increase their numbers—those spells were gone. He'd have to draw on a different spell.

"Density!" he shouted, pulling the spell from the *Codex*. The blast sent Puff backward midflight, and the dragon barely managed to keep himself upright. Max directed the spell at the ice bridge, and as the force of the spell hit, the structure cracked. The crossing Shadekin began to run, but too late. An explosion of gray sent the bridge tumbling into pieces, and as before, hundreds of the Maelshadow's warriors fell into the storm below.

"Princess!" Puff cried, suddenly thrusting his wings and spinning his great bulk around. A black form swept past them, barely missing Max.

"Hey!" Dirk called out to her. "It's me! Your honey bunny!"

"*Honey bunny*?" Melvin repeated over Dirk's shoulder.

But Max had other things on his mind. "Captivity!" he yelled, aiming at Nightmare-Princess as she prepared to attack again. There was a blast of power as the Prime Spell hit her, and suddenly she was wrapped in silver chains that pinned her wings back and bound her hooves and feet. A silver mask covered her horn and her mouth was wrapped in the magical chain so that all means of movement were taken from her. Nightmare-Princess screamed in outrage as she began to plummet downward.

"Max!" Dirk exclaimed as she fell. "Save her!"

Max drew the next spell from the *Codex*. "Gravity!" he commanded. A sudden flash of lightning exploded around the edge of the storm as the Prime Spell ripped into form. He steered it toward Princess, wrapping the magic around her and stopping her fall just feet from the boiling clouds. He heard Dirk sigh in relief as he lifted Nightmare-Princess into the air and carried her back to the portal, where the others stood guard.

"Max, I can sense the spells leaving you," Puff said. "You can't get them back, can you?"

"No," he admitted. He had used seven of the Prime Spells already. Puff didn't have to warn him that bit by bit he was losing the one thing that gave him power over the Maelshadow. But he knew he couldn't have lived with himself if he'd let Princess fall—not when *he* was the reason the Cataclysm had come in the first place.

"Look over there!" Melvin shouted.

Max turned to see the remaining Shadrus necromancers gathered on a smaller block of floating ice.

How they had gotten there, Max was unsure. But he could hear their chanting over the din of the storm and battle. Then he saw the outline of a giant serpent tracing itself in the air, long enough to reach from one side of the churning storm to the other.

"Dude, major boss alert," Dirk exclaimed. The necromancers were summoning a monster from the depths of the Shadrus, if "monster" was even an adequate term for something so big.

Puff yelled at Max, "That is a Schritan—an eater of worlds! You must stop it!" Max didn't need any more convincing.

"Fixity!" he yelled. *Fixity—to hold fast and unchanging.* He flung the Prime Spell at the materializing Schritan, and when it struck the enormous creature, it let out an ear-piercing hiss, thrashing its massive head and body. The Prime Spell had stopped its materializing, but had left the creature split between the umbraverse and the Shadrus. The enormity of the pull between the two realms tore the creature apart, and it burst into a fiery shower of bright flame that filled the massive eye of the storm with streaks of light. The necromancers howled with rage as the creature's remains flew across the sky before burning out.

Max wasn't about to let them have another shot at summoning something else, however. "Vacuity!" he yelled. *Vacuity—to empty.* Max had used the spell in a very subtle way once before to plant a suggestion in the minds of the students at the Wizard's Tower. This time he raised the spell like a giant hand, sweeping it across the ice where the necromancers were preparing their next spell. Like so many toys cast off a child's table, they were flung into the air until they fell from view.

"I'd say those guys got a little *carried away*," Dirk exclaimed. He turned and lifted a high five to Melvin. Melvin slapped palms, but without much enthusiasm. Dirk frowned. "Classic eighties movie line—adds insult to injury."

"What now?" Puff yelled back to Max. The dragon had been circling the two armies below.

"Take me higher," Max replied, a new idea forming in his head. There were three or four huge floating islands of ice, the largest serving as the battleground where the knights fought with the Shadekin. The spectral knights had taken the upper hand now that the enemy was deprived of reinforcements, leaving the bulk of the Maelshadow's army spread across the other islands.

And as long as they remained, the techrus was at risk.

"The knights have won," Melvin announced as he watched the last of the battle below. "Too bad they're stuck there."

"Not for long," Max replied.

CHAPTER TWENTY

FACING THE MAELSHADOW

MAX WISHED HE KNEW HOW MUCH TIME HE HAD LEFT. IT COULDN'T BE much, he figured. He just needed a little longer to do what he intended.

"Max!" Dirk yelled. He turned to find that one of the islands had drifted close enough to the portal that Shadekin archers were firing on his friends.

"Panoply!" Max yelled. The Prime Spell flew from the *Codex* and followed the path Max directed. The world buckled for a moment, before the Prime Spell fell across his friends, covering them. *Panoply—to cover and protect.* He watched as the enemy arrows bounced harmlessly from the invisible shield—large enough to protect them and the bound Princess. *Only five spells left.* Max hoped it was enough.

"Be ready to head to the portal," Max called out to Puff. The dragon nodded.

"What are you doing?" Dirk asked.

"Endgame," Max said. He reached into the *Codex* and found the remaining Prime Spells. "This is going to be a big one," he announced to his friends. "Hang on."

"Careful," Puff cautioned, sensing what Max had in mind.

"Unity!" Max shouted. In his mind's eye he envisioned the spell around all the floating islands of ice. He stretched it further than any spell he'd attempted before, willing it to do as he commanded. The very power of it nearly swept him away, and he was reminded just how powerful the Prime Spells truly were.

The shock wave that exploded from him ripped across the eye of the storm between the worlds, slamming into the churning clouds and scattering them for a moment. For an instant Max saw a blackness devoid of stars or light. A sudden cold filled him before the clouds rushed to fill the gaps, pinching off whatever nothingness lay beyond. The storm redoubled as lightning crawled along the spinning clouds, but was moving faster now, growing in intensity. Max remained focused on the Prime Spell

as it encircled the islands of ice. Then the great floating islands began to move, slowly accelerating toward the
black castle.

"Max?" Dirk asked, watching in astonishment.

"He's bringing them together!" Melvin shouted.

Max continued to drive the islands forward, bound
by the power of the Prime Spell. They watched as the
first two collided into each other with an explosion of
snow and frost. Then the spell wove through them, seal-
ing them together. Max continued to steer the massive
islands, and one by one they crashed and joined together,
gaining speed with each collision.

"Now!" Max shouted. "To the portal!"

Puff dived toward the portal, which was moving
like everything else, floating just above the ice island
where his friends waited. As they passed over the spectral
army, Max drew another spell: "Parity!" *Parity—to balance and make equivalent.* Max wrapped the spell around
his remaining forces as the island of ice crashed into one
containing a sizable contingent of Shadekin. He stretched
the spell to the space between the Shadekin and the portal, and suddenly the knights were split into two equal
groups. The second half materialized on the ice and

immediately moved forward, unfazed by the maelstrom of magic happening around them. The ranks of Shadekin were in disarray, however, and the knights fell on them with a deafening clash of steel. Max felt the spell leave as he leaned toward Puff, his heart racing. "Hurry! Take me to the castle!"

The dragon raced across the moving islands of ice as they continued to career into one another. They were moving fast—maybe even too fast. But Max couldn't help that now. He was about to try something as dangerous as he'd ever attempted with a Prime Spell.

"Futurity!" he shouted. He flung the spell away from him, and even through his armor he could feel Dirk tense behind him. Futurity was the spell he'd accidentally cast so long ago when they'd first brought the *Codex* to Dwight. They'd had no idea what it was then, or all that would follow. Futurity was the spell that had moved him and his friends forward in time—and they very nearly hadn't made it back.

The resulting explosion echoed all around them, like the sound of a jet crossing the sound barrier. Puff was tossed in the air so violently that Melvin was forced to drop his bow in order to grab hold of Dirk.

"Hang on!" Dirk shouted, struggling to keep himself from sliding off the dragon's back. But Max kept his focus on the two armies. It was a dangerous move, but he needed the path cleared to the Maelshadow's temple and there were too many of the Shadekin scattered about to contend with. Max focused the Prime Spell on the thousands of Shadekin ahead of him, and in the blink of an eye they were gone.

"Whoa!" Dirk exclaimed, looking around the now empty fields of ice.

"What did you do, Max?" Puff called back to him.

"I sent them forward in time."

"Very dangerous," Puff warned. Max understood, but the existence of everything he cared about was at stake.

"Couldn't you have just done that from the beginning?" Dirk asked him.

Maybe, Max thought. *Maybe if I was more experienced and knew what I was doing. Nobody seems to realize I'm having to figure this out as I go.*

Dirk accepted the silence and didn't press further. "You're probably not going to be really good at this stuff until you're like level thirty," he added, hoping it made his friend feel better.

It didn't.

Only two spells left, Max counted to himself. *Will they be enough?*

They arrived at the Maelshadow's castle just ahead of the massive ice island barreling toward them. Max didn't need to tell Puff to stay in the air—getting on the ground before the impact seemed a dangerous proposition. Max's mind raced as he tried to think about what could go wrong. It made sense at first, but everything was happening so fast. And before he realized it, he was out of time.

The impact almost seemed to happen in slow motion: The massive new island struck the ice castle island with a tearing sound like the very fabric of the universe had been rent apart. Great blocks of ice exploded, and the impact caused a massive fissure to erupt, crawling its way toward the black castle like cracking glass.

Max's friends were thrown forward, and with them the portal took flight as well. Another explosion sounded as a great portion of the castle split away, the expanding fissure ripping through the structure and sending it tumbling into the storm. For a horrible second Max feared the whole castle would collapse, taking Sarah with it.

But what remained of the Maelshadow's temple held fast, despite being ripped in two.

Max drew the next Prime Spells from the *Codex:* "Gallimaufry!" *Gallimaufry—to create a mixture of diverse things.* Earlier he'd filled his mind with images of weapons but now he thought of mattresses—hundreds of them. They popped into existence all around the base of the castle, four or five feet thick, just as his friends careened into them. They bounced several times on impact, only Ricky somehow looking graceful as their flight came to a sudden end. The portal kept going, however, tumbling end over end and growing to the size of a highway billboard. It smashed through what remained of the castle's entrance and disappeared inside.

Max shuddered, whether from adrenaline or nerves or the fact that he'd only just managed to save his friends. Even Princess bounced safely across the mattresses, her eyes burning at the indignity of being captured and tossed around. Puff gently landed on the thick pile of mattresses—he was too large to get through what remained of the castle's entrance.

Max and the others slid off the dragon's back. Puff folded his massive wings and regarded the gray-haired boy in wizard's robes. "If I were to put the fate of the world in anyone's hands, I would choose you, Max Spencer."

"Sounds like a compliment at first," Glenn said from Dirk's back, "until you realize he doesn't know anybody else."

The dragon scowled, an expression considerably more impressive coming from a giant, fire-breathing dragon than a sheep-sized ball of fluff. "I will prepare the transformation to my human form," he announced. "I am too big to go further."

"I understand," Max replied. *If I fail, I need you to protect the others.*

Max strode toward the ruins of the castle, climbing several steps and turning to address his shaken but otherwise uninjured friends. "Ricky, you and the other wrestlers take Princess to the portal and get her through. Dwight and Dirk, I need you to come with me and find Sarah. While I deal with the Maelshadow, get her free and take her home."

"You can count on us," Dirk replied.

"Well *me*, anyway," Dwight added.

"What can I do?" Megan asked, stepping forward with her staff in hand.

"You go home with the others, okay? Keep your sister safe."

"Okay, Max," Megan answered, barely managing to keep her emotions in check. She had a dark suspicion that she might never see him again.

"What about me?" Sydney asked, joining her sister.

"I need you to do something very important," Max said. He motioned to Moki who was jumping up and down on one of the mattresses. "Watch over my friend here, and when Ricky and the others have gone through the portal, you follow right after them. And once you're home, stay by Ricky and Puff—they'll protect you."

Sydney smiled. "Come on, Moki."

"And Melvin, I know you'd follow me in an instant, but I can't be worrying about you when I face the Maelshadow. You have to return with the others and keep them safe."

"Without a bow I wouldn't be much good to you anyway," Melvin said. "Max, I just want to say I misjudged you. You are more a hero than anyone I've ever known."

"Again, just his imaginary friends we're talking about," Glenn piped in.

Max ignored the lute and looked over the ragtag group. Here they were, living the roles of the characters they'd only imagined before, caught between two realms and about to face the greatest evil imaginable. And Max knew each of them wouldn't hesitate to follow him—no matter the danger. They weren't just a bunch of nerds who played fantasy games for fun, they were the very essence of those characters: brave, heroic, and honorable. It just so happened they'd been born in a world of technology. Totally not their fault.

"Follow me, then," Max said. "I guess it's all or nothing now."

The Maelshadow sat on his throne, his temple split in half and open to the churning storm outside. He was in the form of a man, but his features were lost in the folds of a long, hooded robe. Nearby, the portal lay wedged between two massive pillars, its smooth surface a pattern of red swirls. Max walked toward him, down the center of what remained of the Lord of Shadow's shrine.

Then Max saw Sarah, bound to one of the throne's jagged spikes and looking defiant. Wayne stood over her, his shield in one hand and his axe in the other. And for some reason there was a monkey watching them from a small black cage.

"I thought the girl should witness your demise," the Maelshadow announced.

"Max, is that you?" Sarah called out, seeing him in his armor for the first time.

"Yeah," he answered. "Are you okay?"

"I will be when you get me out of here."

Max heard the sounds of Ricky and the others dragging Princess into the room. He turned his attention to the Maelshadow. "Close the portal and return to your realm," he demanded. "I've destroyed your army and I will do the same to you." *One spell,* Max thought. *And my sword—it's all I have left.*

"You have merely helped pass the time until the Cataclysm is permanent," the Maelshadow answered with a dark laugh. "And as for my army, what you have destroyed is but a handful of what I possess. There are legions that serve me in the Shadrus, despite your most entertaining efforts to the contrary. You did not defeat an invading army. All of it was simply a test to see if you were worthy to face me. And look what it cost you. Did you not know you would lose the Prime Spells here? What have you left? Anything?"

"I don't need them," Max continued, hoping it was true. He drew Penumbra from its sheath. "One form of shadow to destroy another."

The Maelshadow laughed again. "Old words, but their meaning is lost to you. You are an infant with a wand, knowing not what you do. But you have fulfilled your purpose and done all that I needed. Farewell, Max Spencer. Go to your grave knowing you have doomed your world." The Maelshadow turned to Wayne, pointing at Dwight and Dirk. "They will try and free the girl. As you have served me well, so as a reward I give you the pleasure of killing them."

The Lord of Shadows rose from his throne, and Wayne put his shield on the floor and shifted the axe from one hand to the other. The large boy stepped down from the dais where the throne rested and moved toward Dirk and Dwight.

"My good ogre," the Maelshadow continued. "It was so easy for him to deceive you. Why? Because you, Max, had already deceived yourself. You thought the Magrus would welcome you as a hero? You thought that was who you really were? The heir to Maximilian Sporazo's throne?"

"I made a mistake. I thought I couldn't be happy unless I was a wizard," Max replied. "But I was wrong. Magic isn't who I am—it's just something I can do."

"Not for long."

"Leave him alone!" Sarah yelled. "Cut me down and face me yourself, you coward!"

"See? I was right to bring her here to watch me break you," the Maelshadow continued. "Because that is what you truly care about, isn't it? That is what will wound you the deepest."

"I don't want to talk to you anymore," Max said, tightening his grip on the sword.

The Maelshadow smiled, turning his hooded head toward the storm outside. "We are heartbeats away, Max, and there will be no going back. I will try and keep you alive long enough for you to know you have failed."

Wayne started across the floor and Max chanced a quick look behind him. Ricky and the others had pushed Princess through the portal. *That's one,* Max said to himself. Then he saw the wrestlers climb through and disappear after her. Ricky was the last.

"Take him out, Spencer," Ricky shouted, then he turned and followed the others. Meanwhile, Wayne was closing the distance with Dirk and Dwight. Dwight stepped forward with his axe, but Dirk put his hand on the dwarf's shoulder and announced, "Dude, I got this." He swung Glenn around and strummed a chord, clearing his throat:

> *Stupid Wayne, fighting the dwarf and me,*
> *But did you forget that you can't see?*
> *At least not us, 'cause you're big and dumb,*
> *And we be fading with each new strum!*

"'We be fading with each new strum'? What kind of stupid lyric is that?" the dwarf grumbled. But suddenly Wayne froze, his eyes wide. Dirk and Dwight were invisible!

The Maelshadow walked forward, extending his arm. A sword grew from it—a smoldering crimson blade that reflected off of Max's armor. Then he leapt forward and Max brought his own weapon up to block the blow. The impact nearly knocked Penumbra out of Max's hand, and he spun around, the tip of his sword inches above the floor. Max barely managed to bring the blade up again as the Maelshadow lunged. The Lord of Shadows drove past Max's defense, and the crimson sword struck Max's helm. The blow sent him sprawling backward, his ears ringing. The Maelshadow walked over to him as Max struggled to his feet.

"Rezormoor's armor is well conceived," the Maelshadow said. "But it assumes the wearer knows how to fight with a blade."

Max had had just about enough insults, and he lunged forward in a series of frantic attacks. But he was off-balance, and the Maelshadow easily parried his blows, finally stepping to the side as Max stumbled forward, bringing his own sword around and striking Max on the back.

"No!" Sarah screamed as Max flew toward the edge of the room. He reached out and grabbed a column, barely saving himself from going over the edge. Max turned, leaning against the column for support. His arm already burned and his breathing was fast and heavy. He caught a glimpse of Wayne, who was walking around the room cautiously as Dirk's song continued:

> *And don't think you'll find us by the sound of my voice,*
> *'Cause it's everywhere and you've got no choice,*
> *So think on that as you stumble around;*
> *You've been owned by the Bard of renown!*

Max stood and brought the sword up, moving away from the edge of the room. The Maelshadow came at him, easily beating through his defense and striking him again and again: in the arm, across the chest, in the head, on the other arm, across the thigh. Max teetered this way and that as the Maelshadow hammered away at his armored skin, finally knocking him to the floor with a vicious blow to his leg. Max lost his grip on Penumbra and the sword slid across the floor. The Maelshadow leapt, landing on Max's chest and driving the point of the crimson sword to his breastplate. Max could feel the heat of the weapon through the armor, but he was helpless as the Lord of Shadows pushed the unholy blade harder.

"Max, get up!" Sarah cried. "Do something."

Max was exhausted. He closed his eyes and hoped the armor would hold. After what seemed forever, the Maelshadow spun away, throwing the blade across the room in disgust. "This is pointless!" the Maelshadow cried, and it was the first time Max had ever heard emotion in the ancient and horrible voice. "I cannot penetrate your armor."

Max rose to see Dirk and Dwight standing beside Sarah. The dwarf swung his axe and cut Sarah free, causing the Maelshadow to whirl at the sound.

"Fool ogre!" he bellowed. "Your mind is weak to be so easily deceived, and I have grown weary of this." He raised a hooded arm at the trio of friends.

"Wait!" Max cried. "Don't hurt them! I'll surrender to you! I'll remove the armor!"

"Max, no!" Sarah cried.

The Maelshadow hesitated. "On what condition?"

"That you allow them through the portal."

The Maelshadow lowered his arm. "And what do you think to accomplish in the moments we have left? Don't you know I'll simply walk through the portal after them?"

"I'll take that chance," Max said, climbing to his feet.

"So be it, then," the Lord of Shadow replied. He moved his hand and Max's friends launched through the air toward the open portal. Sarah just managed to reach out and grab the cage with the monkey in it before she flew past.

"Max, I—" she shouted, but she was through the portal with the others before she could finish. To Max's relief the temple was empty now—his friends had made it home. That left him with only one thing to do. Max raised his arm and touched the blue symbol. It glowed for a moment before the armor retracted, collapsing into the wristband.

"Clever," the Maelshadow said. He walked over to Penumbra and kicked it. The weapon slid across the floor and off the edge. He then turned to Wayne.

"Come and join me, ogre."

Wayne walked to where Max stood, unarmored and defenseless. Max looked at the amulet hanging around Wayne's neck—it glowed black. Evil. Max turned to him. "I don't know why you did this," he said. "But I have to believe you were used somehow. Maybe you didn't know it at the time, or maybe you still don't. But you were good once. And you were my friend. And so no matter what happens next, you should know that friends don't turn on each other. I don't know what the Maelshadow promised you, but I'm pretty sure friendship wasn't part of it. So I forgive you—even though you might have destroyed everything that matters to me."

The Maelshadow threw his head back and began to laugh. "So naive. So *human*. How have you survived so long? But it doesn't matter. We are mere moments now from a new beginning. How does it feel, Max, to have failed so completely!"

"Irony!" Max shouted, reaching into the *Codex* for the last Prime Spell. The power of it shot out from Max, cracking already damaged columns. He had used the spell before, unpracticed and afraid when the robot unicorn and her hunters had threatened his friends. But he wasn't the same person anymore, and he imposed his will on what would happen. He reached between the realms with the only spell powerful enough to do so, and found what he was looking for. He brought it back, and suddenly the gracon was standing before Max. Peaches saw the

Maelshadow at once, and lunged at him. Peaches, a creature born of shadow, was now free to exact its revenge.

"What?" the Maelshadow cried as the gracon smashed into him, driving the lord of Shadows to the floor. The lava that seemed to run across the gracon's skin burned bright red as it delivered blow after blow. The Maelshadow shrieked, and the world suddenly dimmed. Monstrous shadows flew from the form of the Maelshadow, slipping along the walls and crawling out of sight.

"Ogre!" The Maelshadow howled. "Help me!"

A blade suddenly sprang from one of the Maelshadow's sleeves, but the gracon grabbed hold of his arm and brought his great horn across it, severing it easily. The blade melted into a pool of black as it fell to the floor, seeping into the cracks. Then the gracon sprang to its feet and tossed the Lord of Shadows into a far wall. The impact cracked the stone itself, and dozens of shadows leapt from the robed figure and scattered across the walls and ceiling.

Wayne stepped toward Max and grabbed him. "I could force you to call him off."

"I wouldn't even if I could."

"I know." Then Wayne shoved Max hard. But not

toward the edge as Max had feared. Instead, he stumbled toward the portal. Max reached out and grabbed hold of the frame, barely catching himself as his legs slipped through. He hung on, fighting against the pull of the vortex.

Across the room Peaches drove the Maelshadow into one of the ragged edges of his throne. The Lord of Shadows howled in rage and pain as shadows flew from him. Hundreds of them, flowing across the floor and walls like a black river running off the edge of the world.

The gracon turned to Max. "Justice." Then Peaches pulled the Maelshadow free of the spikes and walked him to the edge. He didn't hesitate before leaping off, carrying himself and what remained of the Lord of Shadows into the nothingness and beyond.

The Maelshadow was gone, but the portal remained open. Max could still lose everything unless he found a way to seal the breach between the realms—but how? He struggled to hang on, watching as Wayne approached. The big kid's amulet pulsated a dark gray. *Still mostly evil,* Max thought. And then he understood, and a smile broke out across his face. Wayne reached up and grabbed the frame of the portal and began to pull. It shook in his giant hands, but it began to close!

"Hurry!" Max called out, watching the portal shrinking around him. Wayne quickly compacted the portal to about the size of a window, but then he struggled, the effort growing more difficult with each passing second.

"It's getting harder!" Wayne grunted in frustration.

"Your amulet!" Max exclaimed. Wayne looked down and saw that his Amulet of Alignment had turned a much lighter gray. "You're becoming *good*."

Wayne pressed harder, the portal closing to about the size of a school desk. Max continued to hold on, feeling the frame diminish under his fingers. But then the portal froze, and Wayne was forced to let go, exhausted.

"There's no more I can do," he said, sounding defeated.

Max hung there, the impossibility of it threatening to drive him mad. They had come so far! If they didn't close the portal now none of it mattered. He knew there were only seconds left—only a matter of moments before all would be lost. He looked at Wayne and suddenly had an idea.

"Kick me!" Max yelled. He watched the surprised expression on Wayne's face turn into understanding.

Max had hoped for a moment to prepare himself, but the big kid didn't hesitate, delivering a well-placed boot to Max's face. Stars exploded around his vision and he fell backward, frantically reaching out to grab the rope. He felt it fly past, then landed on something softer than he'd expected.

"Told you he wouldn't find the rope," Ricky said.

Max raised his head to see that he was lying on a mound of wrestling mats. Then a much larger body landed with a thud next to him, nearly launching him back into the air. It was Wayne, clutching the Shadric Portal in both hands. The magical tempest that had been its center, however, was gone.

"I closed it!" Wayne exclaimed. He turned to Max. "Sorry about the kick to the face."

Max managed a smile even though his eyes were watering from the pain in his nose. "Probably the least I deserved," he said.

"How'd you do it?" Dirk asked, eyeing Wayne suspiciously.

Sarah was on her feet and headed toward the one-time Ogre, payback in her eyes.

"No!" Max shouted. "He saved me—us."

"He's the one who started it," Dwight added.

"Maybe," Max admitted. "But he also finished it. He was the only one who could do it."

"Bad Ogre," Moki chastised.

"And the kick to the face?" Megan asked, her eyebrow raised.

"I needed a little more evil to finish the job," Wayne admitted.

"Good Ogre," Moki said, changing his mind. The others began laughing in spite of themselves.

CHAPTER TWENTY-ONE

FRIENDS

THE SCOREBOARD READ EAGLES 56, PANTHERS 7. MAX WAS SITTING BESIDE Sarah on the football-field bleachers, watching as Wayne smashed through the offensive line and sacked the quarterback—again. Dirk was next to Princess, while Melvin, Megan, and Sydney sat in the row directly in front of them. Sydney was holding Moki, who had no idea what the rules were for football but liked all the whistle blowing. Even Dwight had shown up, with his strange-looking dog in tow. It turned out that while Puff had learned to shed his scales and take on his true dragon form, he'd lost the ability to become a human. When he tried, he ended up a fluff dragon again—but with a gap in his scales just large enough that he could make the transformation to full-sized dragon any time he wanted. Max had cautioned that doing so in Madison might not be the best idea.

It had been two weeks since the Cataclysm—but only Max and his friends knew that was what the strange event was called. To the rest of the town it was simply known as the Lost Weekend. After Wayne closed the portal in time, the town slowly reverted to its old self. That didn't mean Max could look at Mrs. Frankelburt quite the same, however, finding the image of the howler with the rolling pin hard to shake.

After much debate as to the cause of the Lost Weekend, it was Mr. Magar, the high school chemistry teacher, who announced that the loss of consciousness and accompanying hallucinations had been caused by a gas pocket that had ruptured underground. Many of the citizens of Madison recalled strange visions as a result, including militarized squirrels and a tornado on top of the school. But with the mystery more or less solved, the town went about its normal business.

Max and his friends had been able to forgive Wayne, although Sarah looked like she wanted to toss him around a couple of times for good measure. The former ogre decided to stay in the Techrus, and found the football coach more than happy to put him on the team. Dwight offered to let Wayne stay at the Dragon's Den, so that the town's fantasy game shop was home to a dwarf, a dragon, and an ogre. Not that anyone else knew the truth—it was a secret shared by just Max and his friends. That included Ricky and the handful of wrestlers who had joined them in their fight against the Maelshadow. Max had even been offered the job of manager for the wrestling team, and to everyone's surprise he had accepted. He figured it was the least that he could do.

There was a roar from the crowd as Wayne picked up a fumble (he had caused it) and ran for a touchdown. Ricky shouted the loudest; he and the other wrestlers were sitting just above Max, cheering Wayne on. Max smiled and took a look at his friends, both old and new, and for the first time in a long time he realized he was truly happy. He might be a magic-wielding wizard and last living descendant of the arch-sorcerer who created the *Codex of Infinite Knowability*, but none of that compared with how he felt with his friends. He looked at Sarah and she tilted her head in response, eyeing him with a curious look.

"What are you thinking about?" she asked.

"I was thinking that life is pretty good," he said.

"Yeah," she agreed. "It is."

Two seats over, Princess leaned toward Dirk. She had no memories of her transformation and was bothered by the stories she'd heard. "Was I really a hybrid *nightmare-unicorn*?" she asked, not for the first time. "It just sounds so . . . horsey."

"Oh yeah, totally. You were a pretty bad nightmare thingy, but I like you better as a bad unicorn." Princess arched an eyebrow.

"I'm still not your girlfriend, you know. Even though I tried to eat you again and you're not holding it against me."

Dirk shrugged. "We could always just hold hands."

"Let me think about it." It was about as encouraging a response as Dirk could hope for. He was also working on an "epic" love song. Glenn had transformed back into a dagger (nobody complained about *that*), forcing Dirk to pick up an old guitar and begin teaching himself how to play. Glenn was very supportive of the whole thing.

Later that night Max sat on his bed. He opened

the nightstand where he kept the *Codex of Infinite Knowability*. There was something different about it without the Prime Spells. Max had used every one of them in his battle with the Maelshadow and his army, and now he supposed they were floating somewhere in the umbraverse, free to do whatever Prime Spells did.

Suddenly there was a swirling of lights and Max's old mentor materialized.

"Bellstro!" Max called out. "I didn't know you could appear here!"

"Why?" the spectral wizard asked. "Is it illegal?"

"Er, no."

"Then listen, because I have something to tell you. When you go against the Maelshadow . . ." But Bellstro paused, studying Max closely. "You already did, didn't you?"

"Yeah, pretty much."

"And you defeated him?"

Max shrugged. "I had some help from a very angry gracon named Peaches."

Bellstro sighed. "I don't think I'm very good at this otherwordly mentor thing."

368 Platte F. Clark

"That's not true," Max replied. "What you said about the spider was really helpful."

"It was?"

"I mean, you could have just come out and told us about being trapped in a dream world, but you kept it all cryptic and mysterious like a good mentor is supposed to." That made Bellstro smile.

"I ruined the *Codex*, though," Max said with a sigh. "It still talks about stuff and all the normal spells are there, but it's different now."

"The *Codex* has been home to the Sixteen Prime Spells for centuries. It will take some time to get used to not having them around."

"I suppose," Max said, and then something his mentor had said caught his attention.

"You mean the *Fifteen* Prime Spells," Max said, eyeing the old ghost.

"Isn't that what I said? Oh, of course, the *Fifteen* Prime Spells. You're right . . . fifteen."

"Bellstro . . . ?" Max asked carefully.

"Max, that's not something you're supposed to know about, so just forget I said anything."

"Too late."

"You, young man, are going to get me into a lot of trouble."

"So there really is a sixteenth Prime Spell?" Max pressed. Bellstro sighed and took a seat on the bed next to Max.

"Yes. Or so the rumors go. But it's missing."

Max frowned. "Does anyone know what it does?"

"No. And perhaps that's the reason it was hidden. Or, some believe that the true purpose of the *Codex* is to gather enough information to find it. Either way, it's not important right now."

Max thought it over for a few minutes. "Did my father look for it?"

"Yes, Max, he did."

Max nodded. Later that night as he lay in bed with Moki curled up on the pillow beside him, his mind kept going over the possibility a hidden sixteenth Prime Spell. It was just the sort of thing that a band of bat-tle-proven adventurers might be interested in looking for. *Or,* he thought as he flipped off the light, *we could just play an online game instead.* He and Dirk had never finished the quest to find the Sword of Spectacular Swishiness.

"Either way, we'll do it together," he said, as he pulled the blanket up. Moki yawned in agreement and then went back to sleep.

Outside, a dark figure with ivory tattoos walked by. It coughed once, enjoying the germ-carrying capacity of the warm evening air. It would be a good year for strep throat, it decided.

ACKNOWLEDGMENTS

Writing a book is like writing a bunch of little books and then squishing them together. Actually, that's a horrible analogy and you should probably forget I even brought it up. Writing a book IS about a team of amazing and talented people, however, including first and foremost my editor, Fiona Simpson. My sincere appreciation and gratitude goes out to all the folks at Aladdin and Simon & Schuster, and to my agent, Deborah Warren. The cover comes courtesy of the talented John Hendrix, and hats off to Jessica Handelman for another terrific jacket design.

Thanks to my fellow Story Monkeys Eric Patten, Dave Butler, Erik Holmes, and Michael Dalzen for your help and insights. And to my wife and family, thank you for all your love, support, and willingness to put up with a dad who enjoys nothing more than long bouts of laughter with his kids.